NOBODY GETS OUT ALIVE

Stories

LEIGH NEWMAN

SCRIBNER

New York   London   Toronto   Sydney   New Delhi

Scribner
An Imprint of Simon & Schuster, Inc.
1230 Avenue of the Americas
New York, NY 10020

First Scribner hardcover edition April 2022

For information about special discounts for bulk purchases, please contact Simon & Schuster Special Sales at 1-866-506-1949 or business@simonandschuster.com.

The Simon & Schuster Speakers Bureau can bring authors to your live event. For more information or to book an event, contact the Simon & Schuster Speakers Bureau at 1-866-248-3049 or visit our website at www.simonspeakers.com.

Interior design by Wendy Blum

Manufactured in the United States of America

1   3   5   7   9   10   8   6   4   2

Library of Congress Cataloging-in-Publication Data

Names: Newman, Leigh, author.
Title: Nobody gets out alive : stories / Leigh Newman.
Description: First Scribner hardcover edition. | New York : Scribner, 2022.
Identifiers: LCCN 2021059421 | ISBN 9781982180300 (hardcover) |
ISBN 9781982180324 (ebook)
Subjects: LCSH: Alaska—Fiction. | LCGFT: Short stories.
Classification: LCC PS3614.E628 N63 2022 | DDC 813/.6—dc23/eng/20211214
LC record available at https://lccn.loc.gov/2021059421

ISBN 978-1-9821-8030-0
ISBN 978-1-9821-8032-4 (ebook)

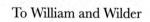
To William and Wilder

Contents

HOWL PALACE

THIS SEPTEMBER, I FINALLY PUT Howl Palace up for sale. Years of poor financial planning had led to this decision, and I tried to take some comfort in my agent's belief in a buyer who might show up with an all-cash offer. My agent, Silver, was a highly organized, sensible woman who grew up in Alaska—I checked—but when she advertised the listing, she failed to mention her description on the internet. "Attractively priced teardown with plane dock and amazing lake views," she wrote under the photo. "Investment potential."

I am still puzzled as to why the word "teardown" upset me. Anybody who buys a house on Diamond Lake brings in a backhoe and razes the place to rubble. The mud along the shoreline wreaks havoc with foundations, and the original homes, like mine, were built in the sixties, before the pipeline, back when licensed contractors had no reason to move to Anchorage. If you wanted a house, you either built it yourself, or you hung out in the parking lot of Spenard Builders Supply handing out six-packs to every guy with a table saw in the back of his vehicle until one got broke enough or bored enough to consider your blueprints. Which is why the walls in Howl Palace meet the ceiling at such unconventional angles. Our guy liked to eyeball instead of using a level.

To the families on the lake, my home is a bit of an institution. And not just because the wolf room, which Silver suggested we leave off the list of amenities, as most people wouldn't understand what we meant. About the snow-machine shed and clamshell grotto, I was less flexible. Nobody likes a yard strewn with snow machines and three-wheelers, one or two of which will always be busted and covered in blue tarp. Ours is just not that kind of neighborhood. The clamshell grotto, on the other hand, might fail to fulfill your basic home-owning needs, but it is a showstopper. My fourth husband, Lon, built it for me in the basement as a surprise for my fifty-third birthday. He had a romantic nature, when he hadn't had too much to drink. Embedded in the coral and shells are more than a few freshwater pearls that a future owner might consider tempting enough to jackhammer out of the cement.

Silver brought me a box of Girl Scout cookies to discuss these matters, and so I tried my hardest to trust the rest of her advice. When she said not to bother with pulling out the chickweed or flattening the rusted remnants of the dog runs, I left both as is. But then I started thinking about what people say about baking blueberry muffins and burning vanilla candles. Buyers needed to feel the atmosphere of the place, the homeyness. Fred Meyer had some plug-in tropical air fresheners on sale. I bought a few. I shoved them into the outlets. Within minutes, the entire downstairs smelled like a burning car wreck in Hawaii.

*   *   *

SILVER SCHEDULED THE OPEN HOUSE for the first Saturday in September. "Noon," she said. "Before families have put the kids down for a nap." The night before, I lay back in my recliner and thought how every good thing that had ever happened to me had happened in Howl Palace. And every bad thing too. Forty-three years. Five husbands. Two floatplanes. A lifetime. It felt as if I should honor my home, that strangers shouldn't come around poking through the kitchen or kicking the baseboards, seeing only the mold in the hot tub and the gnaw marks on the cabinets from the dogs I'd had over the years, maybe even laughing at the name. "Howl Palace" was coined by Jamie Donovan, Danny Bob Donovan's little daughter during a New Year's Eve party in 1977. She said it with awe, standing in the middle of the wolf room with a half-eaten candy cane. "Mrs. Dutch," she said, "this is so beautiful, I think I need to howl a little." And howl she did, cupping her hands around her mouth and letting loose a wild, lonely cry that endeared her to me for forever.

Howl Palace was still beautiful, in my mind. And could be to other people, given the right welcome. Silver had said to just relax, to let her finesse the details, but buyers needed to experience how the house would feel if they lived in it—friends coming over, kids in the backyard pitching mud chunks at mallards, a little music going on the speakers. I went to the locker freezer and pulled out fifty pounds of caribou burger, plus four dozen moose dogs. All we needed now were a few side dishes. And some buns.

* * *

THE NEXT MORNING WAS BUST a hump. The menu for the cookout had expanded to include green bean casserole, macaroni salad, guacamole, and trout almondine. Trout almondine requires cream for the cream sauce, which I forgot on my eight-thirty run to Costco, leading me to substitute powdered milk mixed with a few cans of cream of mushroom soup. My fifth husband, Skip, used to call me the John Wayne of the Home Range, not in the nicest way, until he got dementia and forgot who I was or that he had to follow me around explaining how I'd organized the produce drawer wrong or let too much hair fall off my head in the shower or failed to remove every single bone from his barbecued salmon because I didn't fucking ever think. Shipping him off to a facility in Washington near his daughter wasn't exactly something I struggled with.

The pool table, where I planned to lay out the buffet, was coated with so much dust it looked as though a fine, silver fungus had sprouted over the felt. I dragged an old quarter sheet of plywood from the snow-machine shed and heaved it on top. If you are looking for a reason to split five cords of wood by hand each year for forty-odd years, consider my biceps at age sixty-seven.

The air had the bright, whistly feel of coming cold. Even as the grass on the back lawn lay in drunken clumps, flattened by twenty-hour days of summer sunlight. Out in the garage, I found a flowery top sheet from a long-gone water bed. That went over the pool table. Soon followed the side dishes, the salads, the condiments. On went the grill, the meat at the ready on the little side table that folded up, with an indentation to rest your tongs and spatula. All that was left was the guacamole. Which was when Carl's pickup pulled into the driveway.

Carl wasn't my husband. Carl was the beautiful, bedeviling heartbreak of my life. His hair had thinned, but not so you saw his scalp, and age spots mottled his arms. His smell was the same as ever: WD-40, line-dried shirt, the peppermint soap he used to cut through fish slime. For one heady second, I believed he had come back to say in some soft, regretful voice: Remember when we ran into each other at Sportsman's Warehouse? It got me thinking, well, maybe we should give it another try.

As Carl told me long ago, "Inside you hides a soft, secret pink balloon of dreams." He wasn't incorrect, but the balloon had withered a little over the years. And it was not a reassuring sign that Carl had a dog in the back of his vehicle.

"I thought you might need a new Lab," he said. "She's pedigree, real obedient."

I had some idea what he meant: She jumped ducks before he got off a shot and went after half-dead birds in the rapids despite the rocks he threw at her backside, trying to save her from injury. Once, she had eaten a healthy portion of his dishwasher.

Over my years at Howl Palace, I'd had a lot of dogs, all of them black Labs with papers proving their champion field-and-trial bloodlines. I loved every one of them and loved hunting with them, but no matter how you deal with these animals at home—stick or carrot—they just can't deviate from the agenda panting through their minds, an agenda born of instinct and inbreeding, neither of which suggests that they sit there wagging their tails when a bumblebee flies through a yard. Or a bottle rocket zooms by.

I have seen my share of classic family retrievers on this lake—black or yellow Labs, dumb, drooling goldens, the occasional hefty Chessie—who live only to snuggle up with the kids and ignore the smoked salmon you are about to insert into your mouth. But I have never had one in my kennel or my house. My last dog, Babs, was a hunt nut, willful, with a hole in her emotional reasoning where somebody yanked out her uterus without a fully approved vet license. I picked her up for free from an ad in the Pennysaver, and maybe that had something to do with it. She drowned after jumping out of a charter boat to retrieve the halibut that I had on the line, unaware of the tide about to suck her into the Gulf of Alaska.

Still, I enjoyed her company more than Skip's and Lon's combined. Babs slept not just in my bed but under the covers, where we struggled over the one soft pillow. When she died, I was ready to retire from a lifetime of animal management. I was sixty-three years old and single, and I vowed to myself: no more Labs, no more husbands, no more ex-husbands either.

The kennel in the bed of Carl's truck only confirmed the wisdom of my decision. The whole thing lay flipped on its side, jumping and heaving from the campaign being waged against the door. Nuthatches flickered through the yellowing trees, made frantic by the sound of claws against metal. Squirrels fled for other yards.

"Carl," I said. "I'm about to have an open house. I can't take your dog."

He looked over at the woodpile, where the remains of the chain-link runs sagged along the ground. "You could put her in the basement. In the clamshell grotto," he said. Then laughed. He had a wonderful laugh, the kind that tickled through you, slowly, inch by inch, brain cell by brain cell until you were mentally unfit to resist him.

"No, Carl," I said—not even talking about the animal.

"She can drink out of the fountain."

"No," I said. "N. O."

"I'm not a dog," he said, his voice quiet.

Wind riffled through the aspens, exposing the silverish undersides of the leaves. A plane buzzed by overhead. Carl jammed his hands in his pockets. "Besides," he said, "you can't sell Howl Palace."

I looked at him, daring him to tell me that he and I needed to live here together. The way I had always wanted. He had a suitcase in the back of his cab.

Carl looked back at me—as if about to say all this. Then he said, "It's your home, Dutch. You love it." He smiled, the way he always smiled. Time drained away for a few moments and we were back in the trophy room at Danny Boy's, thirty-five and tipsy, his finger laced through the loop of my jeans. The Eagles skipped on the turntable and my second husband, Wallace, ceased to exist. Tiny, dry snowflakes clung to the edges of the window like miniature paper stars. Carl kissed me and a dark, glittery hole opened up and I fell through, all the way to the bottom.

"I hate you, Carl," I said, but as so often happens around him, it came out sounding backward, fraught with tenderness.

The kennel creaked all of a sudden. We both looked over and, blam, the door snapped off. Seventy pounds of black, thundering muscle shot out of the truck and into the alders.

"Oh boy," he said. "Not good."

"Hand me the zapper."

"She doesn't have a shock collar."

I tried a two-fingered whistle. Nothing. Not a snapped twig.

"I hate to say it," he said. "But there's this appointment—"

"Carl, I've got an open house."

He toed something, a weed. "It's a flight," he said. "To Texas. I'm fishing down in Galveston for a few weeks."

All the dewy romance inside me turned to gravel as I watched him move toward his vehicle. When he bent down to pick up the door to the kennel, his shirt twisted. The shirt was a fly-fishing model, with a mesh panel for hot Texas days, through which I caught a glimpse of the pager-looking box strapped to his side. It was beige. A green battery light blinked on top.

Everybody our age knew what that box was. Carl was not here in my driveway to romance me all over again. Or even piss me off. Carl needed someone to dog-sit while he went off to get fancy last-ditch chemo down in the Lower 48. Houston, probably.

7

I took a minute to organize my face. "Get your animal," I said. "Get her back in the goddamn kennel and take her with you."

"Or what?" he said. "You'll hang her on a wolf peg?"

The cheapness of his comment released us both. I turned and went inside to not watch his truck peel down the driveway. Carl and I had always disagreed about the wolf room, which was the only thing that he, Lon, Skip, Wallace, and my third husband, RT, might have ever had in common. None of them liked it, and I respected that. But it didn't mean I had to rip it out. I was proud of it. It was beautiful. It was mine.

* * *

BACK IN THE KITCHEN, A case of avocados sat on the counter, waiting. People wail about chain stores ruining the views in Anchorage, but if you lived through any part of the twentieth century up here, when avocados arrived off the barge, hard as the pits at their centers, you relish each trip to the vast cinder-block box of dreams known as Costco. All forty-eight in the case were packed with meat. Out each one popped under my spoon like a creamy, green baby butt headed to the bottom of the salad bowl.

Next came mayonnaise, then mashing. I didn't hurry. Carl's dog needed to run off her panic and aggression. And I needed not to envision a wonderful, loving couple arriving for the open house—the husband in dungarees from the office, the wife in beat-up XtraTufs because she wanted to wade around in the shallows and check out the dock for rot. Across the lawn they went, admiring the amazing lake views, telling Silver that the place was underpriced, actually, and sending their polite, unspoiled toddler to go catch minnows. At which point Carl's dog came charging in, fixated on a dragonfly she believed might be a mallard, knocking over the toddler and grinding him into the gravel beach.

I also needed not to think about Carl being sick, Carl not getting better, Carl having left, and how I had acted on the steps. He didn't have the money for a kennel, I suspected. Or for cancer.

Mashing avocados helped. I mashed away, thinking how RT—a man I yelled at daily for three years just because he wasn't Carl—once said, "Maybe the reason you shout so much, Dutch, is that you really long to whisper."

RT was an orthodontist, a World War II model airplane builder, and an observant man. But all I thought at the time was that if Carl had realized about the shouting instead of RT, he and I might still be together.

Luckily, I had moose ribs in the freezer. Labs are not spaniels or pointers, they don't have the upland sense of smell, and Carl's was deep in the alders. I couldn't call her over to my hand and grab her collar. She didn't know my voice, and I didn't know her name, and even if I had, a few hours in a kennel had no doubt left her suspicious of my motives. A rib tossed in the bushes and dragged in front of her nose, however, might kindle some interest.

All I needed was something to spice up that rib. My neighbor Candace Goddard was at home; I sighted her with the scope I kept in the kitchen. Candace's decor scheme is heavy on the chandeliers. Every room features at least one upside-down wedding cake made of cut lead glass, and this was generally how I found her when I needed her. Where the crystals wink.

It was ten a.m., two hours before the open house, and she was still in her nightgown, bumping into furniture. By the time I got over there, she was playing acoustic guitar. The guitar was supposed to help with her anxiety when her husband, Rodge, flew off to go sheep hunting and forgot to check in by sat phone every three hours. Stopping to call home while halfway up a shale-covered peak under a sky so blue you taste the color in your lungs pretty much ruins the moment. Not surprisingly, Rodge often forgot.

Candace was fiddling around on the guitar, picking out some prelude number by Johann Sebastian Bach. Like more and more of the younger wives on the lake, she had dealt with turning forty by investing in injections that left her with a stunned, rubberized expression. Her hair was many, many shades of high-voltage blond. Her guitar playing, however, told a different story. Listening to her was like listening to butterflies trip over each other's wings. You wanted them to flit around inside you for forever. This was one of the many reasons why we got along, and drove to book club together.

That day, unfortunately, the anxiety had gotten the upper hand. Her eyes were two dazzles of pupil. When I asked her to borrow a little medication from her supply, she answered me in her floaty voice. "Pills?" she said with a kind of delicious enjoyment of the word. "What kind?"

"The sleepy kind," I said. "Enough for a seventy-pound—well—female."

She looked out the window, as if the world beyond the glass was just one vast, sparkling diorama. "I think it's going to be fine, flying through the pass," she said. "What do you think?"

What I thought was that Rodge didn't put in enough flight hours, but had a great touch with short landings. The odds of him smashing his Cub into the side of a mountain were the same as anybody's: a matter of skill, luck, and weather.

It wasn't as if her concerns were that far-fetched. Flying in the wilderness, all your everyday, ordinary b.s.—being tired, being lazy, trusting the clouds instead of your instruments, losing your prescription sunglasses, forgetting to check your fuel lines—can kill you. And if it doesn't, a door can still blow off your plane and hit the tail or your kid can run between a brownie and her cub or your husband can slip on wet, frozen shale and fall a few thousand feet down a mountain, lose the pack and sat phone, break a leg, and that is that. Which is something you've got to live with, chandeliers or no chandeliers.

"I made him a checklist," she said as I rummaged through the bottles at the bottom of her purse. "Mixture. Prop. Master switch. Fuel pump. Throttle."

By the time she got to cowl flaps, I had long stopped listening. One of the biggest shames about Candace is that she still has a pilot's license. Her not flying, she said, started with kids, strapping them into their little car seats in the back and realizing there was nothing—nothing—underneath them.

Sometimes I wish I had known her before that idea took hold.

"Play me a song, Candace," I said. "It'll make you feel better."

"You know what Rodge doesn't like?" she said.

"Natives," I said, because he doesn't. He got held up for a "travel tax" by one random Athabascan—on Athabascan land—and now he is one of those cocktail-party racists who like to pretend to talk politics just so they can slip in how the Natives and the Park Service have taken over the state. He and I nod to each other at meetings for the homeowners association and leave it at that.

"Anal sex," she said, her voice as light as chickweed pollen. "He won't even try it."

"Look," I said, holding up a pill bottle. "How many of these things did you take?"

"I could live without him," she said. "I know how to waitress. I could get the kids and me one of those cute little houses off O'Malley."

I had some idea of what she was doing, only because I had done it myself, which was leaving her husband in her mind, in case he did die out in the Brooks Range—which he wasn't going to—so that, hopefully, she'd fall apart a little less. But the thing about having gotten divorced four times and widowed once is that people forget you also got married each time. You and your soft, secret, pink balloon of dreams.

"If you want anal sex, Candace," I said, "just drive yourself down to Las Margaritas, pick some guy on his third tequila, and go for it. Just don't lose your house in the divorce like every other woman on this lake. Buy him out. Send him to some reasonably priced, brand-new shitbox in a subdivision. Keep your property."

Beneath her bronzer, Candace looked a little taken aback. "Gosh, Dutch," she said. "I didn't mean to make you upset."

I shook a bunch of bottles at her. "Which are the sleepiest?"

She pointed to a fat one with a tricky-looking cap. "Was it Benny?" she said. "Was it because I brought up crashing in the pass?"

"I'm having a bad day," I said, but only because there was no way to explain how I felt about Benny, my first husband, crashing his Super Cub, or about the search for the wreckage, that smoking black hole in the trees. Even now, forty-one years later. The loneliness. The lostness.

Not to mention what it had been like, being the first and only female homeowner on Diamond Lake. If I had been cute and skinny and agreeable like Candace, it might have been easier. But I was me. The rolled eyes during votes, the snickers when I tried to advocate for trash removal or speed bumps, the hands, the lesbo jokes, the cigars handed to me in tampon wrappers—which I laughed about, seething, but smoked—I got through it all. What hurt the worst were the wives, all of them women I had known for years, who dropped me off their Fur Rondy gala list every time I was single. And stuck me back on when I wasn't.

Benny was a world-class outdoorsman and an old-school shot-gunner who did not believe in pretending that everybody got to make it to old age. On trips he took without me, he always said, "Dutch, if I don't come back, hold tight to Howl Palace."

Four-plus decades later, I still had my property, and it had come at a sizable cost. Wallace put me through a court battle after I left him for Carl. RT needed an all-cash payment to make him run away to Florida. Add to that Lon's rehab and Skip's long-term care. The Cub and the 185 were gone, all the life insurance money, the IRA. Howl Palace was all I had left. And now I had to sell it in order not to die in a state nursing home, sharing a room with some old biddy who liked to flip through scrapbooks and watch the boob tube with the volume cranked up high.

You can't cry about these things. But you can't sit around and contemplate them either.

Luckily, Candace's youngest boy, Donald, turned up at the top of the stairs. His electronic slab was tucked under his arm. "Where's the charger, Mom?" he said.

"Donald," I said. "Let's go fish for a dog."

"Donald has asthma," said Candace. "He can't handle a lot of dander."

"Get your boots on, Don," I said. "You, too, Candace."

"Really?" she said. "I get to come? Do I get to see the wolf room, too?"

For all the obvious reasons, I didn't like people on drugs in the wolf room. Or people with drinks, food, or mental issues. Despite our friendship, Candace had never seen it. "If you help me with these safety caps," I said. "And fine-tune the dosage."

* * *

DONALD WAS A LITTLE WHEEZY fellow with glasses attached to a sporty wraparound strap. He knew how to hustle, though, and stuck to my side as I laid out the plan. Your mom's job, I said, is to crush up some medicine and roll the moose rib in it. Your job is to take the spin rod I give you and cast the moose rib at the end of the line into the bushes. Then slowly, slowly reel it in. The minute the dog bites on the rib, you sit tight, play her a little. We'll have only a few seconds for me to grab her by her collar. Then we'll stick her in the kennel with the rib. Nighty-night.

Fifty feet from the house, I got a feeling. It was a sucker-punch feeling—my meal prep left on the deck. I started running. Donald ran, too, the way kids will, without asking questions, as if there might be matches and a box of free Roman candles at the end of it.

"Hey, guys?" said Candace. "Wait up." In her peaceful, free-wheeling frame of mind, she had put on Rodge's size 12 boots.

The last, short stretch of the path, I kept telling myself that I would not have taken the meat out and left it by the grill, that I would have not put the dishcloth over it to keep the flies off, that I could have, for some reason, left the meat in the fridge, even though everyone knows that meat can't be slapped cold on a hot fire, it needs to mellow out at room temperature. Except that I knew exactly what I had done and why I had done it—believing, at the time, I didn't own a dog.

I also knew what I was going to find, even as I ran through the backyard finding it: bits of gnawed plastic and butcher paper pin-wheeling all over the grass. Here a chunk of hot dog casing, there a lump of caribou burger. Blood juice dripped down the steps. The grill lay on its side on the deck, blue propane flames still burning.

I knelt down and turned off the valve. The birches were in their last, tattered days of September green. A leaf whirled down and landed by my foot. It was small, the yellow so fresh and bright it belonged on a bird.

"Dutch," said Donald. "I saw her! She ran right by me."

"Don't chase her," I said. "She'll think it's a game." I stayed down there, delaying the cleanup ahead, folding the leaf along the stem. The edges of it were tinged with brown.

Footsteps thunked across the deck. Carl's footsteps. Carl's boots. He had not taken off and left me with the dog apocalypse. This was so unlike him, it took me a little longer than it should have to understand. "Your animal," I said, "ate sixty pounds of meat."

"Most of it, she threw up," he said. "By the looks of the grass."

"I have an open house, Carl."

The flies were moving in—a throbbing blanket of vicious, busy bottle-green. With the sun out, the smell would be next.

"I could always run to Costco. Pick us up some steaks." His tone was kind, even understanding, but steaks were not what I wanted. And there was no way to explain what I wanted, which was everything the way it was years before. Neighbors in the backyard. Charcoal smoke. Bug dope. A watermelon. People showing up with a casserole, leaving with their laughter and wet hair after a dip in the hot tub. Whatever my private upheavals, there was always that at least.

A duck paddled past my dock, blown over by the current that was ruffling the surface. I missed wind socks. Everybody on Diamond Lake used to have a rainbow wind sock tied to their deck. It added a cheerful note to the shoreline.

"I had her by the woodpile," said Carl. "But she gave me the slip."

"I think you should go," I said. "Just go get your flight."

He shrugged, scratched a bit of dry skin on his neck. "I can get another."

"Right," I said. "The fishing trip to Houston."

He looked at me, as if ashamed, and I felt a little bad about calling out his lie. As far as he, I, and everybody we knew understood Houston, it wasn't even a city, just a mythical, cutting-edge treatment center, the Shangri-La of last-hope clinical trials. You went there to get a few more months to not die.

"Well," he said. "You got me, Dutch." He laughed. I didn't. Another leaf blazed down toward us. Fall lasts for weeks now—which, despite my best efforts, still befuddles me. All my life, fall took about three days in August, the leaves dropping almost overnight, followed by a licorice snow taste in the wind. Global warming, the papers say, though almost all the articles talk about are the dying caribou and the starving puffins, never the less obvious, alarming changes of every day and the guilt about living in an oil state that goes along with it. As if the rest of the country, sucking up all that oil, wasn't also to blame.

Donald ran by us, headed for the water with a moose rib in his fist. Candace followed with my snow shovel and a garbage bag. She was still in her nightgown. Watching her try to scoop raw-meat dog vomit off the grass while wearing a gauzy orgasm of white chiffon was one of the more moving experiences of my life. She really did want to help.

I sat down on the steps. Carl sat next to me, close, then an inch closer.

"Dutch," he said. "What a fucking corner we have found ourselves in."

I smiled. It felt like a small, broken snowflake in the middle of my face. There was a list of questions I was supposed to ask: what kind, what stage, what organ, herbal teas, protein smoothies? Instead an image floated through my mind. His trailer. His kitchen. The byzantine mobile-home cabinetry he built himself.

For each of the six days that we lived together, I lay there in bed every morning, watching Carl make coffee, memorizing where he had stuck the cups, the creamer, the filters, so that I could make the coffee for us one day—an idea that made me so happy I had to shut my eyes and pretend to be asleep.

It was September then too. Mushrooms bloomed in the corners of the walls. Carl scraped them down with a pocketknife he wiped clean with a chamois cloth. We made spaghetti and played gin rummy and dragged ourselves out of bed only for glasses of cold well water. I was careful where I left my clothes, though, careful not to leave them on the floor, where they would take up room. I had left Wallace. And the dog. And even Howl Palace.

On the morning of the seventh day, Carl sat me down and said, in the stiff, unsettled way he had adopted the minute I arrived, "It's just that I didn't know it'd be so close."

"Me neither," I said, still thinking he was talking about square footage.

How lonely it had to be, to realize that the only resource he had left—besides his trailer and a few truly world-class stuffed rainbows—was me. Maybe getting sick had made Carl softer. Maybe this was why he had shown up. Maybe this was why he had not left, despite my need for him, as fresh and pathetic as ever. The idea broke my heart, and into that jagged, bleak crevasse, all my fears rushed to fill the gap. "I'm out of money," I said. "Just so you know. In terms of helping you with your deductibles."

He looked at me—puzzled, or maybe stunned.

"Out-of-network is expensive," I said. "That's how it is, I hear, down in Houston."

"Dutch," he said. "And you wonder why we always go to shit." He stood up. He started walking down the backyard toward the dock, where Donald was standing with the rib tied to a length of frayed plastic rope he had found in the snow-machine shed.

"Wait," I said and stood up. "I'll keep your stupid dog."

"I don't want your money," he said. "And you don't even like her."

"Sure I do," I said. "She's kind of spirited, that's all."

"What's her name?" he said, not stopping, not slowing down in the least.

"Rita," I said. All his dogs were named Rita, one after another. He stopped to scrape some dog puke off the bottom of his boot. But he waved. "I call her Pinkie," he said. "After your secret balloon of dreams."

That was how I knew it was the last time we would see each other. Carl always liked to leave me a little more in love with him than ever.

* * *

EVEN BEFORE THE OPEN HOUSE had officially begun, people were pulling into the driveway. Silver had sprinkled baking soda all over the grass, then hosed down the entire yard. There was nothing else to do, she said, but hope for the best. One of her ways of hoping was to stick Donald down on the dock with his rib and his rope, where he would look like an imaginative, playful boy. Calling to his dog. With all the innocence of a kid in a lemonade commercial.

Candace was subject to a similar redecoration. Silver laid her in a deck lounger under a blanket, so it would look like she was just dozing, enjoying the sun. I sat beside her for a while, wishing she could get herself upright enough to come up to the wolf room with me, the way she had always wanted and the way I was finally ready to let her—high or sober or even just a little brain-dead from the chemicals. Carl was gone. I had no one. All over again.

I did consider pouring water on her face. But she was curled up on her side, her hands tucked under her cheek—not because her high had brought out the child in her, I saw only at that moment, but because the child kept surfacing despite the pills she took to keep it asleep.

There was nothing to do but tuck her in under the blanket and take the back stairs, which are the only stairs to the wolf room. The air in there is climate-controlled and smells just faintly of cedar from the paneling. I sat down in the middle of the skins and tried to look dignified, as if ready to answer any questions that a buyer might have. Questions that only I knew the answers to.

A young couple with matching glasses stopped in the doorway, looked in—politely, alarmed—and wandered off without a word. Over and over, this happened for the next few hours. A couple with fake tans. A couple with a baby. A couple with matching man buns. Single people and old people, apparently, didn't buy houses at my price point. Every time another couple turned up, I told myself to smile. Or invite them inside. Or leave so they could marvel at it openly. Or disparage it. Or discuss their plans to replace it with a master bath.

Silver had told me that it was better for the closing price

if the owner went out for lunch with a close friend during the open house. Now I knew why. Nobody was being unkind, but you couldn't tell, just by looking at it, that the wolf room used to be a nursery.

That's what it said on the plans that Benny and I ordered from Sears. The baby for the nursery didn't work out, the way it doesn't for some people. And so Benny and I did other things. He was tight with the Natives, as we called every tribe back then, as if they were all one big happy family or we just couldn't bother to learn the phonetics. His parents had been Methodist missionaries in the village of Kotzebue, trying to convert Inupiat until they had stumbled down to Anchorage, confused about their life's agenda. The Arctic Circle is not the place to go if you have even the slightest existential question.

That was something Benny always said. He knew Alaska better than me, mostly because I showed up on a ferry at age five, with a baby-blue Samsonite and a piece of cardboard hanging from my neck: FLIGHT TRANSFER TO ANCHORAGE. DELIVER TO MRS. AURORA KING. My parents had died in a head-on crash outside Spokane. Aunt Aurora was my nearest relative.

Aunt Aurora was a second-grade teacher in the downtown school district. She was deeply into young girls being educated in the ways of our Lord, and I met Benny at yet another Sunday at United Methodist. I was seventeen. He grabbed me the last shortbread cookie at coffee hour and spilled tea on his flannel shirt so we would have matching stains.

A week later he took me to the Garden of Eatin', which was located in a Quonset hut in a part of Anchorage I had never been to. It was the fanciest place I had ever eaten. Tablecloths on every table. Real napkins. We ate Salisbury steak and vanilla ice cream, and I was careful not to lick my plate. Two months later we were married.

Benny loved me, but he also loved men. He was not that different from a lot of guides and hunters at that time. They wanted to be out in the wilderness with another man without anybody seeing. For weeks. For whole summers. He never lied about it, I never asked beyond the minimum, and we never discussed it. We understood what marriage was—the ability to hold hands and not try to forgive the other person, not try to understand them, just hold hands.

After my fifth miscarriage, they removed my entire reproductive system while I was asleep and couldn't stop them. As soon as I was well enough to sit up, Benny dumped his shotgun buddy—a guy he had been affectionate with, in secret, for most of his life—and took me up to the snowfields to go after wolves.

"You have to have a taste for it," he said my first time. How else could he explain why you would shove your gun out the open window of a single-prop plane drilling hell for the horizon, your face a mask of eyes and ice, your hands so cold that when you aimed for the animal fleeing across the white, your fingers did not move the way they were supposed to. Or mine didn't. The first time, I cut my finger on the window latch and had to pull back on the trigger still slick with my own blood.

It was warm blood, at least. And I was alive. Despite any wish I might have had to be otherwise, which was maybe what Benny was trying to show me.

Most of this is to say that despite the local gossip, the wolf room was probably smaller than anybody at my open house expected. There are no windows. There is no furniture save 387 individually whittled pegs. On each peg hangs a pelt, most of them silver, black-tipped fur. Others reddish brown.

The ones staple-gunned to the ceiling are all albino white. The ones laid down on the floor are all females, with tails that can trip you if you don't watch out, though no one watches out. Walking into the wolf room is like walking into a forest of fur. Or a feathery winter silence that lets your brain finally go quiet.

"You'll never trust anyone like you trust your shotgun buddy," Benny told me the night before my first hunt. Though he did not say it, he was speaking about his shotgun buddy and how much he missed him and who I had to be for Benny from there on out.

Our fire was huge and fantastical in the flat, white dark. I was afraid of the morning and what might happen, and I wasn't wrong to be afraid. Shotgunning, as shooter, you have to aim into the wind and snow behind you—the plane going faster than the racing pack—while at the same time compensating for the dive of the plane, so that you not only don't miss the wolf but also don't get disoriented and shoot the propeller. And kill you both.

Up front, the pilot has to get so low to the ground and swoop at such radical angles to keep up with the pack—who keep spreading out over the snow like dots of quicksilver from a broken thermometer—but not stall and crash. And kill you both.

"Think about it this way," said Benny. "We live or die together." I was nineteen by then and he was the age I am now—sixty-seven. I held on to his words as though they were special to our situation, not an agreement you enter into with every person you ever care about. Even just in passing.

* * *

THOUSANDS OF FEET ABOVE HOWL Palace, Carl was on his way to Seattle, where, changing planes for Houston, he bought a balloon for a girl in a gift shop who was being rude to her mother. Downstairs, Candace was stumbling through some demonstration of my dimmers in the dining room, while her future next-door neighbor—Californian, all-cash, above asking—was pretending concern about "the whole hot tub, mold problem." A poorly constructed staircase below, Silver was sitting in the clamshell grotto, dipping her toes in the fountain, surrendering to what she felt, at that moment, was a lost commission.

Outside, at the far end of the dock, Donald went on tossing out his rope, calling across the water, "Here, Pinkie. Here, Pinkie," his voice squeaky with anticipation, his casts surprisingly sure-handed.

Pinkie, I almost told him, was long past coming to anybody. Pinkie was charging down the shoreline, trampling kiddie pools and sprinklers, digging into professional-grade landscaping while mothers chased after her with shovels and fathers contemplated lawsuits and the implications of those lawsuits at the homeowners association meeting—all of which they could avoid if they just jumped in the plane and took off for a few hours to remember why they had moved to Alaska in the first place.

The wind died down. Rainbows slicked along the shallows, bright with the smell of algae and avgas. Donald hardly noticed when I sidled up beside him, so intent was he on his task. He tossed out another cast—a perfect one, ending in a satisfying thunk as the rib hit the surface of the water. He cast again. And cast again. "Pinkie!" he said, unable even now to give up.

HIGH JINKS

THE MORNING OF THE FATHER-DAUGHTER float trip, Jamie's father has the horrors and can't leave the can. Jamie's mom runs Jamie down to the plane dock. Jamie still in her nightgown but with a rain jacket over it and hip boots underneath. Two pairs of ragg wool socks dangle limply from her pocket. A jumbo box of Cheez-Its leans out of the grocery bag falling from her arms.

"Junk food and dry feet!" says Katrina's dad. "What else does a girl in the wilderness need?" He lifts Jamie up into the cockpit of the 185, sliding her into the copilot seat.

In the wayback, Katrina is packed between duffel bags. She has one duffel under her feet and another on her lap. When Jamie's mom sticks her head into the plane, she blows a kiss at Katrina. Then another at Jamie. Then she says, "Don't be a sour sass. Your dad didn't mean to get so sick."

"Did we pack the TP?" says Katrina's dad. "Did we remember the extra tackle box?" Only later, after he climbs in beside Katrina, does he say quietly that she is going to have to share all her gear during the float trip, toothbrush included, as if she and Jamie are sisters. Then he says that since Jamie's dad was supposed to bring half of the dinners and lunches, Katrina will need to get on the stick when they hit the river and catch a salmon for them to eat.

Katrina would like to say that she and Jamie are already almost sisters, since her dad is always taking Jamie to Baskin-Robbins with them or to the movies or bossing Jamie around about honor roll and making her go to sleep during sleepovers. Even when Jamie already has a sister, as well as a three-wheeler, a fluffy white pound kitten, and a pair of diamond stud earrings. None of which Katrina has or will ever have.

Her dad, however, has mentioned more than once that he will not brook any unkindness on this trip. Jamie has to fend for herself in a house full of grown-ups that act like children. Jamie needs understanding, even when she fibs and won't let Katrina pet her kitten.

All this, Katrina knows, is why Jamie gets to sit up front by Jim the Pilot, where Katrina never gets to sit. Her dad settles in beside her, moving around the duffels to make room. One extra head-set dangles from the hook, but before he can hand it up to Jamie, Katrina slips it over her ears. The world goes fuzzed and silent. Dust bits trickle through the sunlight. A smear of slapped mosquito bloodies the corner of the map by her knees.

Before Katrina's mom left for forever, she always got the front seat. Her mom was best friends with Jamie's mom. And Katrina's dad was best friends with Jamie's dad. And Katrina was best friends with Jamie, even if Jamie didn't let her touch her diamond studs. They were twin families and each other's only real family, since their other families, with grandparents, lived thousands of miles away, in the Lower 48.

Now Katrina's dad doesn't want to be best friends with any-body. Or go over to Jamie's parents' big white house, across the lake from their house. Or tell holy-shit-hour stories while the moms all do the hustle on the deck. He wants to sit at home and tie flies. He agreed to the father-daughter float trip only because he and Jamie's dad and Jamie and Katrina have been doing the trip every July since Katrina was six and Jamie was seven. Each year on a different river. This time, their fourth time, they are floating the great and mighty Deshka.

Static crackles through Katrina's headset. Jim the Pilot talks to the tower about a southwest takeoff and another plane with priority at two o'clock. The backseat shudders under her thighs as he buzzes them over the water and up, up, up over the tree line at the end of the lake. The flats of Cook Inlet spread out below, along with the last of the Anchorage houses. Then Fire Island. Which is where Jim the Pilot finally gets on the mouth mike to fill in Katrina's dad on the high jinks that came to pass last night at Danny Bob's.

Danny Bob is Jamie's dad. Katrina keeps her breathing slow and quiet so they will forget she has a headset on too. The high jinks went as follows: Jim the Pilot stole the blue bear out of Danny Bob's living room. Danny Bob had brought down the bear last fall but shouldn't have, since the shot belonged to Jim the Pilot. As they had both agreed at the start of the trip.

The fact that Danny Bob had had the bear mounted and stuck it in his living room so that every blessed guest at the party could ooh and aah, congratulating Danny Bob on the kill of a lifetime, had been too much to stomach. Jim the Pilot waited until Danny Bob was lost to the sentient world, loaded the bear into the bow of his canoe, and headed home. Granted, this was an error in judgment. Somebody on the lake had to have seen him—and the bear—and that somebody was going to call Danny Bob.

"Well," says Katrina's dad, "maybe they mistook it for a dog."

"Buddy," says Jim the Pilot, "it's a blue bear."

"Jim," says her dad, "it's not a blue bear."

"It sure as Sunday is a blue bear," says Jim the Pilot.

There is a long, crackled silence. Then her dad says, "It's a blue cub."

And this is the end of the talking. Katrina's dad, even Katrina knows, has broken the rules, because even though Danny Bob's blue bear *is* a cub and too little to have shot, you are supposed to call it a bear. The blue bear is actually also more of a gray-white-tan color. It didn't eat enough glacier ice or blueberries or whatever bears eat that is supposed to turn them blue.

What makes something what it actually is—or what it isn't—is a subject Katrina has been thinking about a lot recently. Jim the Pilot, for example, really is a pilot. But all the dads on Diamond Lake are pilots. It's just that none of them get called pilots except Jim, because he has his instrument rating and owns more planes than the other dads say is tasteful. This is why he offered to fly Katrina and her dad and Jamie and Jamie's dad out to the put-in site on the Deshka, as a favor among friends.

But now he is so mad, he doesn't even offer to help unload. He stays in the cockpit, slapping at horseflies and picking at a hole in his chest waders. Katrina and her dad have to slosh through the thigh-high water with the raft and coolers and tent and duffels and rods, while Jamie sits on the float of the plane, bouncing her long curly brown hair over her shoulders as if to catch the sunlight in each strand.

Katrina's dad says, "Let's crack open those Cheez-Its."

Jamie holds out the box to him. "Take a few," she says in a drippy stewardess voice. "You need your strength."

When Katrina wades over, Jamie shakes her head. "Cheez-Its go straight to your hips."

"Suck my dick," says Katrina.

"Lesbo," says Jamie.

"Dildo-dingleberry-asswipe."

"You don't even know what that means." Jamie pops a single Cheez-It into her mouth—and sucks on it to make the flavor last, without ingesting calories. Yet another trick she learned from sixth graders.

"See you in a week," says Jim the Pilot, looking at the propeller instead of at her dad. "Noon. At the mouth."

"Seven days," says her dad. "Not five."

"I know what you mean by a week," says Jim the Pilot. "When I discuss the details of a trip, I pay attention. I don't handshake on something, then do something else."

"Seven days," says Katrina's dad. "At noon. At the mouth."

"I'll be there," says Jim the Pilot. "You've got the girls with you. And even if you didn't, I'm your friend, buddy—remember?" He reaches into his pocket and tosses Jamie something round and glinty. A coin. He tosses one to Katrina too. It is the size of a quarter but worth a dollar, with an angry old-lady face on one side. Susan B. Anthony. "Liberty," it says, "1981."

Katrina rubs the eagle on the back side of the coin, feeling the finely raised feathers and talons that make her think of the bumpy, embossed fruit on the edges on her mom's china. The china is broken and her mom is gone now for forever, but sometimes, inside her head, where nobody can see, Katrina wishes her mom would come back. Her mom didn't mind if she didn't fall asleep after books and good-night kisses. Her mom even woke her up sometimes for midnight popcorn. And told her things, grown-up things. Like that women are a woman's best friend. Or that girls like Katrina often blossom in college. And that men with the horrors are worthless. Men can't handle hangovers after age thirty-five. They've never had a baby and they just aren't used to adversity.

* * *

THE FIRST TWO DAYS OF the float are what Katrina's dad calls classic Alaskan summer. A steady drizzle hisses off the river; waves nibble at the sides of the raft. Save for the green of the birches and alders, everything is a thick, gloppy gray: the sky, the water, the rocks, the mud, the weeds where the mud has sloshed up and flattened them into matted lumps. Katrina's dad sits in the backseat of the raft, but the girls have to take turns up front, paddling.

Mostly, it is Katrina's turn. Her arms burn and grow leaden. Jamie sits in back, asking Katrina's dad if he's a Republican, if he thinks nuclear bombs are going to blow them all into black ash, if his parents named him William because they were related to English royalty way back in the past before they came to Alaska, if he wears V-neck or crewneck T-shirts, because the crewnecks are totally more chic.

Driftwood beach after driftwood beach slides by, almost no birds. They set up the tent in the rain and sleep with drops splatting onto their faces from the condensation. Water seeps into the sleeping bags from the seams where the tent sides meet the floor. They eat the bananas and hard-boiled eggs before they go bad. The yolks taste soggy, Jamie says. There is *no* way she can eat them. Katrina's dad orders her to eat them. They are not exactly swimming in food. They will catch a king tomorrow to supplement their rations.

* * *

THE SUN COMES OUT FINALLY, drying their gear. The air smells of spruce and hot new car from the raft rubber. There are no fish, or they are not fishing right, despite the detailed instructions that

Katrina's dad gives them: more weight, less drag, switch your Pixie to a Teaspoon to a big swively Mepps, let your lure bounce along the bottom but not land on the bottom and not float either. "Bump, bump, bump," he says. "Can't you feel it?"

Katrina can't feel it. At all.

"I can feel it," says Jamie, without any extra breathy stress on *feel*, despite her many late-night renditions of Rod Stewart's "Da Ya Think I'm Sexy?"—a song she performs with multiple shudders and all the wrong words, moaning into her hairbrush-microphone as if it was a big, thick, bristly penis, "If you really need me, just reach out and feel me."

Touch! Katrina has almost told her, a million billion times.

"That's the way," says Katrina's dad. "Work the water behind that rock." Katrina studies her fishing line floating down the river, so that she will not have to listen to her dad complimenting Jamie's backcast or praising Jamie's handling of a tricky snag.

"Katrina," says her dad, "ye who catches the first fish shall be the Great and Mighty Queen of the Deshka River."

Katrina watches as her lure pops up to the surface, but she doesn't recast. The water riffles, her lure bobs along. She is thinking about how her mom and Jamie's mom used to do the hustle on Jamie's deck in the summer. They did it barefoot, their high heels kicked off. They wore flowers behind their ears, and lipstick. They got all the other moms to do it with them. But Katrina's mother was the best. She was taller and wore a shimmery peacock dress, with her hair in curling-iron curls. She knew how to wave her arms and swish her hips, on top of all the other moves you did with your feet. Her dad liked to stand there and watch her like she all of a sudden had skin made of moonlight. All the other dads watched too. Until one time, the V-neck of her peacock dress slid all the way off her shoulder and she just kept dancing, and Katrina's dad grabbed her by the elbow and told her it was time to go home. Now. No stops at the bathroom, Diana.

"Tater Tot?" says her dad.

Tater Tot is the nickname Katrina's mom gave her. Her dad now calls her Tater Tot all the time. He makes her mom's zucchini bread and brushes her hair 101 times a night the way her mom used to. She loves her dad, her dad would never leave her, but watching him try to be her mom is harder somehow than when he was burning all her mom's clothes and records in their trash cans and kicking them, still burning, off the dock at the back of their house.

"Do you want to try my fly rod?" her dad says.

"I hate fishing," she says. "I hate fish." But even she knows her dad doesn't believe her. She can tie a blood knot in the dark. She can fish like nobody's business.

*   *   *

THEY PULL OVER AT A gravel bar. It's Katrina who has to sort out the poles and hold the end of the rain fly, putting up the tent. Jamie only has to gather wood for the fire, while Katrina's dad primes the stove. They are having spaghetti, but only because they are saving the Mountain House for tomorrow. After that, they have to catch a salmon.

Katrina's dad does not know that you are supposed to boil the water *before* adding the spaghetti to the pot and Katrina doesn't know this either. Katrina's mom might have known this, but she is in Homer doing coke off the ass of a guy named Derek, which Katrina heard about only because her dad had shouted it to her mom on the phone last winter, saying, "I hope you're doing coke off Derek's ass!"

Jamie heard Katrina's dad say this too. She was sleeping over, on Katrina's floor in a sleeping bag. The bedroom door was open and something jangled and crashed across the living room downstairs. Jamie did not say anything and kept not saying anything, until she finally came over to Katrina's bed and said, "Don't be gay. Move over." Then she slid in beside Katrina and wrote letters on her back—*S*'s, *T*'s, *X*'s, the easiest ones, so easy Katrina didn't need to stop crying to guess.

This is the Jamie that Katrina tries to remember while eating the spaghetti glop and watching Jamie wriggle into Katrina's last pair of dry pants. She slides up the zipper, then announces: "Time for the show!"

The show is a routine that Jamie performs in her room with the door closed, when Katrina is allowed to sleep over. Either she does the hairbrush number to Rod Stewart or a dance routine during which she humps the carpet and leaps around doing full splits. The last few times, it has also included a part for Katrina where she is the lady at the party and Jamie is the stud and they go on a date to a water bed and kiss with tongues until Katrina finally sits up and says she has to pee or she feels like playing Atari.

Out here on the river, the show is different. Jamie sits on a rock with a sad, romantic look on her face and sings, "Sunshine on my shoulders makes me happy. Sunshine in my eyes can make me cry." She has a voice that makes little sparks float up Katrina's spine. Katrina's dad looks at her like she belongs in one of the scrapbooks that he pulled out from the trash-can fire at the last minute. The ones where all the rubber cement melted, leaving the pictures of the three of them smiling on a mountaintop or by the old VW camper bus covered in a honey-colored ooze.

"Katrina," he says, "why don't you sing us something?"

Her favorite song goes "You gotta know when to hold 'em, know when to fold 'em." It's from *The Gambler*, her favorite record. But nothing about Kenny Rogers is romantic. She tries to think of another song, one that makes shivers float up your spine, one that makes everybody cry and think of their old dead hunting dogs.

"Don't worry," her dad says. "I never had much of a singing voice either."

* * *

ON THE THIRD DAY, TWO successive emergencies arise. Katrina gets her boot stuck in quickmud, which is like quicksand only thicker, and pulls out her foot, leaving the boot and sock still stuck inside it. Her dad has to dive around in the frigid, murky shallows trying to find it, which he finally does—just as Jamie announces she needs a new ponytail holder; her hair is naturally thick and will get knots requiring a mayonnaise treatment if she does not pull it back off her face. Katrina's dad is still in his wet clothes. Mud leaks down his face. A whitefly bites him on the shoulder. He shouts that Jamie can pull her hair back with a goddamn twig. A hairdo is not an emergency.

Katrina smiles inside, where no one can see. But for the rest of the day, Jamie sticks by Katrina in the raft, whispering with her like they are best friends again, even if Katrina is only in fourth grade and embarrassing around her fifth-grade friends. They give Katrina's dad the evil-dictator eyes. They call him Sir. Then Admiral Bossy.

He almost notices, but not really. He is fishing all the time. He is a master fisherman. Everybody says so. He is famous back in Anchorage, especially at the fly-tying store. There is a chair by the woodstove that says "Will" on the back of it so he can sit down and tell stories to customers.

All there is for lunch is granola bars and the rest of the Cheez-Its.

"What we really need is a king," says Katrina's dad. But he would take a dog salmon at this point, any kind of salmon. All he brought was food for two people. Back in the plane, in his mind, two girls made one person and he was the other. When did girls start eating so much?

"We're animals," says Katrina. "Me eat meat. Me no want stinking granola bar."

"I don't mind granola bars," says Jamie. "They're really quite delicious."

"Thank you, Jamie," says Katrina's dad. "That's very gracious of you."

Katrina sits in the bow of the boat, pretending to nap, listening to Jamie ask question after question about the lame, boring fishing knots, while Katrina gets sunburn all over her nose. That night, she is surprised when Jamie asks to sleep next to her and whispers, "I wish we really were sisters, don't you? Don't you wish this float could go on for forever with just me and you and your dad?"

Katrina doesn't know what to say. Most of the time, it is her wishing that she could live with Jamie at her house with Jamie's dad and Jamie's mom and Jamie's sister, where everything is still like it was before. Jamie's mom lets Jamie and her sister stay home from school for "snuggle days" and lets them stay up late on party nights, even if they steal people's olives and orange slices and scoop hot tub bubbles into drinks the grown-ups leave on tables.

Jamie's face looks sad and alone, even if Katrina is right there. She tries to comb Jamie's hair with her fingers. "Is your mom on coke too?" she says.

"My mom just sleeps," Jamie says. "And my dad is never there unless people are over."

Katrina is confused. She loves Danny Bob. Danny Bob hugs her. Danny Bob calls her a pistol and says she looks just like her mom, even in front of her dad. Nobody is allowed to talk about her mom. It's not a rule exactly. Except that it is.

"Forget it," says Jamie. "Your dad, like, worships you and tucks you in."

* * *

THE MORNING OF THE FOURTH day, a plane buzzes by overhead. It's a Super Cub—white with red stripes down the sides. It swoops over them, around and around in circles. Jamie is the first to wave. "It's Dad!" she says. "Hey, Dad!" She starts jumping up and down.

"We're on a river," says Katrina's dad. "He can't land on a river."

"He'll land," she says. "He can't bear to be without me."

And just at that moment, the plane banks and starts to lower in the sky, headed not for their gravel bar, but for somewhere behind them, deep in the alders. "There's not enough clearance—" says Katrina's dad. But there is a bump, skid, the sound of branches crashing, the whine and roar of a propeller. Then nothing.

"For the love of Christ," he says, and hands Katrina the rifle, safety on. "The chest," he says, pointing to his chest. "Not the head. And don't shoot at a goddamn bear until you see it—really see it— and only if it charges. Got it? There's no shame in letting it trash the camp and wander off with everybody not mauled."

Katrina nods.

He pulls out a hatchet, sprays himself with bug dope, checks the pistol in his chest holster. Off he goes. For a while, Katrina sits with the gun by the cooler. But nothing comes out of the bushes. She puts the rifle down.

Jamie starts prancing around in her hip boots doing the sizzle, sizzle, burn dance. Then she wades out a little and casts. Katrina throws a rock at her but misses. Just then, Jamie's rod bends. A tail slaps the surface. She has a fish. A big one.

"It's a king!" she yells. "It's a king!"

"Don't let it go down by the ripples," says Katrina. "Pump and reel."

"I know what I'm doing," said Jamie.

Jamie does know what she's doing. She works the fish down the bar, letting it out and reeling it in, keeping her tip up, her drag tight but not too tight. Then she backs up, slowly dragging it onto the beach. It is more than big; it's huge: thirty pounds or even forty—and the first and only fish of the trip. Katrina tries to remember where the bonker is. The bottom of the tackle box. But Jamie just grabs a rock and bashes it on the head, the fish shuddering and trying to bounce off the gravel until she gives it a final smash. Dead. Down to its imploded eye.

"Victory!" says Jamie. "I'm the Great and Mighty Queen of the Deshka."

Katrina slowly goes over to the fish, touches it with her boot toe. Jamie knows it all and has it all, and now she has Katrina's dad too. Some girls get married to old guys. She has seen it on *60 Minutes*. Iranian girls the same age as her.

* * *

OUT OF THE ALDERS COME their dads, crashing through the branches and tossing their hatchets onto the gravel. They pull off their clothes and jump into the water—a black cloud of mosquitoes following them like smoke. "Fuck, fuck, fuck," says Danny Bob. They've been bitten on the eyeballs! They've been bitten on their balls!

Katrina's father says nothing. His face is grim, swollen, and smeared with bug guts and blood.

Jamie holds up her king by the gill cover. "Look what I got, gentlemen," she says.

Danny Bob is the first to see. He spits out a mouthful of water. "Jamie," he says, "there's no need to fib."

"I'm not fibbing."

"Katrina," says Danny Bob, "did you get that fish?"

Katrina thinks a little. Then she says slowly, in the kind, generous voice of her school librarian, "It doesn't matter who caught it. We all can share." The lie hangs there golden and perfect in the silence, and the smile that both dads give her for catching such a huge and amazing fish is like the minute before you go downstairs at Christmas, when all the presents can still be anything you've ever wanted. Even a kitten.

Jamie stomps off down the river. "I know how to fish," she yells. "Katrina's dad taught me when you weren't here. Again!"

"Jamie," says Danny Bob, "did I ever tell you the one about Pinocchio?" The gist of it is, when Pinocchio told a tall one, he got spanked.

* * *

THAT NIGHT THEY GUT THE king—a male, no eggs—and build a fire. Katrina's dad jerry-rigs a grill out of green wood and they eat the fish on paper plates. Danny Bob has a trash bag filled with Irish emergency supplies. He hands both girls two cans of Coke from the trash bag, then takes out a bottle of whiskey that he cracks open with his mouth. He sloshes it into two cups. The dads cheer and tip it back. Then they tip back another one, which Katrina's dad never does, since his rule now that her mom is gone for forever is two half glasses of white wine, period. One before dinner. One with food.

They eat a little of the salmon, then Danny Bob says, "Well, this is one for the holy-shit story hour." He points to his head, where the holy-shit story hour is recorded for retelling later, when it's funnier and the repairs to the plane are long paid off. They drink some more whiskey and talk about what kind of idiot would try to land on a strip of sand and gravel less than 150 feet long, most of it covered in alders.

"Time for the show," says Jamie.

Danny Bob sucks off the bottle, hands it to Katrina's dad.

"Dad!" says Jamie. "Pay attention! You have to watch."

"I'm paying attention," says Katrina's dad. "Me first." His eyes are bright, his hair standing up from the muddy water that dried in it. He does the hula dance that he, Katrina, and her mom learned in Hawaii when she was six: "Along the beach at Waikiki," *hip, hip, hip,* "a handsome stranger waits for me," *hip, hip, hip.*

Danny Bob does a jig he learned growing up in shantytown Oregon. Even with his waders on, he keeps his back very straight and his feet moving. "Take that," he says, and points at Katrina. Katrina blinks, everybody looking at her, the fire smoky and hot. She doesn't know the words to "Sunshine on My Shoulders," except for the chorus. She doesn't know anything. Her mind is a big empty field with fireweed fluff blowing through it—until it comes to her.

"If you want my body, and you think I'm sexy . . ." She wriggles around like Jamie does, raising her hands like the moms do when they do the hustle on the deck. Danny Bob is laughing. Jamie is clapping until, out of nowhere, something hits Katrina, hard and fast.

She falls back a little and looks at her arm. Down on the ground is a can of Coke, a full one. Her dad's face is white and flat and he says, "I don't ever want to see you do that again."

Katrina will not cry. She will not.

"What the fuck?" says Danny Bob.

"She was only dancing," says Jamie.

Something about their sticking up for her only makes it worse. Katrina sits down. She pulls her knees in front of her face.

"Will," says Danny Bob. "You're over the line. You're messed up in the head."

"*I'm* messed up?" says her dad. "You're too hungover to get in the goddamn plane. You threw your daughter at me like a sack of dog kibble. In her nightgown."

Danny Bob stands up, swaying a little. He grabs Katrina's dad and hugs him. Her dad tries to struggle his way out, but Danny Bob is taller, stronger; they both fall over. They roll over and over almost to the river, where Danny Bob sits on her dad and pins his arms down to the gravel. "Give in," says Danny Bob. "Give in, you sadsack fucking fuck."

Her dad turns his head so that Katrina can't see him. He is crying—big heaving sobs unlike any Katrina has seen before. "I'm sorry," he says.

Danny Bob rolls off him. "I miss you," he says. "We all miss you."

The look on her dad's face is strange, distant. "It's not like I died."

"No," says Danny Bob. "You didn't. Let's keep it that way." He pulls out a crooked cigarette and lights it, sucks in, passes it to Katrina's dad.

"Dad," says Jamie, "you promised Mom no smoking."

"This here is a peace pipe," says Danny Bob. "A peace pipe is different. Suck on the peace pipe, Will."

"Time for bed, girls," says Katrina's dad. But he doesn't climb into the tent with Katrina and Jamie. He sits down by the fire and picks up the whiskey bottle. Danny Bob puts his arm around him.

* * *

LONG AFTER DARK, KATRINA HEARS a rustling, a thud. She feels for her dad's back. His sleeping bag is empty. The gun is there and Danny Bob is there but he will not move, even when she shakes him again. He goes on sleeping, just like Jamie. She takes the gun and checks that it's loaded and unzips the front door very slowly, moving with the barrel pointed at the ground. The rustling out there is her dad. He is crouched by the fire, staring up at the sky. Stars glint through the cloud cover. Trash litters the sand at his feet—an oily sardine tin, an empty jar of peanut butter, a package of Nutter Butters. He has eaten almost everything in the dry box, even though he is always the one saying to portion out the food to last the whole trip. Something is wrong with him. Maybe he has the horrors, which Katrina has never seen before, only heard about in the morning. She is a little worried. His eyes are bloodshot.

"I love you," he says. "You know that, right?"

She picks up the paper and plastic, throws them into the fire, just in case of bears. Jamie's king is cached and safe in the locked metal cooler way, way down the beach. "Katrina?" says her dad.

His face is soft, somehow pleading in a way that makes her want to not look at him. "I shouldn't have asked your mom to leave," he says. "Now she won't come back."

The last time Katrina saw her mother, Katrina was in the part of the den near the breakfast bar, where you can see inside the kitchen. Her mom was by the refrigerator. It was so far past bedtime, there was a rainbow on TV.

A milk crate with her mom's records was under her mom's arm and in her other hand, the lamp from the living room. She wanted the china. Her dad had the china. He was sitting on the counter throwing plates to the floor, aiming for her mother's feet.

"It's mine," her mother said. "It was my mother's."

Her dad threw another one. It missed. He threw another one. It missed too. The broken pieces bounced off the linoleum, gold and winky. Her mom had to dance around to keep from getting cut on the ankle. "That's it," he said. "That's how you do it. Take this one!" Smash. "And this one!" Smash. "And this one!" A thud, him jumping off the counter. "Get the fuck out."

There was a pounding on the front door, but Katrina waited a long time before she unlocked it. The guy on the daisy mat was a grown-up only wearing a leather jacket and not old like her parents. He leaned down and ruffled her hair. But didn't go into the kitchen to help her mom. He went into the living room instead and took the stereo speakers, then the chair from Seattle. There was more yelling from the kitchen, more crashes. Each time he took something out to the car, he looked at Katrina and put a finger over his mouth: *Shush*.

When her mom finally ran out of the kitchen, Katrina thought for a minute that she would scoop her up and take her too. Katrina was small. She could fit in the car. Or her mom could leave the records and give her the backseat, in the middle.

But her mom only hugged her. "That china is yours," she said. She handed her a broken piece, as if it were something beautiful and famous. It had oranges on the edge, and apples, and a horn of plenty. Her mother smelled of sweat and rotten pj's. There was a little crackled star in her eye where a vein had broken.

Katrina touched her just under that eye, on the dark circle. "Does it hurt?" she said.

"Autumn," her mother said. "That's the name of the pattern." The guy pulled her on the elbow. The two of them backed toward the car, her mother waving. A little medal on the rearview mirror swayed when they hit the bump of the street and drove away.

The fire pops. Katrina's dad looks up at her.

"I don't want her to come back," says Katrina. She is surprised when she says this, and not sure if she even means it. But it sounds good. It sounds hard and solid, like when you pitch a too-big rock into the river and it lands with a thunk, as if it somehow could break water.

* * *

THE NEXT MORNING KATRINA'S DAD walks straight into the river to dunk his head. Danny Bob is whistling and firing up the propane stove for coffee. He gets the raft loaded, the tent broken down. The coffee boils over and he strains it through one of Jamie's socks, then banks the fire with sand. "Tally ho, darling!" he says to Katrina's dad. "Load up."

"What about the Cub?" says Katrina's dad. "You're not just going to leave it."

"I'll paddle down with you. Jim the Pilot can fly me back later. We'll chainsaw out the Cub, chop-chop."

Katrina's dad drops his head underwater for another dunk.

"That is exactly the kind of detail you might have mentioned before we whacked around in the bush for three hours trying to free your goddamn plane by hand."

* * *

LUNCH ON THE RIVER IS salmon. And salmon fat. And salmon skin. "I had peanut butter in that trash bag," says Danny Bob. "And cookies. Before somebody got the munchies."

They still have twenty-plus pounds of salmon. They have only three days left on the trip. They will be fine. Except that the thickest parts of the king are still half-raw, the skin blistered. Every bite tastes like the bottom of the river. "I'm not hungry," says Jamie. "How far left do we have to go?"

"Eat around the edges," says Katrina's dad. "Protein is your friend."

Danny Bob sighs. There is an inch of Wild Turkey left in the bottle. He drinks it down for the vitamins.

* * *

RIVERS, KATRINA'S DAD ALWAYS SAYS, are moody. They have their up days, their down days, their sad days, their angry days. The Deshka almost stops moving after the next bend. The current is so slow that they have to keep floating until it's dark, just to make up the lost miles.

"Jim will wait a day," says Danny Bob. "He's not the type to panic."

"If you say so," says Katrina's dad. "Our exchange was less than amicable."

"Is there anybody you won't get pissy with?"

"I told him I would be there. I don't make one deal at the beginning of a trip, then change it on a whim."

Danny Bob gives him a look. "Well," he says, "that's good to hear. I wouldn't want you to all of a sudden change your lifestyle and get judgmental about everybody else."

Katrina's dad begins to paddle. He paddles hard. He paddles without singing. He is good at the silent treatment, Katrina's mom used to say. What she used to do is go downstairs and start playing 33 rpm records on the 45 rpm speed until he had to laugh and let her apologize.

* * *

ANOTHER DAY SLUDGES BY. THEN another. The rain kicks in. They eat salmon for breakfast, they eat salmon for lunch, they eat salmon for dinner, and still they float on. Both dads are paddling now. Jamie's dad keeps wondering if they missed the take-out. Maybe there was a tributary that Katrina's dad miscalculated with the map. "I doubt it," says Jamie. "Will is far too conscientious."

All three of them look at her. She makes an innocent face.

"Jeez," Danny Bob says. "What the hell happened while I was back in town?"

"Maybe they're old enough to call us by our names," says Katrina's dad.

"Not to stand on ceremony," says Danny Bob, "but I prefer Uncle Will. Or Mister Will. Or something along those lines with some authority."

"Maybe Will and I know each other better than you think," says Jamie. "Maybe we no longer need to rely on such silly old-fashioned formalities."

Danny Bob pulls back on his paddle. The raft stops, as if shot. He looks at Katrina's dad, who shakes his head. But Danny Bob wheels them around and heads toward the shore. Jamie hunches lower in the seat. "It's not like you even know what my favorite color is," she mumbles. "Or my favorite lure."

Danny Bob paddles. The raft bumps up against the gravel. "In or out," says Danny Bob.

Jamie hunches down. "You never know if I have homework," she says. "Or make me eat hard-boiled eggs."

"In or out."

Danny Bob would not really leave Jamie on a gravel bar, would he? He is her dad. But his face is not kidding. And Jamie isn't even telling him to shut his ugly old piehole, the way she always does. She is looking at Katrina's dad as if he's supposed to tell Danny Bob to stop being so mean or remind him that Jamie's favorite color is orange, which is why she orders the orange sherbet at the Baskin-Robbins, even when Katrina and her dad try to make her order mint chocolate chip.

Katrina looks at her dad too. But he just looks away as if he were in another raft or at a restaurant looking out the window instead of at some table full of loud, embarrassing strangers. Katrina will remember this moment forever. Always hoping that her dad didn't mean not to stand up for Jamie, that he was just about to tell her to hop back in the raft and stop being so melodramatic. And always knowing that he had told her nothing, that he had let her stand there on the gravel shivering, so openly afraid that Katrina couldn't look anymore either. And turned away.

A dragonfly lands on the side of the raft and nobody whacks it off with a paddle. "In or out," says Danny Bob.

Jamie slinks back into the middle seat and doesn't cry and

doesn't cry. And doesn't get out. "Good," says her dad. And pushes off.

Once they are a few bends down the river, Jamie says she has a chill and that "it's probably hypothermia." Katrina only watches the dragonfly, glued to the raft by the rain and wet. She still loves Danny Bob, even if she doesn't want to. How can he not know what Jamie's favorite lure is? It is a Rooster Tail, which she likes for the feathers, even if it is less than reliable at attracting the attention of the kings. That is why Jamie hardly ever catches a king. Until this trip, when she finally listened to Katrina's dad and tied on a Teaspoon.

* * *

THE TALK FOR THE LAST day goes: chicken-fried steak, steak with French fries, fried chicken, lemonade, biscuits with sausage gravy, baked potatoes with sour cream, mashed potatoes, potatoes gratin, potato chips, onion dip, Cheetos, guacamole, ribs, enchiladas. There is no arguing, no conflict, except when Jamie declares that she will not split a chimichanga with a side of beans with Katrina, and Katrina says she's selfish and chimichangas are too big to eat by yourself. And her dad says he will hit both of them on the head with his paddle, except they are all too tired of paddling and sick of salmon and don't know what the hell they are saying.

"A Seven and Seven," moans Danny Bob. "On the rocks."

* * *

IT IS THREE-THIRTY ON THE Friday that Jim the Pilot is supposed to meet them at the mouth. He may have left already. They are six hours late. And for those whole six hours, they paddled and paddled and paddled.

When they arrive, Jim the Pilot is sitting on the float of his 206, drinking a Dr Pepper. He lifts it up at them. Cheers. "Do you have food?" says Danny Bob. "Food that is not salmon?"

Jim the Pilot tosses them a bag of cashews. The cashews are sweet and salty. The most amazing cashews in the world. Katrina eats them by the handful, and so does Jamie. They eat them down to the grease on the bag. Neither of them argues about who is hogging.

It feels good to sit back in the raft, licking slick, rich cashew fat off their fingers. The sun blazes by from behind a cloud and the world is filled with golden gnats. Jim the Pilot holds out his hand, as if Katrina were a princess he was escorting over the pesky puddle between the raft and the float of the plane. She climbs into the cockpit and, as the first one in, gets the front seat. Not just the front seat, but the pilot's front seat. She turns around to get a puke bag from the back in case she has to throw up later.

There is a bear in the backseat staring at her. His eyes are glossy brown glass. His coat is gray but tinged with blue in the sunlight the way her old velveteen comforter looked either yellow or gold depending on the direction of the sun through the window. Katrina pats him on the muzzle. Little tiny bumps pimple his nose.

"My blue bear!" says Danny Bob, knocking on the pilot side window.

Through the passenger's window, Jim the Pilot is giving Danny Bob the finger. Katrina's dad pushes his finger down, saying, "Not funny."

"Kathy wouldn't let me keep it at the house," says Jim the Pilot.

"Because it's a cub," says Katrina's dad. "And your wife is right."

"It's just that attitude," says Jim the Pilot, "that inspired me to take it to your house and store it in the garage. But *somebody* was already there. With a van. And a guy, hustling down the driveway, your microwave stuck under his leather jacket." He does a little dance down the float, demonstrating.

Katrina sinks down in the pilot seat. The blue bear is somehow looking at her, the way usually only normal stuffed animals can. Not ones with real fur and real claws. Snoopy. Sad Giraffe. String Snake. She is too old for stuffed animals, but sometimes they are okay when you are alone and nobody can see you. The blue bear is like this. He is sad with her about the *somebody*, who is really just Katrina's mother, coming over because she just leaves and comes back whenever she feels like it. Or because she doesn't want to see Katrina. Or because Katrina slowed her down the last time and almost got her caught.

A little dead light explodes in her heart. The blue bear sees it somehow. Maybe. Even as her dad kicks the passenger side of the plane. "You didn't stop that somebody?" he says to Jim the Pilot.

"I didn't know I was allowed, buddy. It's not like you tell me what's going on."

Katrina slides down to where the pedals are—right, left, stick for up and down. There is a lot of shouting. "Jim," says Danny Bob, "you didn't have the shot. I did."

"It's my blue bear," says Jim the Pilot. "We shook on it."

"Was anybody with that *somebody*?" says Katrina's dad. "In that van?"

Nobody is listening to him except Katrina, hidden down by the pedals, who is thinking what her dad has to be thinking: how her mom never liked the microwave, because it cooks your brains. And how her mom made real popcorn when she made midnight popcorn, with real butter, on the stove. Or how her mom kissed all her toes in the bathtub. And how her mom smelled like Estée Lauder in the blue bottle on the sink.

One day when Katrina grows ups, she will be like Jamie. Nonchalantly flinging her curling iron curls. She will laugh. She will say to her dad that her mom was only pulling some late-night high jinks. Don't be such a crybaby, she will say. Just steal the goddamn microwave back. Or go over to where Mom lives and fill it with marshmallows, Wild Turkey, and some shotgun ammo. Then turn it on high for three minutes.

Right now, she only climbs back up into the seat and gives the blue bear a scratch. The fur behind his ears is rough and smells like skin. She can't see her face, but she is not an idiot. It looks like her dad's face, soft and weepy. She will always look soft and weepy, she will always be soft and weepy as long she is always around him and always remembering everything that is gone now, not even for forever the way her dad promised. Everything comes back, over and over.

Outside on the bank, Jamie is eating what looks like a 100 Grand bar that Jim the Pilot has just tossed in her direction, while still arguing with Danny Bob. His point is: Three men, two girls, a blue bear, and all their gear will be too heavy for a 206. They will have to make two trips.

Danny Bob will not let Jim the Pilot take off with his blue bear.

Jim the Pilot will not let Danny Bob stay on the water with it.

It is Katrina's dad, they both decide, who will stay with the bear. He is the only neutral party and gets off on being Mr. Responsible. Jim the Pilot and Danny Bob want to drop the girls off in town, together, and fly back faster than you can spit, together, at which point they can all sort this out as friends.

The only person who doesn't seem to understand the plan is

Katrina's dad. He hops on the float, motioning to her to hop down, while Jim the Pilot and Danny Bob unload the bear onto the beach. "Let's get that raft deflated," he says to Katrina through the window.

Before she can get out of the cockpit and not get in trouble for dawdling, the door thunks open. It's Jim the Pilot. "Scoot over," he says to Katrina.

Katrina scoots. She still has a front seat, even if it's the passenger one. And when Danny Bob and Jamie climb in, Jim the Pilot flips Jamie into the back, before she can even try to complain. He hits the ignition, then says to Katrina, "Your dad wants you to stay and help with the raft."

Katrina thinks for a minute. Then she yells over the propeller, "Screw that. Let's go back to Danny Bob's and do the hustle on the deck."

Jim the Pilot laughs. And Danny Bob laughs, too, as he climbs in the back next to Jamie. Katrina is a pistol, he says. Katrina has a sense of humor. He doesn't say that her mom had a sense of humor, too, but only because the side window is open and Katrina's dad can still hear.

Jim the Pilot yells through the window, "We're taking your daughter, buddy! Keep the blue bear! Even trade!" He hits the throttle and pulls out. Everything, for once, is finally perfect. Katrina has the front seat. And Jamie has the back.

Katrina's dad is shouting over the engine noise, waving from the bank. She looks at him, but he is looking at her like *You better hop out right now, young lady*. She hunches down. She slips her headset on. The rubber foam sucks over her ears and she can't hear him. In the wilderness, there is no tower that you have to ask for permission. You can just take off, anytime you want, as long as you go fast enough to get above the trees.

NOBODY GETS OUT ALIVE

GETTING PAST THE MASTODON TOOK planning. The great plated skull was wedged between the fireplace and the credenza, leaving the two ivory tusks splayed across the carpet where a coffee table belonged. To exit the wedding party, guests either stepped over one tusk, then the other—a choice that required skillful footwork and a certain level of sobriety—or jumped over both with an awkward, last-minute leap.

This late in the evening, the leaping had become more frequent. And more flamboyant. Guest after guest soared over the mastodon tusks—feetfirst, faces joyful, landing in the foyer without the slightest injury to their ankles. At which point they hugged Carter. And asked him how he had met the bride. Or what he loved about her. Or if the two of them had considered . . . well . . . little Carters and Katrinas!

Carter improvised a light, evasive laugh, handed them a bag of candied almonds, and thanked them for coming. Though no one seemed to notice, Katrina had not spoken to or even looked at him since the start of the party. Save during the cake-cutting ceremony, when she had fed him a forkful of frosting that had the same cold, white, dead-flavored consistency as her smile.

At this point, she was no longer in the living room. Or anywhere in sight. Carter had said so many things he now regretted, things he would go back and change if only that were possible. Which it wasn't. Time slogged on, as the mastodon well knew. Both its empty sockets were as expressive as eyes—huge, soulful, slightly depressed. No doubt due to the elephant lurking in its genetics. You never saw an upbeat elephant. They were like donkeys: charismatically morose.

The idea of owning such an animal had never occurred to Carter, and his failure of imagination felt more and more as it should have—like a failure. What did a three-piece sectional really say about your understanding of the universe? He and Katrina had a three-piece sectional, plus a matching ottoman that she called a poof.

"Carter!" said Neil by the fireplace, holding up an empty glass. Carter held up a bag of almonds. Cheers!

Several times, he had been tempted to tell Neil about his argument with Katrina. Neil was her oldest friend from childhood. He would know what to do. Or how to make her less upset. He had a swashbuckling kind of generosity, a way of walking through the crowd that inspired laughter or a fresh round of clinking glasses in every group of guests he passed. It was Neil who had dug the mastodon out of the permafrost with a pick and shovel. And Neil who had built his log-cabin mansion—by himself, after work and on the weekends. When he found out that Katrina and Carter had been married in New York—at city hall—he insisted they let him throw a party. In Alaska. With all of Katrina's hometown friends and neighbors.

Now he was heading in Carter's direction. Carter gave the mastodon a little pat. The skull was polished and warm to the touch. Except where a few chunks of missing bone had been patched with soldered bronze.

"Buddy," said Neil. "Let's blow the stink off."

"I'm good," said Carter. "I'm saying our goodbyes."

"Katrina's ice-skating," said Neil.

Carter smiled, as if he knew this already. Then followed Neil across the living room, trying to keep up with his discussion about his stepdaughters: Both were towheads. Twins. Competitive figure skaters.

Neil stopped at a glass door, slid it open, and ushered Carter out to a snowy deck. The cold was soul blasting, fantastical, a gasp of winter in each breath. Neither of them was wearing shoes. Not that Carter mentioned this.

"The two of you need to move up here!" said Neil. "We could be neighbors!"

Carter nodded—and, for a moment, almost agreed. The lake at the back of the house was glazed with moonlight, the sky a dream astronomy of stars.

"Lake ice is too bumpy to skate on," said Neil. "Even if you flood it and refreeze. Plus you have the air traffic." He pointed to the tiny planes on skis that were parked along the shoreline, their noses wrapped in padded blankets. "I put in a practice rink for the girls. Moved the helicopter into a hangar." This was pricey. Inconvenient. But better vis-à-vis the homeowners association. Landing pads in the backyard always upset the neighbors.

Carter's feet were finally numb enough to move. He inched closer to the railing—and could not believe for a moment what he was seeing. Katrina was down on the rink. But skating the way that someone from the tropics might, someone who had never seen a snowflake.

Around the wall she went, shuffling and hunched and hesitant, her arms outstretched. The look on her face was unmistakable.

Carter understood it all too well: She hated ice-skating and hated being lousy at it but hated quitting more. She would go around and around that rink, miserable and forcing herself on for reasons he could only assume had to do with marching up mountains as a child, and conquering foreign equity markets, and believing, above all else, in pointless personal accomplishment. A belief that he did not share, but that did make him feel so tender toward her. She was unlike anyone he had ever met. And he had ruined their wedding party. "Katrina?" he said.

She looked up, squinting through the floodlights.

"Katrina!" said Carter. "I'm . . ." But before he could apologize for what he had said and how he had said it—her eyes widened, her skates kicking out in front of her. Down she went, in a flurry of cocktail dress and flailing limbs.

"Are you okay?" said Neil. The way Carter should have, if only he had moved faster, if he had been able to think when his wife was lying on the ice like a blond broken puppet.

She sat up. She rubbed the back of her head. "Who makes ice this slippery?" she shouted. "I demand a hot toddy."

* * *

ALASKA HAD BEEN CARTER'S IDEA from the start. He had never met Katrina's father or seen where she'd grown up. Anchorage had sounded exotic—a city with five mountain ranges and a reindeer named Star, who lived in a backyard pen downtown. Her father owned a floatplane! Which she knew how to fly!

"Let's wait for summer," she said, "when we can go fishing. This late in winter, all anybody does is ski and watch TV."

He might have agreed. Except for his job. Back in New York,

Carter taught sixth-grade social studies at an all-boys private school. He loved his co-workers. He loved his kids. And yet, one too many Monday mornings, they had revealed the stunning number of Styrofoam ammo packets they had purchased for their Nerf-gun arsenals over the weekend—a total that when researched and multiplied by unit cost (in secret, on Amazon) surpassed his monthly paycheck.

They were clumsy to the point of falling off their stools, these boys—goofy and entitled and egotistical, yet despite the smartphone porn, astonishingly naïve. When Carter had told them he was taking a few weeks off for his honeymoon, they had whacked each other on the arms and rolled their eyes, unable to imagine a future that did not involve marrying your best friend from kindergarten and moving to the desert to invent rocket launchers out of tinfoil and string cheese.

On such dreams hydrogen bombs are built—and tested. Thinking back, he might have tried to teach the boys something useful, for once, and explained what had made him fall so thunderously in love. Except he couldn't. Nobody could. Love was dumbifying. It had no articulation except sex, happiness, and befuddlement. If he had been forced to tell his kids anything, he would have said that Katrina smelled of blackberries from his grandmother's long-sold house in Connecticut, which wasn't possible. And yet she *did* smell of blackberries, dark and heady and warm. He knew the smell, and he couldn't stop smelling her, touching her, doing things like poking her in the ribs when she was trying to brush her teeth.

Add to this: She ate fast-food chicken from the bucket, and flung her drumstick bones on the bedroom floor. She made fantastical amounts of money trading futures for cunt-bag ass toys whom she called cunt-bag ass toys on the phone, and to their faces. Then turned around and wept over obscure Italian cinema. Or bought him a bunch of violets—violets!—and left them on his pillow while he slept.

"Jesus," said his friends when they found out about the wedding. Carter's previous girlfriend of five years had been a yoga teacher. A vegan.

Katrina, on the other hand, had shot into his life like a blond, carnivorous meteor, and he had married her two months later. She was eleven years older. A few days after they met, she took him swimming at her club, a place with failed teenage models as doormen and a rooftop pool like a chip of fallen sky. She sat on the edge and watched him do laps. When he got out, she said, "You passed."

"Of course I did," he said. "I graduated summa from Williams." Then he laughed. But she was serious. She had wanted to see if he put his face in the water. She could not sleep with a man who didn't, and she couldn't or wouldn't explain why.

The outrageousness, the bravado—he had thought this was the Alaskan in her. But her father, who actually lived there, was not this way, not at all. They had spent the past three days in Anchorage with him. He lived in a ranch house that had not been updated—as he mentioned more than once—since 1983. Each morning at six a.m., he ironed his jeans in the kitchen. Each night at six p.m., he barbecued a chicken on the deck wearing a parka patched with duct tape on the elbows.

He served the chicken at the kitchen counter, the only vegetable a bottle of chardonnay. The wine was creamy, French, expensive. The meat was slightly pink with fire-blasted skin. Her father bought both at Costco, which he seemed to frequent hourly. They ate on stools with paper towels for napkins—two half glasses of wine per person and as much chicken as he could load onto your plate.

Dinner conversation followed certain rules. They didn't talk about the mini stroke he had had two years earlier, which had cost him his pilot's license. They didn't talk about how he continued to fly in secret. Most of all, they didn't talk about Katrina's mother and whether or not she knew about Katrina's marriage.

Once or twice, Carter had considered bringing up the subject himself. Katrina's mother had had a coke problem. She had not solved it. Which was how Katrina had phrased it to Carter in her carefully gray apartment. Her mother had been in and out of the house for most of her childhood. There—and then not. A week, a year, an occasional Christmas. The words came out of Katrina in a monotone, the voice of a government form. And for a minute, Carter thought there might be something wrong with her, until suddenly, as if against her will, a small, terrible smile had flitted across her face—a butterfly of heartbreak.

He had waited a few moments, then held her, knowing in that instant that he was going to ask her—fragile and teetering— to marry him, though right then had not been the right time. He asked anyway. While still on his feet, his arms around her, no ring.

Tonight, just before Neil's party, the two topics at dinner had been her father's use of soy sauce as a marinade and his need to put in a beach. Diamond Lake was a man-made lake, basically a liquid runway, and yet the EPA guys were sniffing around now, requiring homeowners to create "natural habitats" for the salmon, to the tune of ten grand in gravel and plants. "I tell you what," said her father. "It's enough to make you want to leave the state." He shook his head.

"Move to New York," said Katrina, her adoration radiating across the kitchen. "I'll buy the condo next door, break down the wall."

"We could do that," he said, shaking his head. "We sure could." Then he laughed and she laughed and Carter got it: The idea of leaving Alaska was preposterous. Talk like this was just a way of painting the air with the last thing on earth you want to do, to ward it off. He served himself another blackened thigh. He thought about the comfort of articulating those kinds of scarecrows—and the danger of them rebelling against your intentions and coming to life. He pictured his father-in-law in a sad velvet bathrobe, looking out their apartment window at the streets of Tribeca. It was spring. Dogs in raincoats paraded down the sidewalks, followed by women speaking to invisible cellphones with such intimacy you almost hoped they were talking to themselves.

"We should get going," Carter said. "Right? The party."

Katrina glanced at him. Her father started scraping plates into the compactor. The metal teeth crunched through bottles and bones. Katrina hopped off her stool. Her father wiped his hands on a dish towel—slowly.

"Aren't you coming?" she said, in a shy voice, almost hopeful.

Her father looked up, startled. "Oh," he said. "I didn't know I was supposed to."

She looked confused. Then Carter was confused. Neil's party wasn't a reception, but it was in their honor. An ice sculpture of a leaping king salmon had been ordered. As well as some kind of punch made with blueberries or birch sap. All of which promised to be more exciting, if not more joy filled, than the lunch in Manhattan they had had with Carter's parents. Both of whom had been too stunned to touch their Cobb salads. His mother had a thing for family weddings, family Christmas cards, family aprons embroidered with each person's name.

"Don't you want to come?" said Katrina.

"It's just with Neil," said her father. "And his . . . however you call them . . . extravaganzas. I wasn't planning on it." The expression on his face was kind, but vague, almost presidential, as if they were talking about parking the car or buying groceries, things he didn't do anymore and had trouble understanding.

Katrina picked up a spoon. She picked up a saltshaker. Carter winced. She could be spectacularly articulate when angry. And inventive. Once, when her boss had failed to back her on the purchase of some unorthodox Russian bonds, she had stapled his suit pants to his chair while he napped off a hangover. An act for which she had been rewarded with the title "vindictive fucktard" and a promotion of two bonus levels.

"Here's what I think," she said. And then she just stopped, midsentence, as if chopping off the idea behind it. She hugged her father. "It's not like it's a *wedding* wedding. It's just some people getting together to celebrate."

Carter looked at her, but there was nothing in her eyes that conflicted with her expression. He sat for a minute. Then said, at a loud volume, "I think you should come."

There was a long, disconcerting silence—save for the grinding of the trash compactor. He washed it away with a gulp of wine. Neither Katrina nor her father looked in his direction.

"It's fine, Dad," she finally said. "Besides, isn't the girl from Nebraska singing *Phantom*?"

"'Angel of Music,'" her father said, his eyes whisking over to the television. "She came in second place last week." Carter could not prove it, but if he had to guess, Katrina's father spent every night just how they left him—sitting at his desk, watching *America's Got Talent* and tying flies for trout he was going to catch when they weren't there. Big ones. Rainbows. Monsters.

* * *

NEIL'S LOG-CABIN MANSION WAS A five-minute walk down the shore-line through the snow. Just past the mastodon, people lingered by the fireplace with sushi hand rolls and one-bite spoons of risotto—people Carter didn't know. He always reacted a beat too slowly, and tonight was no exception. "About the girl from Nebraska," he said.

"Ugh," said Katrina. "I hate a preteen prodigy."

"I'm so proud of you."

She looked at him. "For what?"

"For not reacting when your father blew us off." And yes, he could see by her suddenly cool face, her calm, flat stare, that he should just stop talking. Still he went on, announcing with such easy outrage: Katrina's father was a grown man. So his own marriage had imploded. Was he afraid that Katrina's would too? His staying home from their wedding party—the only one they would ever have—was, if you thought about it, manipulative. A less-than-obvious control tactic.

"Or maybe," she said, "he's an introvert who doesn't like parties." Then she zipped off her boots—with a sound as brisk and dismissive as her expression—and strode toward the kitchen.

Long ago, Carter had understood that some people grasped the power of timing better than others. One of those people was Neil, who swept in at that exact moment, bearing a pint glass half-filled with single-malt Scotch. "On the house," he said. "Felicitations."

Carter examined his drink. Three maraschino cherries floated in the potent-smelling liquor—baubles in amber. "My father-in-law has a tab started. Let's put it on that."

"An amazing man," said Neil. "A giant outdoorsman. Though

slightly rigid." He was studying Carter, though more smoothly than Katrina's Manhattan friends, all of whom seemed to flip through his possible ages before speaking: Forty? Thirty-five? Thirty-three? No, no (no way!), younger.

Neil held up his glass, clinked. "He's still a little emotional with me, I suspect. About last New Year's." This past January, he continued, he had been feeling a little down, a little existential. He had buzzed over to Houston, Alaska, in his helicopter and loaded up on cherry bombs and mortars. Then buzzed back home and set them up in a hole on the lake ice, a tad too close to Katrina's dad's backyard. Regrettable. As was the single fuse he had snaked back to the plane dock.

"What happened?" said Carter.

Neil shook his head, as if implying police, a lost eyeball, a forest fire. Then grabbed Carter by the shoulder, and whispered, "It went boom."

Carter laughed. But Neil only sighed with contentment, the way you might after eating a slice of warm pie. His features were crooked, almost misshapen, his nose a kind of farm potato in the middle of his face. He was not a handsome man, not at all, but you wanted him to be; you were rooting for him in some cosmic way—the cause of which was probably his expression, each freckle a bedazzled star that seemed to convey that he too was knocked out daily by his own good fortune.

Carter had a hard time connecting this Neil with the Neil that Katrina had described on their walk to the party. Neil sometimes got wound up, she said. Too wound up.

"Like a toddler?" said Carter.

"Like someone on an ass-ton of mood stabilizers."

Ten years earlier, Neil's dad—her dad's closest friend—had

shot himself. In the face. At his fifty-fifth birthday party. It was Neil who found him in the laundry room. And Neil who tried to clean it up, by himself, to keep his mom from seeing.

She had a theory about this, a theory that seemed to apply to everyone except herself and her father: Your average happy person didn't last in Alaska. It was too much work not to die all the time.

About this, Carter only nodded. The Anchorage that he had seen was mostly strip malls and bowling alleys, Denny's franchises and icy boulevards—the mountains looming in the distance, but not exactly putting anyone in the position where they had to crawl around looking for food and a warm cave.

And regarding all those happy people, Carter had bipolar twelve-year-olds in his classes, billionaire parents on crack, a fellow teacher who had spent six months at Bellevue because he thought a brown recluse lived in his back molar. It was almost relieving that Alaska was similar, that spruce forests and sunsets that looked as if the entire solar system was melting didn't quite fix the human condition—the way he had believed that nature might during certain darker periods of his life. Periods he had also not mentioned to Katrina.

Ta-da! Neil had made him yet another Scotch with maraschino cherries. "Next time, buddy," he said, "you'll come up and stay with us." He waved to a woman sitting in a leather armchair, knitting a striped, soft-looking blue blanket. "Right, Janice?" he said. "We love to host young lovers. We'll take you out to the Wrangells. Go scout some wild sheep."

A giddy feeling was swelling in Carter, one that dated back to second grade, when you wanted to ask somebody in your class to be your friend—but knew that to do so would destroy any chance of it happening—and so spent your lonesome, sleepless nights nursing that tender wisp of happiness, trying to figure out how to place yourself in the other boy's general vicinity, where if you were stand-offish enough, he'd pick you to be on his team at recess. This was the secret to Neil, maybe; you didn't have to feel any of this. He put you on his team the moment he met you.

His wife perhaps did not. She smiled—warm but with the guarded eyes Carter often saw in his fellow teachers, who under-stood that children waltzed off to the next grade and never came back. She was older than Neil, or looked it, her face weathered, her hair a chopped blondish-grayish afterthought. Neil, he had as-sumed, would be married to someone else, someone tan and ripe and plastic. It was relieving that he wasn't. Carter raised his pint glass. Janice nodded. It occurred to Carter that she had knitted her way through a lot of parties like this, including ones that went boom.

* * *

BY THE TIME KATRINA HAD pulled off her skates and hobbled inside, all the guests had left—a course that Carter and she could have also followed but didn't, for reasons they would puzzle over for years to come. At that moment, however, Neil was back behind the log bar. He was serious about Katrina and Carter moving up to Alaska. Intellectually speaking, the state was underemployed. There was a need for people like themselves, go-getters. Now, while the price of oil was high.

Carter sat down on the sofa beside his wife. She didn't move. He put his hand over hers. She let him. Was their argument finally over? Or was she just distracted by the idea of moving back home? An image floated through his mind: him with a bow and arrow, a sheepskin slung over one shoulder, a glacier in the background, a whole bubble life that would melt into nothing, he realized, when he woke up in the morning with a Scotch-and-cherry hangover.

Neil continued: He had some ventures on the horizon, some opportunities. His first thought for Carter? Central AC. Sure, it was negative three outside, but you had to understand, he said: In the summers, Alaska now saw eighty-plus-plus temps. He had been working with a young engineer in town on an eco-friendly cooling system that was powered by biofuel made from the by-products of commercial fishing. Salmon guts, crab shells, et cetera.

"Uh," Carter said. "I'm not sure that dovetails with my résumé."

Neil filled more pint glasses. "Stem cells, then. I have a doc in town regrowing cartilage for blown knees. Not quite legal, as of now. But promising." He had other ideas: his chain of adult-care facilities, his IT operation, his health-club franchise, the small-dog grooming business. The profit in small dogs was not to be believed.

Carter lay back on the sofa and looked up. Heads and antlers staggered up the log walls to the ceiling, each identified with a brass trophy tag: Dall sheep, mountain goat, gazelle, blesbok. What was a blesbok? And if Carter had been back in New York, wouldn't he have found it upsetting to see one slapped up on a wall? He couldn't say. There was something unicorn in all this carnage, something silvery and make-believe and authentic all at the same time.

What would Carter have been like if he had grown up with the belief that it was natural—and enjoyable—to go after what he wanted, however off-putting or seemingly impossible? "Stem cells?" he said. "I thought you were a hunting guide."

"The lodge?" said Neil. "Strictly a hobby." He guided one or two guys a summer—tech kids, mostly, who paid five grand a day to pop a black bear. "It's a dying industry. But it does cull the numbers in terms of overpopulation."

"Right," said Carter.

"Gross," said Katrina. "You know how I feel about trophy hunting."

Neil balled up a cocktail napkin, threw it at her. "And yet you still eat chicken. Do you know what goes on in a poultry death camp? I've got the YouTube videos."

"Honey," said Janice. "How many cherries did you just put in that drink?"

He looked down. "Nine," he said, and laughed. "I like them."

"Neil," said Katrina. "Carter teaches *social* studies. Like politics. Like government."

"I think of it more as a course in historical-cultural ethics," said Carter. "What the past can teach us about who we are—and who we want to be." He paused. "By now most public school curriculums have cut it." The bitterness in his tone was there, but he was unable to remove it.

"Well," said Janice, back to her knitting. "Both our girls know all the state capitals."

"You can always go back to teaching that mud class," said Katrina. She slid down the sofa, turned to Janice. "Carter makes a *mean* coil pot."

He willed himself to look calm, unaffected. The mud class referred to a steaming, impoverished summer three years ago when, out of desperation, he had stooped to working at a daycare, crafting projects for toddlers out of a chemical substitute for clay called magic mud. Apparently, she was still mad and needed an apology. Which Carter now had zero desire to give her.

Then again, the only helpful point he made about her father

was that sometimes you had to do things for love that you didn't want to do. "Look," he whispered, "I was out of line about your dad."

"Don't worry about it," she said. "He doesn't like you either."

The next thing he wanted to say was that he didn't give a crap what her father thought; her father was self-centered and dogmatic and would not let anybody touch his trash compactor buttons; her mother probably did coke just to escape his god-on-high complex. A complex that, by the way, his daughter had not escaped, huddled down on the ground as she was, in daughterly worship.

Neil, however, was presenting their drinks on a tray lined with twinkling white doilies. Carter wondered how *he* would handle this. But Carter knew. He held himself back for a moment. Then flung himself onto the floor at Katrina's feet and cried out loudly, with great theatrical anguish, "I'm sorry. I was a cunt-bag ass toy! Your dad's a giant."

They all looked at him. Even Janice ceased knitting for a few stitches.

"How much exactly," said Katrina, "did you and Neil drink?" But the fight was over. She had folded. He sat up and kissed her on one bare, waxed, blackberry-smelling knee; her knee always made him think of the inside of her elbow, which always made him think of the inside of her thigh—the soft downy upper reaches.

"Now that's how you run a marriage," said Neil. "Minus the language. We have growing girls upstairs. This house is strictly rated G."

"It's Katrina's expression. She uses it on clients."

"Katrina," said Neil, shaking his head.

And then it happened—Carter saw it happen while still nestled on the lush, creamy wall-to-wall carpet, thinking how wonderful wall-to-wall carpet was, so comfortable on the knees, so cozy, why did no one in New York have it? Neil looked at Katrina and his face went soft and dazed, as if his brain had turned to maple syrup. "You remember that time when you snuck out of the house and jumped off the roof and my brother caught you?" said Neil.

"You were supposed to catch me."

"He was older. He pushed me out of the way."

Janice knitted on, briskly, efficiently.

"I was fourteen," said Katrina. "What an arrogant shit I was. My poor old dad."

"You were wearing that skirt," he said. "With the flowers." The flowers drifted through his eyes, even Carter could see them—light springtime blooms, pink petals, her feet bare in the grass.

All night, Neil had hardly talked to Katrina, save to give the congratulatory toast. He had stayed by Carter. He had introduced him. He had hugged him. He had showed him his archery range in the basement. Which, Carter realized, is exactly what you do when you plan on sleeping with someone else's wife. You seduce her husband.

"I don't remember," she said, but in a way that implied she did. Something—the skirt? a summer? a night? a lifetime?—was glistening in the air between them. They were both looking at it, together, the rest of the world on mute.

"Oh shoot," said Janice. "I need more blue. It's in the basket. Will you?"

Neil got up to get the yarn, but Carter was on the floor, closer. He reached in, cutting Neil off. Then he held up the ball and rolled it slowly to Janice's feet. She had toes that did not go with the rest of her—long and elegant, a braided silver ring on the smallest.

"Did I ever tell you how Janice and I met?" said Neil.

"Neil." She pretend-frowned.

"I pulled her out of a ditch. No exaggeration. There she was stuck in the mud in a Ford Fiesta. Her two girls in back. I towed them out. Escorted them home."

"I made you lemonade," she said.

"The lemonade," he said, his eyes turning to her. Then to Katrina. "I remember standing in that tiny kitchen, thinking how if I could marry a kind, understanding woman like her, everything else would be all right." His voice was husky with feeling.

Carter could not believe it. Did she not see that Neil was showing her his tender side? Heroic, sensitive Neil, so emotionally in touch. "You know how we met?" asked Carter. "At a party. We left in a taxi. Ten minutes later we went at it, right in the backseat."

The silence that resulted was majestic, velvety, absolute.

"Well," said Janice, coming to the rescue. "Sex *can* bring two people together." Carter was not sure if she was dumb or simply possessed an almost inhuman ability to forgive anyone, himself included.

"It's not like it's a secret, I guess," said Katrina. "I've always been easy."

"No," said Neil, with gravitas. "You've never been that."

A light came down from on high, a light that Katrina basked in like a Dutch girl from the seventeenth century with a basket of apples. Everything was quiet, except for the pleasant clicking of knitting needles, the soft creak of the house as it shifted against the cold outside. Carter sat there carefully. His hands looked odd to him, as if they belonged to somebody else.

"I'll tell you what we didn't do," said Neil. "Give you two a wedding present."

"Absolutely not," said Katrina, still aglow. "That was the rule, no gifts."

Carter looked back down at his hands. He wondered what his face was doing. He felt as if he were sitting on the rink while they raced around him on diamond ice skates, faster and faster. Going home was not an option. Should Carter suggest it, Katrina might just tell him to go ahead, she'd meet him, later. Ditto to Janice. She had surrendered to her knitting coma years ago. An understandable decision. She had been a single mom with two kids and a compact car to get her through Alaskan winters, a life that was long behind her.

"I bet," said Neil, "you don't have one Alaskan thing in that fancy New York apartment."

"I bet," said Katrina, "my apartment is tasteful and understated."

He pointed to a fluffy white skin on the back of the sofa.

"It's yours," she said.

"Correct. And it's still mine to give."

"Don't be silly. Besides, they shed."

"I already ordered them something," said Janice. "Williams-Sonoma."

"A waffle maker," said Neil. He threw back his Scotch. He pulled a leather armchair over to his trophy wall. He took down some antlers—thin, crooked ones. He looked at them as if they were cheap, diseased. He set them on the top of a bookcase. Then pushed the chair over to a set of horns, twisted into thick, lavish curls. They were too high up on the wall. He jumped, as if to swat them down with one hand.

"Stop!" said Janice. "Please?"

"A waffle maker," said Neil. But his face was red, his voice agitated.

Janice looked at Carter. There was nothing in her expression. Not a plea for help, not an acknowledgment of their crappy circumstances. "It's heart-shaped," she said to the whole room. "Nonstick."

Carter walked over to the mastodon, ran his hand down the front plate of the skull. It was comforting almost, how the bone warmed under his fingers, as if a vestige of life still beat inside. "What about the mastodon?" he said.

All three of them swiveled their heads—and burst out laughing.

"Just a tusk, then," he said. "The left one maybe. It's shorter."

More laughs.

"And there I was thinking you were relaxed," said Neil. "You're a go-getter, Carter. An alpha where it counts."

Carter smiled—kind of—and started picking up plates. Katrina followed, targeting napkins. It was strange how suddenly a moment could bloom, then just as quickly shrivel up and vanish, poof. So Neil and his wife had possibly screwed their heads off for a teenage summer. Or for a year after college. So it hadn't washed off. Everyone had their young, misguided loves, bronzed by the memory of sex on the family sofa. Every now and then, sometimes even while he was with Katrina, he slipped back in time to Jennifer Larchmont from sophomore year and the hand she used to keep in her lap when she drove him to band practice, the slender possibilities of those fingers, so fluent in clarinet.

The kitchen was a blinding arrangement of stainless steel and granite. Carter placed the dishes on the counter, then stopped at a window above the sink that opened onto the living room. Over by the fireplace, Katrina was snapping open a garbage bag. She tossed in a plastic glass, a smashed bit of cake. Neil bumped into her. Obviously not by accident. And obviously, unaware that Carter was watching—though he moved slightly to the left, just out of view.

"Cut it out," she said.

"Katrina brought a boy home," he said, in a teasing voice.

"Shut up," she said. Then paused—for a beat too long. "It's not like he's a teenager," she said, finally. "He's almost twenty-nine."

"He's an odd one. Dark. I like him."

"I want you to."

Neil tossed in a handful of used napkins. And stopped. "He'll never leave you, Trina," he said. "You know that, right?"

Katrina nodded, as if not only did she know this, but she also thought it was a wondrous thing, even when she also knew—or should have known, as Neil so clearly did—that there was no love between anyone without the slight unspoken fear that that love might vanish, or be snatched away by someone else.

Carter was younger. He was taller. And stronger. All of which would only work against him if he gave in to the impulse to punch Neil in his supportive, caring face.

A door stood next to the refrigerator. It did not look as if it led to the pantry. Carter yanked it open. He walked down a long hallway, opening door after door until he found a bathroom. He sat down on the toilet. He didn't have to go, but just sitting there with his pants down, all that cold porcelain against his skin, was calming. Underneath every toilet was an invisible river. You just had to focus on it and float away.

He reached over for the toilet paper. A baboon stood in his way. It was stuffed and upright and dressed in a loincloth—holding the roll in its leathery, humanish fingers. Of course Neil shot monkeys. He flew over African savannas in his death chopper, lions running from him like a herd of blesboks.

The door opened. Carter jerked and clapped his thighs shut. It was Janice. His pants were on the floor. "I'm in here!" he said.

But she already knew that. She was in the bathroom. She slid up on the edge of the sink. In the opening of her blouse, the bones on her chest were visible, the skin flecked with sunspots.

"Carter?" she said. "What are you doing?"

"I'm on the toilet?"

She cocked her head. She might not recognize his identifiers: prep-school hair, thrift-store sweater, scholarship parents, younger (anorexic) sister enrolled in grad school for life—but she suddenly seemed well equipped at flicking off a person's packaging with her eyes. "Neil isn't well," she said. "And Katrina isn't helping."

"He's trying to fuck her."

"He doesn't know what fucking is," she said. She said this without emotion, as if reading a prescription bottle. She got down on her knees. She wedged her hands between his thighs and pried them open. She looked at him—clinically, expressionless—and moved closer. He almost shoved her back into the baboon, but worried about the noise, Katrina hearing, how to explain. Her hands were cold and she was cold and there was something horrible in her, something musky and calculated and authoritarian. His hard-on arrived without his desire—or consent. He pulled her hands off his legs, held her by the wrists. "I feel sorry for you," he said. "What you've had to do to survive."

"Please," she said. "Don't play grown-up." She whisked his hands away. He let her. She turned and looked at herself in the mirror, fluffed her dull, practical hair. "You know the sad thing about weak people?" she said. "They fall in love with strong ones, thinking they'll get stronger."

"Get out," he said.

"But it's weakness that rubs off," she said. "On everybody." Then she smiled—not at him, but at herself, in the mirror, with such hatred. From her pocket, she pulled out a tube of lipstick and smoothed it over the contours of her lips.

"Get out," Carter said. "Get out right fucking now."

Janice, however, was already at the door. "I guess you've already looked underneath the loincloth." She slid into the hall with a quiet click of the knob. Carter stood up, zipped, tucked in his shirt. Then went over to the baboon, lifted the loincloth. There was nothing there, whatever had been there—male or female—had been chopped off or patched up and you'd have to dig around to tell.

"See?" said her voice from the other side of the door. "It's just that easy."

"There's something wrong with you," he shouted. The vomit slid out of him softly into the toilet. When it was over, he rubbed soap on his finger and brushed his tongue. It tasted both horrible—blackened chicken—and better.

*   *   *

AT THE DOORWAY TO THE living room, Carter paused. A vast cathedral of windows led up to the log ceiling, where the mountains slept on—contented giants, their faces slashed with ice and moonlight. Katrina sat on the sofa, her feet stuck in a bowl of water. Neil held up a mask. It was leather of some kind, with two round eyeholes and a circular trim of feathery white fur. It was the mouth, though, that gave it all its sadness—curved downward with the sucked-in look that old people have when they've lost their teeth. "It's Yupik," said Neil. "Old school. Dad got it from a Native buddy."

He knelt, actually knelt, at her feet. "Here," he said. "You take it."

Carter willed himself not to charge into the room. Was this

weakness? Or strength? Or some cockroach longing to see how far Katrina would go when she thought he wasn't there to see?

"I'm fucking married," she said. "I'm fucking happy."

Neil stared up at her, his expression softening until it looked strange, molded, as if smeared across his skin. "It's a son-of-a-bitch world," he said, in a quiet voice, a broken voice. "And nobody gets out alive."

She shook her head. "Your dad was sick. He didn't mean it."

"I think about that night," said Neil. "That's what he said, in his toast. Remember?" He picked up the mask from the sofa, tucked it under his arm. "You could have stayed to help me clean up."

Neil was crying by now. Carter didn't exactly want Katrina to comfort him. Then again, he didn't expect her to do what she did next. Which was to stare past him, out the window, her face a blank, as if Neil no longer existed. And she were far away, sucked out into the night.

Carter stood there, so very aware that he should not move. He had never seen her afraid before. If this was fear as she knew it—or something more terrible. He gave himself a minute. Then another. Though perhaps it was his stillness that caused Katrina to finally glance over.

"Carter?" she said.

"Buddy!" said Neil, his voice snapping back to jovial. "Your wife has blisters. The ice skates. We made her an oatmeal bath."

Carter watched as his wife, a woman he had married in less time than it took to learn to drive or recover from mono as a teenager, looked down at the carpet so as not to meet his eyes.

"We should go," she said.

"You don't have to," said Neil to her and her alone. "Not unless you want to."

"Not without our gift," said Carter. He walked over to the mastodon, slowly, and yanked on the closest tusk. It didn't move. It was soldered on, perhaps with bronze.

"Carter!" said Katrina. "Stop."

"Buddy," said Neil. "If you want a tusk, take one." He flung open a door beside the bar. There was a long walk-in closet behind it, piled high with ivory. "What's mine is yours," said Neil. "Take any one you like."

"Carter?" said Katrina.

"Most of them are mammoths," said Neil. "Bigger. Easier to find." He gestured to a tusk at the back—deeply curved and thick as a human thigh.

Carter picked it up. It was lighter than expected. Slick with polish. He dragged it across the carpet. Stopping only at the mastodon. There was no way around that skull, not alone. He waited. Then waited a little longer—not looking back, even when Katrina finally grabbed the other end of their wedding present and lifted it up. They cleared the first tusk. Then the second. Gracefully. As if they had planned their steps. Was this marriage, he wondered, how well the worst in you worked with the worst in the other person? Or was it something else? He and Katrina had years to find out, a lifetime, once they staggered home through the snow together. There was no stopping for boots, no time to grab coats. Even as Neil called out from the doorway that they could take another tusk, a better one. They could have as many as they wanted. The glaciers were melting, buddy, bones and ivory surfacing. It was almost a little too easy. Everything was right there, lying on the ice. Exposed. Ready for the taking. You didn't need a shovel. You didn't need a pickax. You didn't even need to dig.

ALCAN, AN ORAL HISTORY

1. Janice: Idaho Falls, Idaho,
to Sweetgrass, Montana

MY BROTHER AND I DIDN'T grow up religious. Still, we were kids. We believed in the sad, dead people trapped inside the eyes of stray dogs and mysteries of rocks that appeared one day in our pockets, only to show up the next in an ashtray or back of a closet. Signs and wonders turned up all the time: a slingshot you could hit a backyard squirrel with, an Easy-Bake oven that shot out a tiny, warm toy cake. Almost always, though, that sign belonged to somebody else. A kid at school with a dad and a tree house. Those kind of people.

Not so for the bottle of gold that Mom passed back to us on the drive out of Idaho Falls. We were done with that dusty, russet town, done with Idaho all together. But the gold, Mom said, was mine and Kevin's. We could keep it for forever. It was from Alaska. A gift from her and Richard.

My brother and I held it between us, both gripping on tight with one hand. The bottle was slender, glass, and topped with a real cork stopper. Inside it was filled with water—or a clear liquid that mimicked water—where a slow, luxurious autumn of gold leaf drifted down. The size and fineness of those leaves, the nonchalant way they floated like chips of frozen sunlight, reduced us to a brief, dreamy stupor in the car backseat. We were kids from a fairy tale for a few minutes, blond siblings who ate bits of leftover marzipan for breakfast and slept side by side, their heads on goose-down pillows.

Until I grabbed the bottle and held it just far enough above my brother's head. I was older and prone to thievery in general, my act justified by Kevin's less than admirable exit from the Saddle Up motel. He had gone rigid, the way he always did when we had to move on, and refused to jump from the bathroom window. The housekeeping cart was broken on the back wheel, the maid was clunking down the hallway toward us. Mom had to throw our bags down and lift Kevin off the sill, at which point she gave up on my suitcase, with all my clothes inside and my lucky mountain bluebird feather.

Only now, outside of Red Rock, did Mom tell us there had been a second bottle of gold that had broken in her purse when she dropped it. Richard had sent her two, she wanted us to know. One for me. And one for Kevin. Richard had always wanted a family. We would see this when we met him in person. We would all go fishing. We might even get a dog. A husky or something. As long as it didn't shed.

Mom's speech, though similar to others she had given outside Salt Lake City and Pocatello, was freeing to me for the moment. The broken bottle was now officially my brother's, the one in my possession mine. I held it up to the sunlight, directing random spangles over Kevin's face.

Kevin shut his eyes. He was a test taker and fought like one— pinching in places too embarrassing to point out to grown-ups, arranging for his forehead to meet yours with a hard, accidental-looking smack. I locked in my grip, kept my elbow at the ready, even when he seemed to give up on the gold and me and went back to breaking down Mom.

She was driving. If she felt him staring at her from the backseat, I couldn't tell. His whole body had already turned stiff and furious. He jammed his thumb into his mouth and began to suck away with these kinds of strangled, spitty noises that made you think he was choking on his own thoughts, thoughts that were so obvious and ugly, you could almost fill them in: Richard did not want a family, Richard did not want us to come for a visit, Richard was not the reason we had to leave Idaho Falls and miss Kevin's seventh birthday at the bowling alley.

Mom met Kevin's look in the mirror, then glanced back at the traffic. She had a soft, startled face that glazed over when people yelled. This confused the yellers, mostly because no matter how loud they got, how many names they called her, she would stand there dazed and vacant until they finally threw a bottle at the TV, at which point she would snap back and pick her way through the pieces of broken glass, as determined as ever to go to the Chinese restaurant with the tablecloths instead of the take-out place with the bags.

Only Kevin really knew how to get to her. It was his thumb sucking, the ridicule in his expression, the way he never said one word. By Butte, her eyes had turned into jumpy brown deer—on him, off him. She had to have known where this was going; we all knew where it was going; it had gone there so many times you would think I wouldn't mind. Instead, I almost told Kevin that I would give him the gold when we got to Canada, as long he started talking or stopped looking at Mom. Then I almost told him I would take him on a camping trip for his birthday instead of bowling—and that I actually didn't mind Mormon Carol or her burnt-black molasses cookies.

Back in Idaho Falls, Kevin had scored in the 107th percentile on a special statewide test—which wasn't possible, and yet had happened. Inspired by the news, his first-grade teacher had stayed late and run off dittos and set a time after school for the two of them to do advanced math worksheets together, during which Kevin refused to give a single answer and sucked his thumb, pulling it out only to ask if she was doing this because she was lonely, slow at triple-digit multipliers, and nobody liked her very much. He said this in a soft, curious voice, as if he really wanted to know the answer. I was there. I saw her crumple. Off went Kevin to the beanbag corner with a stack of chapter books.

Six months later, Mormon Carol found him in that corner—half-scowling, half-asleep. Unlike the other grandma volunteers, she skipped the homemade Play-Doh and the build-your-own bird feeders. She read to Kevin from her *Little Golden Book of Bible Stories*, flipping straight to the good ones about sacrificing sons or plagues of crusty sores. Then she crocheted on her blanket with a plastic hook and refused to explain how she did it. One week later, Kevin was doing all her crocheting for her—slip stitching, doubling, solving whole algebras of yarn. He burned through her crossword puzzles and made worksheets for her to practice her long division.

Kevin loved Mormon Carol, so much that he forced the other kids in kindergarten into making her Popsicle-stick bookmarks until she found out and stopped him. She had a kind of brusque, cinnamon authority that neither of us had ever encountered. When some girl's charm necklace went missing and I was supposed to report to after-school detention every day for a month, it was Mormon Carol who met with the principal and got me out.

Still, I knew better than to bring her up to Mom. Kevin was

smarter than me, smarter than any of us. He knew how Mom got about teacher meetings, hand-me-downs, government cheese. And yet, he had bragged to her about the Cadillac that Mormon Carol drove, and the promise she had made to take him to the bowling alley next month for his birthday.

"Wow," said Mom. "Isn't that generous."

Not even an hour after his mention of the bowling alley, both of us all of a sudden had to pick our crap off the floor and clean the whole room. Including vacuuming. Kevin didn't snap to and help out the way he was supposed to, Mom and him had a blow-out in the bathroom, and after that we were headed up to Alaska in search of a new, exciting life with Richard.

Richard was Mom's friend through a pen-pal newsletter. Richard was single and worked in construction. He liked pancakes but only sourdough. He printed his sentences, no cursive. You could tell a lot about a person by their handwriting, Mom told us. Especially their choice of ink. Black was too professional. Red creepy. Blue had some thoughtfulness to it, some sensitivity.

Just past the exit for Deer Lodge, I wondered—idly, only for a moment—if I should offer to sell the gold. All total, Mom had thirty-seven dollars in her wallet, minus the seventy-five cents I had skimmed from her change purse the day before.

But Kevin was through with staring and on to rocking. Off he bounced from the backseat upholstery, only to fall back and bounce off again—over and over, timed with exquisite irregularity, as if modeled after a dog barking when you are trying to nap: the dog barking and barking, then stopping long enough for you to think it had stopped for forever. Then barking some more.

Mom tried to hum over the thudding and tension—all the old lullabies, plus Carole King. I started doing something I would do for the next fifty miles, squeezing the bottle of gold, hard and harder, just to see if the thin, wavy glass would hold or break under the pressure. Each time I did this and it held, I felt better. Then I counted to thirty and tried it again.

Miles of dry, jagged landscape slashed by. Flocks of starlings raced the sky and splatted into rolling fireworks of birds. Outside Helena, Mom offered to buy us both sodas. Her voice was tired, uneasy, and she didn't turn around: It was hot. We all needed to cool off. We had days of driving ahead of us. The Alcan was a long highway, longer than any we had ever been on before. It went all the way through Canada. We had to get to Sweetgrass, at least, and cross the border.

"I want a Sunkist," I said. "Orange."

Nothing from Kevin—flat face, thumb suck, rage.

She kept driving but wondered if we ought to splurge on a motel.

"I like camping in the car," I lied. "Let's pull over."

Kevin shut down and went quiet. His kind of quiet was terrible, spreading through the car like something foul and chemical poured on a field by the side of the road. Mom tried to talk us through it: In Alaska, people fished for their own food! We could get a woodstove! We could run out in the morning and make snow angels!

I stuck the gold in my pocket and slunk down. Mom swerved off the highway and into a parking lot. The neon signage of a steak house chain blinked blankly down. Even then, my hopes were not entirely dead. It was possible, wasn't it, that Kevin might just go inside and eat the rib tips we couldn't afford and toast a soda to our future? That's all he had to do really, order a soda and pretend to drink it.

Rolls of dust blew over the windows. Mom thunked the gear into park, the keys clinking against the ignition. She got out, I got out, and Kevin went rigid, the way both of us knew he was going to, his whole body stiff and unresponsive, his hands gripping the seat belt. Mom tried to pull him out by his ankles. One of his sneakers fell off, but he held on. And she held on. Until his arms gave way and he was sitting on the asphalt with one sock foot, one sneaker.

He stood up, his eyes like two dead bits of black at the end of a match. Go ahead, the dead bits seemed to say, smoking at her.

Mom smacked him once, the easy way. Then again, the other way, harder. Time glittered to a stop. Kevin didn't cry; he never cried. He just stood there—stunned, relieved-looking that the buildup was finally over. A tiny kit plane whined across the horizon. Clouds blew by, loose as kites. Kevin popped his thumb back in his mouth, looking at the ground, sucking on it silently the way other kids did, as if it might help.

Mom wore a lot of turquoise back then, most of it rings in shapes of sunbursts and eagles. He couldn't see the red, mangled bird shapes surface on his cheeks. But Mom could and I could and so could the people in the parking lot with their doggie bags and purses. Her face scrambled. Then she got down on her knees in the gravel and bawled and hugged him.

I just stood, my arms at my sides. I had this idea, at the time, that if I looked at the dust simmering in the distance or the tree standing raggedly by the parking-this-way sign, then people would mistake me for an onlooker like themselves. Luckily, it was a Sunday. The after-church crowd had thinned out. Cars sped by on the highway. Mom kept crying. The air smelled of charcoal and burnt fat and snow from the mountains so high above us, they were part cloud.

Kevin pulled his thumb out of his mouth. "I forgive you," he said, the way that Mormon Carol had taught him—with a Jesus look on his face, like he meant it.

Mom shook her head. She hugged him one more time. She said he didn't have to use a booster seat at the table if he didn't want to. He could get a chocolate pudding off the menu. She was sorry. She had lost her temper, even when she had promised not to.

Kevin sniffled. Then asked if she really meant it about the pudding, which surprised me, though it shouldn't have. I knew how the two of them were, how the two of them would always be. I knew it so well that I wished it had been me who had gotten hit instead of him, not just then but all the other times. Not so much to protect him, but to sop up all the love from Mom that came right after.

The pudding he was going to get at dinner was just the beginning. For the next two thousand miles, Kevin would get to pick the radio stations, Kevin would get to drink Mom's coffee creamers, and Kevin would get to cuddle up with her at night in front, while I shivered in back alone. Everything he wanted, she had to say yes to now. And sooner or later, he would want the gold.

A Kleenex floated by us, freewheeling on a gust of wind from the traffic. Kevin sighed. He wouldn't mind a soda. Or some rib tips. Mom agreed. As we walked toward the entrance, I shoved the bottle deeper into my front pocket, as if to hide it not just from my brother but from myself.

2. Maggie: Peace Arch Park, Washington, to Johnson's Crossing, Yukon Territory

WE WERE FILTHY, FEMALE, AND fresh out of ag school at Ithaca, New York. Two ladies of the Great Eastern Wild who had slogged it across the entire United States in a VW Bug with a slipping transmission, only to careen north at California—a dazzle of Alaska in our eyes, a crumpled guide to the Alcan on the dash.

At the crossing booth in Peace Arch, a border service guard leaned into our window: What did we plan on doing in Canada? Did we have enough money? Enough gas? Enough food?

We had twelve ounces of homegrown sewn into the backseat upholstery and $1,136 American packed inside a half-full jar of Folgers crystals. Plus, the cherries. Even then, we knew to declare the cherries. But they were Bings, a six-pound sack that we had picked at an orchard on the outside of Spokane. The smell inside the car was so rich, so overwhelming, it had an almost animal heft—part perfume, part hormone, part velvet.

The guard ran through the dangers that foreign produce posed to Canada's food supply. "Surrender your fruit," he said finally. "Or turn around your vehicle and remain in the United States."

I looked over at Danielle. She looked up at the guard—a boy in blue and gold, a boy with a swoop of thick, bristly man hair across his upper lip. She shrugged at him. He stiffened, then marched around to the back. "Pass me the sack," I said to Danielle, nodding to a bin piled with outlawed grapes and oranges.

"No way," she said. "And who's he kidding with that mustache?"

For a minute, her fury was almost reassuring. The Danielle I knew from Ithaca had fought about everything, including gravity: jumping off the thirty-foot-high gorge at Second Dam, freeing a black bear cub from a legally set trap, keying the station wagon of our plant and soil science professor after he asked her out during class. A fight with border service, however, was going to get us banned from Canada.

Unless—and I loathed to even think this—that was what she secretly wanted to happen. Ever since our stop to see her family in Carmel, California, Danielle had holed up in the backseat of the

Bug, smoking homegrown and floating her hand out the window as if it were some wondrous windblown moth that had attached itself to the end of her wrist. There was no more camping by the side of the road, no more stops at swimming holes. When the sun went down, we pulled over at a motel and bickered over the cost of a double room until I folded and she got the key from the desk.

All night, splayed out on a ratty twin bed, she smoked yet more homegrown and fed nickels into the ten-minute TV, while I suggested in a casual-sounding voice that we call Eileen. Who was her mother. Who had given her life. Maybe to see how Eileen was doing. Maybe to let her know we had found her going-away present.

"Only I get to call Eileen, Eileen," Danielle said, her eyes fixated on an episode of *Hawaii Five-0*. "And besides, it wasn't a present. It was a bribe to keep me from coming back."

I disagreed. Maybe because I was the youngest of five siblings. Maybe because I was a Holy Cross girl from Rochester with a mother of my own who had spent significant time during my years at ag school perfecting molded margarine and writing me long letters starring my old high school boyfriend Dennis. As in: Dennis showed up at Star Market! Dennis still bowls at Olympic Lanes! Can you imagine?

My mother was lonely, I had only recently come to understand. As were most mothers, including Danielle's mother, however difficult this was to picture or point out. Not that I had to. The guard was back, spangled with purpose and bearing an official clipboard.

Danielle stared down at the sack of cherries in her lap. "Officer," she said, "is that like glued on? Or do they like assign it to you, officially, along with the hat?"

The mustache. The guard stared back at her, confused, but growing less so with every second. Against my better instincts, all of which were telling me that whatever my proof of cute white American girlhood, I wasn't a guy and would end up strip-searched or arrested or worse, I reached over, grabbed a handful of those cherries and smashed them into my mouth. Then chewed. And chewed. Marching some kind of fuck-it-all smile across my face, willing Danielle to remember all the adventures that we were going to have once we finally made it to Alaska—the cabin we were going to build, the creek out back, the mules and garden and free frontier land, if she would just stop ruining it before we even got on the highway. Please?

Something lit up in Danielle's eyes, something reckless and familiar. She dug into the sack, grabbed a handful, and smashed it into her mouth. Then smiled back at me. Same smile, only wider. I laughed. She stuck out her tongue, stained with juice. The guard suddenly nothing to us, the guard weepy with frustration behind his clipboard, as the two of us continued, handful after handful, pound after pound, interrupted only by our laughter and the rich, syrupy vomit that rose to the back of our throats.

Cars in line behind us began to honk and flash their brights. Our stomachs seized. Our lips turned purple. Still, we chewed and swallowed and spit and laughed until there was no fruit for us to declare, save for a wilted sack of pits. That, we surrendered.

* * *

A STORM HAD MOVED THROUGH most of British Columbia the night before, knocking over whole stands of trees right where the asphalt ended. Potholes deep enough to have a current swirled between sunken branches. For the first time since Carmel, Danielle took over at the wheel, easing our cheerful yellow Bug through water lapping right up to our tail pipe, babying the clutch on downhills and popping it past second straight into third, to keep the gears from sticking.

My best friend and mountain sister was back. The transmission was holding. We shuddered up the gravel highway at Dawson Creek, our engine revving like a hand mixer. By Prophet River, transport rigs plowed right up to our bumper. Danielle stood through the sunroof, steering with her bare feet, blowing kisses off the tips of her middle fingers. I laughed, aware of the gun racks that hung in every cab, but too comforted by the return of her bravado to tell her to cut it out.

Towns popped up from the trees—bar, bar, steeple—and still, we drove. And drove. And drove. We skipped the happy hippie camp sites, the flash of rainbow lanterns hanging in the trees. We had jug water and tinned sardines, homemade jerky and rolling papers. We sang along with the radio: country fuzz and Neil Sedaka. In the distance, the mountains smoked with ice.

At night, when we finally did pull over, I dug inside my pack and pulled out the jar of Folgers crystals. Even with what we had wasted in the days since Carmel, we still had $1,136. And $1,136 was more money than I had ever seen in my life. I counted it bill by bill, then recounted it just to make sure we hadn't lost a ten somehow or that it hadn't turned into $11.36 while we weren't looking.

Danielle refused to even acknowledge the money on my lap. Then again, she didn't reach for the homegrown either—instead flipping open her buck knife and whittling the bark off a branch she had picked up that day, the way she used to after classes in Ithaca.

Save for the occasional kid who had been born on a working farm, most everybody at Cornell's ag school was there for the cheap tuition and the artsy-crafty attitude. All of us did woodwork, weaving, basketry. Most of us, myself included, had tried to build a bamboo fishing rod or bluegrass instrument. Resulting in stitches and a pile of gluey mangled scraps.

Danielle was different. She carved on everything—tables, logs, the massive stumps behind our campus cabin. Listening to a lecture on seed genetics, she would sit there, idly flicking the tip of her knife into the surface of her desk, only to leave behind a face in the polished surface—someone you recognized but had never really looked at: the novel-reading girl who plopped oatmeal into our trays at the cafeteria, the gossipy old guy who dropped off manure for community gardening. How she did it, I could never figure out. Except that she distilled them down to just a few features—a nose, eyes, a sadness in the tilt of their head—the rest left blurred and dreamlike, as if she'd carved it out of rainwater.

On our trip up the Alcan, we stopped so infrequently and saw so few people that I could predict who she was going to do that evening: the toothless gas attendant, the exhausted van driver wearing a pom-pom ski hat. She worked quickly, throwing each finished face into the fire as soon as she was finished. Sometimes before I even got to see it.

Just once, outside of Muskwa, did I catch her carving me. My eyes were exactly my eyes, my nose exactly my nose, but my expression so unlike myself that for a moment, I wondered if what she had really been capturing about people was less what they looked like and more who they wanted to be—one day, if they could just figure out how.

On that slender spruce branch, I looked wistful, distant, a crown of milkweed on my head. The opposite of the real person I had been this whole trip, sitting beside her, counting our money, never entirely unworried that if I didn't hold on tight and pay attention, Danielle might reach over and toss the jar in the campfire. Just burn the last of Carmel down to ash.

* * *

ALASKA, IN MY FAMILY, WAS the name of the coveted way-way back of the Buick station wagon. Only the hardiest of us got to sit in that distant, spacious section of the car, meaning my sister and my two older brothers. Tommy, the oldest, got shotgun until Mom picked up Dad at the Kodak plant, at which point he was booted into the middle with me, the youngest, and whatever nose-picking neighborhood kid Mom had offered to watch for the afternoon.

Little did I know that in ag school, everybody would be talking about the real Alaska, where due to the combination of rainfall and endless summer sunlight, cabbages grew the size of pumpkins—sixty-pound pumpkins!—and salmon grew even bigger. You could homestead in the real Alaska, the way the pioneers had in the olden days of the wagon-train West. All you had to do was farm a frontier site for five years until the state signed over ownership.

Free acreage—without the pesky rules of a commune—was over-the-rainbow stuff to kids who spent their days studying Husbandry 101 and integrated pest management. But unlike the ax-and-flannel guys in our class who sat around the bonfire, drinking home-brewed beer and planning caravans up the Alcan that faded off in the morning along with their hangovers, I wondered if I didn't have the skills to make it happen. Back when most of the faculty were still snobby about any field animal other than horses, I had helped develop the mule program. Then came first in our class in soil science. And Husbandry 101. And Husbandry 201. And, to my surprise, chemistry.

Still, I stuck to what I had done for most of my good-girl life: worry, research, and hope in secret. I looked up weather patterns, water tables, growing seasons. I sent letters to officials in a town called Palmer, asking how you staked a claim. No one ever responded. Little did I know that 1975 was the heyday of the pipeline construction. Workers were pouring into the state—not to homestead but to build the pipeline. Men with wrenches and union contracts, not a girl with a torn, secondhand tent from Eastern Mountain Sports and a plan to build her own cabin, farming the acreage and trapping mink and martin until she saved enough cash to buy mules for a pack line.

Only Danielle knew the full extent of my wild, deluded ambitions. The wildest of which was my using that pack line to ferry hunters into the mountains, returning a few weeks later to pick them up and haul out the moose and wild sheep that they had harvested—saving them the agony of lugging out all that meat on their backs. Mules were cheaper than boats and planes, tougher than horses, and almost as fast as goats.

When I gave up a few months later, Danielle was the only one I told. My reasons were hardly a surprise: I was the first in my family to graduate college. I had decades of student loans ahead of me and zero job prospects, save for a job at Higbie's feedstore selling dog kibble.

Still, we cycled through the same routine each night: the two of us stacked into our bunk in our rented room off-campus; me adding to the pack train, me building miniature cabins for the hunters, me creating Alaska's first mule breeding program; her listening until I crashed back to reality and flicked out the light.

Danielle's nonchalance as to how she was going to make a living, her refusal to keep any of her carvings, her silence about how the hell she had ended up in Ithaca—from California!—was a maddening, glamorous mystery to me and the rest of our class. We were upstate kids from upstate families. The only time we had ever left New York was on a school field trip to the Canadian side of Niagara Falls.

Though I had no proof, I believed that my lifelong training as a little sister had earned me her friendship. Unlike the greasy grad students and bloodshot professors who hovered around Danielle, inventing corrections to her exams or nonexistent internships they needed to discuss with her right now, I knew how to kiss up to her smoky disdain with a kind of helpful, less slobbery version of worship. Or so I told myself.

"You know what they call a gnat in Alaska?" I said one night, fall semester of our senior year. "A no-see-em." She listened to me as I ran through all my statistics: the state flower (the forget-me-not), the state bird (the ptarmigan), the state motto ("North to the Future!"). Then listened to me conclude, once again, that I wasn't actually ever going to go that far away from my family. And home. And everything I had grown up with. Especially not when I had finally found a job for the following summer rubbing down trotters at Tioga Downs.

We both knew what that involved—the track owner drooling on my boobs, the trainer making me spike horses when the licensed vet refused. All of which I readied myself for Danielle to point out. Instead she smiled—halfway, which was the only way Danielle ever smiled. "Or," she said, "we could fuck it all and head to Alaska together."

Inside me, a tiny handful of tinder sparked to life: We! *The two of us!* Together! And yet I tried to ruin it. "But you don't even want to go," I said. "At least you never said you did."

"Maggie," she said. "You're the talker in this relationship."

* * *

THAT LAST NINE MONTHS OF school, I put us on a budget that discouraged even me. We ate nothing but rice, odd lot apples, and fifteen-cent cafeteria lunches. We worked the orchard season and lamb season. We picked up shifts at the library and sold seeds from our senior project. Still, our total savings, including what we needed for fees, was only $352.25. Which shriveled to $351.50 after I cracked and bought us brand-new shoelaces for our boots.

In April, when I got my first official statement about my loans and told Danielle I had to back out on Alaska, I expected ridicule, maybe a cutting remark. But she nodded. Then lay down on her bunk with her back to me and did not speak or move.

"Okay," she finally said as if we had been arguing all night long and she was giving in to my ultimatum. "I'll guess we'll have to stop by Carmel."

Carmel, I had gathered over the years, was where Eileen lived, Danielle's mother. With Danielle's stepdad. There were no step-dads or stepmoms or divorced anybody in Rochester. There were no kids who called their mother by her first name either. And there were certainly no bright-eyed, twenty-one-year-old girls who woke up one day and decided to go to Alaska and the next day decided to swoop across the entire United States in order to drop by some town in California that sounded drizzled in suntan oil and stuck on a cake. Secretly, I wondered if she was crazy. Not crazy-crazy, but just not exactly in touch with reality.

"Eileen will give us the money," Danielle said. "Then we'll head up I-5 and catch the Alcan in British Columbia."

We were adding on another thousand miles. The transmission was already slipping. My youngest older brother had handed down the Bug so I could go home and see our mom and keep her from worrying. "Great!" I said. If Danielle was with me on this last-minute gambit to jump-start our lives, we might possibly survive.

* * *

TWO HOURS AFTER GRADUATION, WE left my parents weeping in the parking lot, their only solace my diploma and the receipt for the return of my rental gown. The drive out took us four days, 2,887 miles, $125 on gas, and an under-budget $22 on food thanks to the commercial-grade cans of tomato soup that we had borrowed from the school cafeteria. All this left us $205. Plus the pennies in the change holder.

At that point, thanks to the welcome sign, I had figured out the real name of Carmel was Carmel-by-the-Sea. "It's just a suburb," Danielle said. "With a golf course and a shit ton of Spanish tile."

Right, I thought as we drove through its sunbaked streets. Bougainvillea spilled off balconies. Morning glories spiraled up traffic signs. Driving up to the house, I was relieved to see that at least she lived in a rancher. Upstate New York was one long endless cornucopia of ranchers.

Only once inside did I understand that the California version split into a kind of panoramic, single-floor mansion overlooking a golf course and the ocean. Nothing in my happy, limited life had prepared me for that long slope of grass that crumpled into black cliff at the bottom—sea foam spraying up as if shot out of the mouths of playful backyard dolphins.

In Danielle's room, every stick of furniture was white wicker with coral pink upholstery. Whole stacks of wooden-handled purses lay on tidy, built-in shelves at the back of her closet. "Bermuda bags," she called these purses. Rolling her eyes at the rows of pearl buttons where she could attach different covers to match the different prints of her sundresses.

I rolled my eyes too. Or tried. But it was obvious: I loved those Bermuda bags. I loved the Vaseline smoothness of her dresser drawers gliding in and out. I loved her tiny stupid pillow that had no purpose except for ruffles. I lay down on her bed and smashed that pillow over my face. It smelled like rose petals. And rich people.

Her dead grandfather, Danielle explained, had founded an oil company and an airline. Her dead father had gambled away his part of the trust, which was why Eileen had left him for Gib, Danielle's stepfather, an SAE buddy of her uncle's at USC.

"SAE?" I almost asked. "USC?" Only then understanding that the world we had sailed into was one long, impenetrable monogram and that the Danielle in that bedroom was no longer the Danielle who refused to buy dish soap when she could steal a free bar of hand soap from the chem lab and get everything just as clean.

I slid her ruffle pillow off my face. And looked at her.

She slid her eyes to the carpet, not to look at me. I wished for a minute that she were my real sister and we could just get into a stupid fight that involved us rolling around and pulling hair until she admitted she was phony and a liar. But as we both knew, she wasn't my real sister or even related to me in any way. Did she understand how worried I had been—about breakdowns, accidents, driving at night? Did she even care that I had pushed my poor, beleaguered Bug through the heat of Kansas, praying as I poured water into her radiator? At any point, Danielle could have let me know that if our engine did melt on the side of the road, she could fix it for us with one of her big, fat Californian sacks of money.

She smiled at me—a tight smile, the kind I knew from junior high, from girls who had kissed one of my brothers and all of a sudden worried that I hated their guts. It wasn't like I could forgive her or make her feel better. But it did occur to me, for the first time, that I might not be the only one of us who had banked her happiness on the two of us staying friends.

"Maggie?" said Danielle. Her voice worried. A first.

I marched my mind through the weekends we had spent last winter, chasing owls in the Adirondacks, shining flashlights into trees. And my birthday my sophomore year when she gave me wild honey in a jar, harvested from a hive by Banfield Creek. "Oh, shut up," I said—not kindly, but not completely unkindly either.

Eileen wafted into the room, straightening the wicker loveseat, fluffing the cushions. She looked exactly like Danielle, only with her smile somehow sprayed into place. "Honestly, Danielle," she said. "Dinner is already served. And you know how I hate to yell."

* * *

DINNER IN CARMEL CONSISTED OF tomatoes and cottage cheese, plus the booze and ice cubes. Once we all were seated, I realized I was shorter than everybody on the patio, including Gib—a lean, fit, baldish man who wore shoes without socks and managed to keep one of those shoes dangling from his foot without it ever falling off. The big topics between him and Eileen were an upcoming bridge game and a thing on Friday for a neighbor who got a little too enthusiastic about saving endangered ocean birds.

Somewhere during their negotiations, I leaned over to Danielle and asked her to please pass me a dead pelican. My accent may have been English. Or somehow related to Julie Andrews in *The Sound of Music*. The two of us fell off into a giggling so relentless, we never recovered.

"Girls," said Eileen in her crisp, official voice that, despite my best intentions, somehow thrilled me. "I'd really wish you would consider being more responsive to the dinner conversation."

"Let the girls have fun," said Gib. "They're young."

Another slice of that tomato. "Yes," Eileen said. "I am aware of my daughter's age."

A long acidic silence followed. Wind flickered through the candles. Invisible sprinklers ticked on. "Are you settled in?" Gib said finally. "The guestroom has the best view in the house."

I looked down at my cottage cheese. Nobody had mentioned a guestroom. Was I supposed to go find it? Was that what guests in Carmel did? "I brought a sleeping bag?" I said. "Danielle's room has carpet. I just rolled it out on that."

Gib nodded, as if irritated. And pinched out the nearest candle.

"The sheets in the guestroom are filthy," said Eileen.

"That's too bad," said Gib. "As we have a guest."

"I'm fine," I said. "I don't mind."

"Maybe we *all* should sleep on the floor," said Gib. "Danielle's room! Pajama party!"

Danielle laughed—a hard blistery laugh, so ugly sounding I was a little embarrassed for her. Eileen patted my hand. More silence, an entire night's worth of silence. "Consuela only comes on Tuesdays now," she said finally. "I had her focus on the closets. I didn't know we were expecting Maggie. Or Danielle."

I studied the candle on the table, the lick of blue under the flame. Our plan, which was Danielle's plan, had been to ask for five hundred dollars after the second round of cocktails, once everyone was relaxed. Not that she was asking. Or that anyone seemed relaxed. The ocean smashed against the rocks like spattered moonlight. There was too much salt on my food, and I didn't know if you were supposed to eat the skin on the tomato or not. Eileen ate hers. Danielle didn't. Gib drank.

"I'm just saying," said Eileen, "I could use a little help."

Another laugh from Danielle, just as ugly as the first. She reached over, grabbed Gib's glass, and took an elaborate sip. "Did you miss me?" she said, not to him but to her mother.

Eileen turned to me. "Nothing too taxing," she said. "Just some pitching in."

"I can do the laundry," I said. "And mow the lawn. Back in high school, at my house, I mowed the lawn all the time."

"Did you?" said Danielle.

I swung around, thinking she was questioning my ability to cut grass, realizing, only at the last second, that she was talking to Eileen.

"Did I what?" said her mother.

"Miss me?" said Danielle.

Eileen looked across the patio, smiled, and brushed a finger over her collar bone as if feeling for a necklace that wasn't there. "Danielle," she said. "I think we all know why you're here."

Gib took back his glass and sucked down what was left. "Well," he said. "Let's leave it at: Your mother missed you and she's had too much to drink."

"Yes," said Eileen, looking down at her glass, which was still full, marked only by an imprint of lipstick where she'd had her first sip. "Time for bed."

* * *

LATER THAT NIGHT BACK IN her room, Danielle told me in a tight tone-less voice, "Eileen isn't going to help us, okay? Don't kiss up to Eileen." Gib had cut off her allowance, probably. That was why

Consuela only came on Tuesdays, if she even came at all. Gib did things like that. Just to remind Eileen who was paying for her lifestyle.

Eileen had no real money of her own. She lived off Gib and his polyester knitwear business. His factories were all over the South, supplying shit sweaters to shit chains like Sears and JCPenney. Plus The Limited, some store in the Midwest. "He just can't shut up about his bootstraps," said Danielle.

I looked up at the sparkle ceiling, which oddly was the same sparkle ceiling as in my and my sister's bedroom. This latest update to Danielle's family only made me more confused. Why couldn't she just tell me what was going on? And didn't she realize that my whole family shopped at Sears? We took our Christmas picture at the portrait studio—the whole family lined up by a fake mantel with fake stockings.

"You'll see," she said. "Sometimes he cuts off her memberships or her credit cards. Or sells her car without telling her."

"Okay," I said. Memberships.

Some questions I didn't ask: If Gib was so crappy, why did she drink out of his glass? Why didn't she hate him, instead of Eileen? The one question I did: "Did she do something to him?"

"She doesn't leave him," said Danielle. "That's what she does."

I shut my eyes. I felt tired all of a sudden. I wanted to go home, but not really, maybe just sleep in the Bug for the rest of our visit.

"I'll get us the money, Maggie," she said.

And she did. Though not the way I imagined. For the next two weeks, I ran around doing exactly what she said to avoid: vacuuming and lemon waxing for Eileen, scooping leaves out of the pool, unable to resist the allure of her cool, electric disapproval.

Danielle, on the other hand, blew off her mother's designated tasks to make sandwiches for Gib. Gib loved sandwiches, she informed me, and sauntered back from his knitwear empire to eat them every day for lunch. The jamboree of planning that went into her grocery orders; the last-minute calls to request this-or-that toothpick or this-or-that can of albacore tuna packed in oil, not water; the assumption that a man from the store would drive the food to the house instead of her getting in a car and buying it herself seemed laughable at first.

Until I tasted one of her sandwiches—sliced in crustless, geometrically exact triangles, layered with a wisp of smoky ham, accessorized with just a shaving of pickle. Still others came with olives cut into flowers or pinwheeled slices of lemon or a second tier of translucent pink salmon that Danielle promised didn't make you puke, even if it was fish and mostly raw. And the mayonnaise that she made—made! with a whisk!

Danielle's mayonnaise tasted like freshly buttered cloud.

I had to wonder if some meticulous nutjob had taken over her personality—or if all that prepping and finessing was how she secretly did everything, including her carvings.

The last day we ever spent in that house, I almost asked her. The two of us were in the kitchen. Danielle was toasting bread over the stove, then pulling it off just before it browned—when Gib showed up in the doorway. He pulled out the chair beside me and sat down. That had never happened. We had eaten together, but even since the guestroom mix-up, he had never addressed me directly again. I wasn't even sure if he knew the Bug in the driveway was mine.

"You should try her chicken salad," he said. "She puts almonds in it. Not whole ones, just the slivers."

I nodded, still sweaty from pruning Eileen's bougainvillea and worried that I smelled. Central AC, I had learned, could do that to you. The cold on your hot open skin.

Danielle took out a bunch of celery, started peeling off the leaves.

Gib leaned closer as if about to share another sandwich secret. "Maggie," he said. "Maybe it's time for you to go home." His face was bland, no expression. Just like his voice.

Home. I laughed, but only a little. Then looked at Danielle, who had her back to us, who was not laughing or even looking at me, just slicing that celery. Slowly, evenly. As if plowing through a scale on a broken piano. Time thickened somehow. Along with my mind. "We're going to Alaska," I said. "We're building a cabin."

"You're a practical girl. Hard-working," said Gib. "But everyone sees how you look at Danielle. It's disconcerting."

A smell boiled off me, one that had nothing to do with air-conditioning and everything to do with stink and fear. I wanted to hide behind it. I wanted it to burn off the weak, wobbly look on my face that showed him that even if I knew nothing about the world, I knew what he meant. I didn't look at Danielle anyway. Unless I did. And I didn't know it?

I shut my eyes. There was the smell of cooling toast, the sound of Danielle's knife. Why wasn't she helping? Why didn't she say something, yell something, get him off me?

"Maggie," said Gib. "All I'm saying is that Danielle doesn't like when people fall all over her, besotted. She gets bored. She runs away. And then there you are—alone and heartbroken."

"I didn't fall all over her," I said. "I mean I don't—"

He tightened his hand, over mine, his grip furious, dry, hateful—and I understood, finally, that it was Gib who had fallen all over her, Gib who she had run away from. "I'm her friend," I said, but this time in a calm clear voice, the very first adult voice of my life.

"Wonderful," he said. "Then you won't end up left behind on the side of some highway." He smiled. It was a terrible smile—wrinkled and defeated, so much so that despite the fear curdling through me, the bile at the back of my throat, I almost felt sorry for him. And that, more than anything, scared me enough to yank back my hand.

"It's a long road to Alaska," he said. "Isn't it, Danielle?"

Danielle set down her knife.

"Go ahead," said Gib. "You might as well ask."

"Just give it to me," she said. She was shaking. Her finger was bleeding. She didn't seem to notice. I didn't know what to do, how to help her. Luckily the patio door slid open. In breezed Eileen, whisking open cabinets, sticking fresh-cut freesias into a vase. "Girls," she said. "Let's use the butterfly plates!"

How long she had been there, how much she had heard or already knew, I couldn't tell. And yet, with her bright cool directive, the world lurched back to life. The butterfly plates had little scalloped edges. The ice-tea pitcher needed more ice. Danielle had cut her finger—just a little. Eileen bandaged it up, threw the bloody celery in the garbage. Nobody needed celery in egg salad, said Eileen. As long as we added a little relish, it would all be fine.

"Danielle is upset," said Gib. "She didn't get what she wanted."

"Honey?" said Eileen.

"She needs to go lie down," he said. "Somewhere not so loud, not so crowded. Maybe in the guestroom where it's quiet. Once you change the filthy sheets."

Nothing changed on Eileen's face—her expression smooth, glossy, unreadable. She folded a dish towel. She patted it and placed it on the counter. "I have an idea!" she said. "You girls can take your lunch with you. On the road! You can have a picnic by the beach."

Danielle looked at me. I looked at her: Time to go. We went

into her room and began packing up our gear as if that had been the plan all along: jeans, toothbrush, some laundry I had forgotten about in the hamper. Danielle was grabbing stuff but the wrong stuff, sweaters, hairbrushes.

Gib circled in behind us. He sat down on her bed and picked up the ruffle pillow, studying the satin pleats, the little button at the center like it was some tender young flower.

"We're leaving," said Danielle "Just like you wanted."

"I believe that's what your mother wanted," he said. Then shrugged, as if overcome by the sad, complicated truth of the matter.

I grabbed her arm, I grabbed our packs, and we ran for the car. As I was backing down the driveway, Eileen flagged us down. She had a hamper. Inside were sandwiches and melon balls and some of those lacy chocolate cookies Danielle had always enjoyed. Plus a jar of instant coffee and a little coil that you could plug into your cigarette lighter, then dunk into a cup of water to heat it up.

Danielle didn't get out of the front seat, not to hug her mother, not to say goodbye.

Eileen hovered around the back of the car. I loaded the hamper. I admired the little coil, just to make her feel better. "Wow," I said, "it just heats up?"

"I ordered it for you," she called out as we drove off. Danielle rolled up the window, stared straight ahead. "From a catalog!" she said, waving. "Mail order, Danielle! Horchow!"

* * *

TWO MILES OVER THE CARMEL town line, I hit a chipmunk—not even a stupid squirrel—and had to pull over. I leaned over the steering wheel, trying not to throw up on my own lap. I shut my eyes. I breathed.

"At least we didn't let him give us the money," said Danielle. "He just goes on like that, talking shit. Until he gives you the money. And then he cries." She looked out the window.

What was wrong with crying? I was crying. For her, mostly. And she was not. Across the parking lot of the car wash where we had stopped, there was a pay phone. I swept all our change out of the holder. I shoved it in the slot, not listening for one coin to rattle down before adding another.

"Mom?" I said, waiting for the operator to ask for extra dimes.

"Call on Sunday!" Mom said, panicking already about the long distance. "After dinner! When everybody's here!"

"Mom," I said. "Remember when you didn't let me go to that sleepover at Alice Avery's? Because Dad saw her dad kick the Franklins' dog?"

"Honey?" she said.

"I'm fine," I said. "I'm—"

"Mary Margaret," she said. "Are you crying?"

"I hit a chipmunk," I said. "That's all."

Before she could bring up the Saint Christopher medal she had hung on the rearview mirror, I told her about the ocean, how beautiful it was, how I wished she could see it.

Back at the car, Danielle had the window open, a foot slung out. She was eating one of the sandwiches. Somehow. I plugged in the coil into the lighter to make some coffee and inside the jar— rolled up very tightly, packed into the instant crystals—I found a roll of money. One-hundred-dollar bills. I yanked them out but they were stuck together. I counted. Then recounted. There were ten, eleven. "Wait," I said. "Eileen?"

"Her runaway money," Danielle said, her voice breaking. But only slightly.

A fly landed on the dash. A car honked at another car in the line for the car wash. I waited for her to admit how crappy she had been to her mom, how mean she had been in the driveway. Instead, she climbed into the backseat, curling into our sleeping bags.

My homegrown was exactly what it sounded like—a weak crumble that I had cultivated back in Ithaca between tomato seedlings. Danielle hardly ever smoked. And now I knew why. She got zonked out of her mind, begging to pull over at every drive-through on the side of the road. California, as I soon found out, had a lot of drive-throughs.

Nothing much changed through Oregon or Washington. The math began to add up: fifteen a night for the motels where Danielle insisted that we sleep, more for onion rings and cheeseburgers. Add to that, all the days slipping by, days we would need later to build some kind of cabin and get settled. I wanted to scream at her. I wanted to slap her once or twice. But I couldn't. I knew as well as she did that she had gone back to Carmel and made Gib his sandwiches for me. To get me to the real Alaska.

* * *

TWO DAYS AND SOME THIRTEEN hundred miles away from Peace Arch and the cherry showdown at the border, Danielle and I were almost back to the way we had been at Cornell. Laughing. Cannonballing off rocks. Sitting on the bottom of frigid glass lakes, our breath bubbling up, teacups lifted to our lips. I shot up to the surface first, as always. Danielle shot up second, never mentioning that she had lasted longer. We pitched the tent. We bickered over the stakes and rain cover. And never, not once, did we mention Carmel.

Still, just past the bridge at Teslin River, Danielle forgot about skipping from first to third and jammed the gearshift into second. There was a grinding noise. A thunk from the undercarriage. When I crouched down, fluid was pooling all over the road, a twist of metal in the middle. "I guess we better find a garage," she said. "And get it fixed?"

The look on her face was unmistakable—relief. So much that I wondered if she had made the mistake on purpose. A new transmission was going to eat up most of the Folgers money. Not all of it, but enough to set us back again. Was that what she was after? Still?

I wanted to shake her. I wanted, just for once, to stop worrying about her, to worry instead about everything ahead of us and how to pull it all off before the ground froze and the weather turned. We didn't need a car. We had Alaska. We had a whole life. For a minute it occurred to me that I could leave her—not the other way around, the way that Gib had brought up in the kitchen. All I had to do was pick up my pack and start walking.

"Maggie?" Danielle said.

The jar was in my pack. It was Danielle's jar, really, Danielle's money. Not that she would fight me for it. She would make me take it. And that I couldn't live with, even in my mind, where nobody could see me turning over the idea, polishing it with reasons and excuses until they outshone the ball of shit-ugly truth at the center.

"I guess we better catch a ride," I said. Like the sky had planned it, lightning broke above the tree line. The rain started. Danielle tossed me a poncho and slung on her pack. I slung on mine, my betrayal washing away along with the dust and gnats.

When a car pulled over, we were deep in the Yukon forests.

There was a woman at the wheel. She had kids with her. I felt a little weird about it. We hadn't seen a single kid on the Alcan. Still, a family had to be safer than some guy in a rig. We got in—both of us in the backseat, on either side of the oldest one, a girl.

3. Laurel: Fort Nelson, British Columbia, to Whitehorse, Yukon Territory

YOU HAD A STYE IN your left eye, thickening under the lid. The fix was simple—ice or an ice-cold can of soda held on to the swelling knot. Soda cost forty cents Canadian, thirty-five cents American. This was all you could think of, once you got to Fort Nelson. The aluminum coolness. The frost on the throb. The quarters you didn't have in either currency, except to save for gas.

Little black moths blew up in the dark and fluttered through the headlights. They were not real. They were exhaustion. You drove and drove and drove—one-eyed, pus in your tears, both hands gripped. Outside Lower Post, storm clouds ghosted over the moon. You were on this highway for the rest of your life, you realized. Anywhere you went, some part of you would always be here in the Cutlass, your kids slumped over the seats like piles of limp pajamas. They were sleeping all the time by then, the way babies do in loud places, to make it all go quiet.

You had done this to them. Once again.

As the town and trees and miles clicked by, you heard Richard in your head on the pay phone. This was back in Prophet River, where you had known not to stop and call him, especially not collect. But Janice had insisted and you were already too tired to fight. The first few seconds, he had almost sounded excited. Then he went straight to distant: "A visit, wow, would be nice," he said. There was a motel he knew about, one safe and not too expensive. He would give you the name, you should book a room for you and your kids.

So. He was married. You should have known. Then again, you did know, or you knew enough to ask, and even if you had asked, there was a vase of flowers in your heart that only people who like breaking things could see.

This had been going on since you were a child. You were not stupid, but you were blind. At this point, almost literally. The stye was getting bigger and you wondered why you hadn't just turned back after the pay phone, why you had driven faster and faster past Fort Nelson then Steamboat then Liard Hot Springs. Kevin had his head in your lap, his mouth open, his lashes thick and heavy on his cheeks.

Whenever a car blew by, you got a flash of Janice in the rear-view mirror, her fingers closed tight around the gold that Richard had sent—a dime's worth of cheap, shiny flake. She met your eyes sometimes and smiled a pleased, shy smile as if she had won an award at school and was worried that the teacher had somehow made a mistake.

Just past Teslin, at the gas station, the old man owner let you use the washroom. Washroom was what they called it in Canada. You splashed cold water on the stye and found the kids by the register, lusting after bright, twinkly cakes in cellophane wrappers. Neither of them whined or pleaded. They knew better and so did you: Coffee was twenty-seven cents, soda forty, aspirin a distant, cotton-packed dream.

The old man at the register smelled of diesel and the kind of loneliness that might somehow help you. He had an office in the back. A TV on the file cabinet, crackling with cowboys and static. You opened the freezer, just to feel the cold on your eyes and get yourself ready. It would be like the night with the manager at the Saddle Up. You would do it and it would be over, save for the taste in the back of your throat. Three dollars could not get you to Alaska and there was nowhere behind you left to go. Not after Mormon Carol's visit to your motel room.

There she had stood in the doorway with her sad vinyl handbag and her pamphlets, warning you that she had seen the marks on Kevin's arm. By law, she told you, she had to tell the teacher. Morally, though, she thought she ought to let you know before anyone showed up asking questions. Maybe she could help? She had resources. From the church.

You knew to be careful about women; women were not your friends, especially women without kids. They didn't understand. They didn't want to. They only wanted a kid that wasn't even a kid—only a cartoon of one, drawn in Magic Marker, who listened when you said to clean up and hugged you instead of pulling away, embarrassed.

Mormon Carol offered you a Wet Wipe. From a travel pack inside her purse. Why didn't you just shut the door then? Why didn't you throw her Bible at her? Why didn't you say Kevin had fallen? Or had a fight with his sister?

You knew why.

At that moment, the cool from the freezer blew over your eye. You leaned in, you let yourself drift. Janice slid past you, eyeing the canned food on the bottom shelves, about to lift something from the middle near the baked beans. She was fast, too fast for even you, and even if you had caught her, you didn't have it in you to parade her up to the counter and make her apologize. Much less offer to pay for whatever she had taken and hope the old man refused.

"Why does only Janice get to hold the gold?" said Kevin.

So he had seen her too. You leaned against the cool, smoky frost from the cooler. Your eye throbbed. You were wearing cutoffs and a peasant top, with a tear in the Mexican cotton. You were not beautiful anymore. A realization that flickered through you like the broken porch light above your mother's old front door. Your mother waiting up after dances, smiling her defeated smile at what she knew weren't punch stains on your taffeta.

"Happy Canada Day," said the old man at the register. "Help yourself to a pop."

You smiled. You had never heard of Canada Day and you wanted to thank him, but what you needed was gas. You put your hand on the old man's hand and tilted your head. All he had to do was nod and walk back into his office. You would follow. The kids would still be fighting over the gold by the time you both came back.

He stared at you. Then slid his hand from underneath your hand like your hand was a spider. "We get lots of people coming through here," he said. "None of them understand how slick that gravel gets."

"We'll be fine," you said, your stye swelling, your humiliation a hot open hole in your face.

"Don't forget to take that pop," he said in a kinder voice, though maybe this was pity. "Or a coffee. We have creamer."

You took a Sunkist for Janice. She was lying down in the back of the Cutlass, the bottle of gold held tight in her hand. On the driver's side, right under your steering wheel, lay three cans of green beans. "Janice," you said. "Where did you get green beans?"

"Maybe somebody left them," she said. "Or didn't want them."

Three dollars and a quarter tank was all you had left. Plus the green beans. And no can opener. You leaned your forehead against the wheel, the molded grips in the plastic almost comforting under your eyelid.

"How come only Janice gets to hold the gold?" said Kevin, his voice tightening.

All you had to do was hand him the glass tube, hand Janice the Sunkist. It was easier. She was easier. Except that you had seen those baked beans on the shelf beside the green ones. You loved baked beans. Janice knew you loved them. She still remembered that long-ago motel in Pocatello with the hot plate—your warming up the sweet, soupy liquid, pouring it into Styrofoam cups so nobody burned their fingers. Rainy day beans. She had moved too fast, trying to make you happy and had grabbed the wrong can.

"Mom," said Kevin, "how come only Janice gets to hold the gold?"

You sat up. You turned the key and pressed the gas. "Because she got us dinner," you said. "Mommy loves green beans. Go to sleep."

*   *   *

ALL THE WAY TO JOHNSON'S Crossing, rain slashed over the windshield like melted glass. Gravel spit and sang beneath the tires. You pushed the pedal down, right to the point where the driving felt like skating on smooth, oiled ice. Your hands on the wheel were spiders with rings and there was a spider in your mind now too—dangling there, whispering that if you crashed, the feeling would be over, the scrabbling terrible feeling that made you try and try and try and try and try even when you would always do it wrong with Kevin's teacher or the mattress-store manager or the head receptionist at the dentist's office who said that all support staff—even those with children—needed to arrive by eight a.m. Regardless of when school started.

It was you who had told Mormon Carol that yes, Kevin had a bruise on his arm, and yes, you had given it to him because he had said he was embarrassed to be seen with you on his birthday: Your shorts were too short and you didn't have the money to get into the bowling alley and you didn't smell like cookies or mommies.

He said it all without meanness, like he was reading the motel room rate posted on the back of the door. You told him to go to the bathroom, which was where you sent him when he was in trouble—and when he wouldn't go, you dragged him in there and sat him on the toilet and held him down for a minute by his arms, wanting so very much to slap the blank, hateful look off his face. But you didn't. You took a breath. You drank a Dixie cup of water. You left the bathroom and shut the door and spent the next half hour picking up dirty clothes and folding them as if they were clean and needed putting away.

Fifteen minutes later, when you walked by, Kevin was sitting on the toilet, his legs swinging, too short for his feet to touch the floor. There he was again—your baby, your little, little boy. You hadn't hit him. You had tried and it had worked. You told Mormon Carol all this—crying into her Wet Wipe like she wasn't taking notes to use on the phone with Social Services later.

* * *

RAIN DRILLED ACROSS THE ROOF. Your stye grew thicker. The world narrowed down the wormhole that your one good eye allowed, a tunnel inside the tunnel of the road ahead. Two lumps of poncho—two girls with backpacks—flashed up on the shoulder and you fishtailed to a stop.

"Tok?" the first girl said, when you rolled down the window. You nodded, though you had no idea where Tok was, nor would you until you got there 1,314 miles later and had enough cash to finally buy a map of the trip you had already taken.

The girl was sturdy, with boots that looked as if she could walk the rest of the way to Alaska if she felt like it. She slung off her pack and started rummaging around for something hidden deep inside, under the clothes. Money.

Her friend stopped her—smarter maybe or just more cautious— and held up a wet ten. "We'll pay for the gas once we get to the station," she said. Then tucked the bill back in her pocket.

You looked at the friend. She was sleek and beautiful in an animal way, tall as a man. You waited another minute, pretending to decide. "Get in," you said at last. "But no ponchos on the upholstery."

The smell of wet plastic and fresh-smoked weed gusted through the Cutlass. The girls were rain-greased, young, so alive. You touched your own hair as if there was a bug stuck in it and told yourself not to check your face again in the rearview mirror.

You had ten dollars now. Almost. If you could make it to a gas station. Plus the three you already had. That gave you three hundred miles. Even if the needle was hovering right at empty. The girls would never notice the gauge. Or think to look. They had sat in the backseat all their lives, eating bologna sandwiches, going to college. You coasted on the downhills, prayed, drove on.

"Cool rings," said the first one. Her name was Maggie. Mary Margaret really, she said, but only around her family. You looked at your hands on the wheel. They were hands again, not spiders. The glint of silver. The turquoise eagles. Kevin's face was healed almost and normal looking. When you flipped on the heater, he didn't flinch.

He was watching the needle. He knew about the gas. If only you had that ten already, you could give it to him. He loved the long busy little numbers in the corner of bills. Whenever you had one, you gave it to him to play with.

Maggie's friend kept staring at the back of your head.

"*Danielle,*" said Maggie, as if telling her to stop.

"It's a stye," said Janice. "Mom gets them when she gets too tired." She went on: Did Maggie like Sunkist? Had Maggie ever found a mountain bluebird feather? Was Maggie a teenager? Did she have her own room—with, like, posters?

All that need Janice had, rolling through every question. You fiddled with the radio. Then snapped it off. The gas in the tank was so low, the needle started to twitch.

"I can whistle," Janice said. "With two fingers."

"I can throw a baton," said Maggie. "And, one time, I delivered a baby mule."

"Not the mules again," said Danielle. Followed by "Shit!" Something had whacked her on the ankle. "Green beans?" she said, holding up the can.

"I love that casserole," said Maggie. "With the onions."

"We have other stuff," said Janice. "For when we stop to eat."

Nothing from the backseat. You just kept driving. Past Jake's Corner. No gas. No houses. No lights. Whitehorse, you decided. You could make it. You floored it, the tires on the Cutlass shuddering over the wooden planks of the bridge, the whole car rumbling as you pushed it faster and faster. Water surged to either side, gray with moon and storm.

"Are we okay?" said Danielle.

"We need gas," said Maggie. "Don't we?"

You said nothing. Neither did anyone else. They were trying to figure out what to say. Gravel spun up in the headlights, little sparkling black stars. Wet white sky. You gained a few miles, a few seconds, another dark parade of trees. There was light on the wet road ahead, a sign blazing at you almost too perfect to trust: Sunoco.

"Hey," said Maggie, pointing over your shoulder. "Let's fill up."

You eased the car over to a pump and tried not to study the dull click of numbers. Or the attendant leaning on the back of the trunk as if he could stop it with his body weight if you tried to drive off without paying. The fill-up cost $9.40 American. Maggie passed him the ten and you couldn't help it, you turned around and stared at it the way every woman in the world knows to never look at money—ready to snap off the fingers that held it. Danielle was staring at you. Maggie was staring at you. You knew why. Your eyes were spiders.

You had to do something. Inside their matching packs, they had allowances and travel money from Grandpa, birthday checks from Mom and Dad. You could not let them get out of the car. And you could not look at Janice. Janice loved them. Janice read every thought spinning through your mind as if it had started inside her own.

Across the highway, directly opposite from the Sunoco, blinked a sign: CHOPS. PASTA. COCKTAILS. The windows were fogged with steam, the curtains lacy invitations. There had been a story you had read when you were a child. In the story, a little girl without shoes had looked through the windows of a bakery and longed for the hot cross buns inside on the tray, the bright sticky frosting in the X of bread. You had never seen a hot cross bun. You were not sure if they even existed. But that was how you felt about those windows, the promise of a candle at the table, a little pottery pitcher of wine.

"Mom," said Kevin in a voice that made you believe for a moment he was thinking of the same story. That was impossible. Or was it? Maybe you had told him about the hot cross buns one rainy day, before bed. You ran a finger through his soft, sleepy-smelling hair. His father's hair.

He looked up. "Janice didn't really get us dinner," he said. "Green beans aren't dinner."

You shook your head, confused. And then you got it. If you were going to eat at the restaurant, then Janice hadn't stolen the green beans for dinner. And if Janice hadn't stolen the green beans for dinner, then Kevin didn't have to let her have the gold. A thought sliced through you, a thought that you felt sharpening inside you for so long and resisted—that Kevin saw the vase in your heart, that Kevin liked to break things too.

You shrugged, just the way you had done when you were talking to Richard, as if he could see over the phone line how good you were at looking unshaken, unbetrayed. Before Kevin could say, "I want spaghetti," before Janice could say, "Kevin, shut up, we only have three dollars," before Danielle and Maggie looked at each other and confirmed that now was the time to hold on to their packs a little tighter and get out of the car, you said, "Are you guys hungry?" in a bright, tinseled voice that invited the whole car to listen. "Why don't we all go inside and have a nice hot dinner? My treat."

4. Danielle: Whitehorse, Yukon, to Hudson, New York

Dear Mags,

How I miss you, Miss Maggie. My lady of perpetual laughter. My first and only friend. I see you everywhere, but never for long enough. A woman swings her backpack off her shoulders on the ferry and there you are for an instant before a seagull cries or a man says, "Ticket, lady. Please." You have nodded at me from a streetcar stop in West Berlin and called my name while boarding a bus outside of Mexico City. You are either in front of me in line, ordering a mango Popsicle, or on the side of the road loading a kayak into a pickup. You turn up at my show in Tokyo and whisper to a woman beside you who is not me.

Last summer, I saw you striding over the tidal flats and despite my sixty-seven-year-old knees, I ran toward you, crying out your name. Whoever I was chasing was a young, upright woman in a Patagonia rain jacket. She moved with purpose through the high grass, unaware, stopping only to dip her feet into the creek.

* * *

Over the years, my assistant, Cheryl, has sifted through the internet, unearthing pictures of your wedding in Rochester and your four boys from Ethiopia, all of them taller than you, a different skin color than you, but with smiles that are entirely yours. After the purchase of your farmhouse in Millerton, New York, she showed me a printout of the entire property, including the barn. Every fall, I imagine you harvesting chanterelles in the woods behind the garden and in the winter, running a syrup line along the maples by the creek. In the summer, you grow

*medicinal herbs and can enormous vats of ketchup from
the last of August tomatoes.*

*Your boys are adults now, Maggie. But they must
still visit, along with their children. Did you ever tell
them about the time we made snowshoes from scrap sheet
metal and two fraying bungee cords? Or about the night
you took me owling? How you dragged me through the
forest with a flashlight and a battered guide to nocturnal
animals? How we ducked and clung to each other under
the great meaty rush of the bird you summoned?*

*That it was me, not you, who finally made it to Alaska
seems almost grotesque. You were smarter than me. You
worked harder. Of the two of us, you had all the ideas and
drive, though you never seemed to realize this. There were
so many times I almost told you and so many times I never
did. Envious, I suppose. Or perhaps just grateful.*

*Not even ag school was really ever mine. Deep in
her undiscussed past, Eileen had grown up on a failing
almond farm in Chico. I went to Cornell to snub her,
possibly humiliate her, goals that Gib encouraged. Until
he found out that I didn't need his financial support.
He thought it was the real Cornell, not the one with a
teaching forest and state-subsidized tuition.*

*Our senior year, my secret plan was to follow you home
to Rochester and find us an apartment where your mother
could come over for coffee and help us make slipcovers for
our secondhand couch. After work—someone eventually
had to hire us—we could play basketball with your father
and brothers. Some nights, I even let myself imagine
trooping along for the annual Christmas picture, an*

event I saw so clearly in my mind, as if I had carved it out of your memory, all of us lined up by the fake mantel under the fake stockings, until the photographer gently reminded me that I wasn't actually a member of the family . . . maybe I could help him with the light meter?

It's a little embarrassing, how I used to belittle myself in my mind. Though I always wondered if you didn't do it too. That's what I saw every time you brought up Alaska, how quickly the dazzle in your eye withered into a smile that wasn't quite a smile, how you shrugged as if to free yourself from what you most wanted.

*   *   *

If you're reading this letter, you've already received the piece I shipped to you in Millerton. It is larger than I had originally planned; the installation more invasive to your daily life than I had anticipated. Some issues with the Fondation Beyeler, the Swiss museum which originally commissioned the piece, may also complicate matters, though Cheryl has informed me that most of these legal disputes have been resolved.

It was not easy, Maggie, informing the curatorial staff that I was not going to deliver my work as promised. But I knew that it belonged to you, almost from the first moment I discovered the fallen spruce on my property and decide to carve it.

All that said, if the piece makes you uncomfortable

*or if you wish to avoid these issues in favor of a quick,
profitable sale, I will understand. Please use the proceeds
however you like. The Dia Beacon—whose collection is so
glaringly, so geometrically male—has already reached out
about the acquisition, as has a private Korean collector.
Cheryl can help you with these negotiations, though I
doubt you will need her. You have always had excellent
judgment. Even now, I regret not listening to you at
that restaurant in Whitehorse. Remember how you told
me to stay at the table while you went to the salad bar?
Remember how I laughed? How I made you promise to
bring me back a few croutons and a cob of baby corn?*

*That I was still trying to prove how cavalier I was,
how reckless and untouchable is laughable. After Carmel,
even I knew the jig was up. You had seen through me.
I had seen through me. But somehow I believed I could
fool the mother, or at the very least keep up with her.
Everything about her was so bleak and alive, so glittering
with a flat absolute lack of fear. Already I wanted to carve
her—or be her.*

*As we sat at the table, I began to memorize her
cheekbones, the hard narrow angle of her neck. She must
have felt the strangeness of my attention. She leaned in,
pushing aside the pitcher of wine and nodding to the bar.
"I've been dreaming of a White Russian," she said. "For
the last three hundred miles."*

"You've got dinner," I said. "I can get you a drink."

"Mom?" said Janice.

"You're in charge," she said. "Watch your brother."

Off she swayed through the tables, men looking up,

*wives looking up, her looking straight ahead as if the
room were made of paper about to burn and blow away
behind her.*

*It wasn't as if I didn't check first, Maggie. The
mother's back was to me. The kids busy fighting over
breadsticks. Only then did I reach into your pack, unscrew
the lid of the jar, and slip out a five.*

*Considering everything I had stolen in my life—all the
add-a-beads from sleepovers, silverware from diners, soap
from the chem lab, the buck knife that I slid out from the
display case at the True Value in Ithaca—you might think
I would have simply taken the pack with me. And yet I left
it at the table, in order to catch up with the mother by the
hostess stand.*

*There, next to a stack of menus was a bowl of chalky
mints. As she passed by it, she scooped up a handful and
funneled them into her pocket. Then turned to me, her
finger over her lips as if the two of us were in on some
wondrous, outlaw secret—the look in her one good eye
so young, so pleased, so unlike the rest of her that I was
almost disappointed. And I looked away, back to the
dining room, where you were still picking through the
lettuce at the salad bar, our pack still leaning against our
chair. All fine. All as I had left it. A busboy began to work
his way toward our table, slumped under his tray. A man
followed behind him. The man was older, thick, wearing,
of all things on the Alcan, a shiny collar shirt. He said
something to Janice.*

*"Mom?" she said—too loud for the mother to ignore.
The mother shrugged. I followed.*

"Lobster tails," the man said. "That's a prepay item."

"What do you mean?" said the mother. "We haven't even eaten."

"Restaurant policy," he said. "With the lobster. Your waitress is supposed to ring you up before it's served."

An argument ensued, as I'm sure you remember. The man went on about all the fast-talking Americans who tried to take him for a ride. The mother said it was just rude, accusing her, she wanted to speak to the manager. He said she didn't need the manager, she had the owner right there. Janice looked down at the floor. "I forgot something," she said. "In the car."

"No you didn't," said Kevin.

"Go pee," she whispered. "Just go pee, okay?" Off Janice went, out to the car. Kevin hesitated, looking over at the mom who was only looking at the owner. Then did as Janice said.

I thought they were embarrassed, Maggie. I was embarrassed. The mother said she must have forgotten her wallet. You came hurrying over with your salad, but the owner grabbed her purse, dumped the contents on the table, and there was the wallet—a few bills, some change.

"I'm calling the Mounties," he said.

I glanced down at our packs. They were there. They were fine, except for your top strap. It was twisted. You would never, ever buckle a twisted strap. I understood what had happened only as a sear of bright panic: The jar inside was gone, Janice had gone to the car, Janice had taken it.

I ran out, just as you started telling the man there was

*a mistake. You had planned on paying all along. It was
you who had invited everyone to dinner. There was no need
to speak to the mother that way, not in front of her kids.*

* * *

*Thirty-nine years later, my life in Alaska isn't even
close to what we planned—or rather, what you planned
for us, with such exuberance and imagination. I live
on a three-acre compound with a cabin, a studio, and
a semifunctional bathhouse, no fields, greenhouses,
livestock, or garden. Last summer, Cheryl did convince
me to try raising chickens—everyone in Southeast
raises chickens—but after I forgot to feed them and a
bloodthirsty marten dug his way into the coop, we both
gave up on fresh eggs.*

*At this point, the only animals on the property are the
dogs inside my electric fence and the brown bears outside
it, the latter of which lumber through alders, endlessly
puzzled by the lady with long gray braids who marches
around with a chain saw, muttering to herself. My
generator provides relatively stable power, but landlines
and Wi-Fi are still impossible this far off the grid.*

*However it may sound, it's not as if I conquered
some corner of the vast Alaskan frontier without your
guidance. All that was accomplished over a century
before, in the late 1800s when thousands of stampeders
built Dyea overnight, seeking gold on Chilkoot trail. Only*

to abandon their makeshift city just as quickly over rumors of bigger, wilder riches to be found farther north.

Today, the road outside my compound is paved, the postman delivers. There is a chat board, Cheryl tells me, for all thirty-seven full-time residents. When the cruise ships unload their passengers in Skagway each summer, hundreds of them flock to Dyea for walking tours of the boomtown ruins or eco-adventures down the Taiya River. Every once in a while, an oddball art devotee slips in through the throng, ringing the cowbell on my gate, alarming the dogs.

I should be grateful, I suppose, that anyone cares about my work enough to drop by, invited or otherwise. Had I not been white and educated I would have been considered an outsider artist and profiled in a charming yet disturbing documentary. As it is, I am merely a local eccentric who hisses at neighbors and hands out whole bags of candy on Halloween. Or would, if any of the local children risked a visit to my door.

* * *

To research you on the internet, poor Cheryl had to drive fourteen miles over the mountain and use the Skagway library. She was able, however, to confirm that the barn behind your farmhouse is unused, all the farming on your land done by a neighbor who rents the acreage. That your home is only a weekend property, that you live in a town house in Brooklyn with an elevator and a five-hundred-bottle wine cellar did leave me a little speechless. Some part of me believes that you still must laugh at all that largesse, that it hasn't changed you. Except to relieve you of the worry you felt when we were together.

I, however, do have one concern. The picture Cheryl gave me of your husband was taken for his work on a hospital board. He looks like an intelligent, trustworthy person, but considering his career in hedge-fund management, can I ask you one favor? If he sees your piece as an investment or suggests you store it in one of those warehouses where collectors shelve their works in panic-room obscurity, can you simply have your farmer haul it outside to one of your fields? It will melt down eventually. The gold has no value, the wax is nontoxic, the wood was salvaged from my acreage. It's enough for you to have seen it, Maggie. The piece is a Kevin, my first and my last.

*   *   *

After I left you in Whitehorse, I would not be surprised if you had refused to look me up. But as this information may help you, I will say that in the small, insular land-art world, I am best known for Janice 121, *a series of living portraits that I completed during the summer of 1978, three years after I continued on to Alaska and you went back to Rochester. As I have noted to the press*

*before, my work is not autobiographical. Her face is not
a real face or even Janice's face. It's a face that my mind
composed and arranged—based on her features but even
more so on feelings that are entirely mine. I never knew
Janice. She was just the girl who vanished into the rain,
only to reappear on the shoulder, hanging out of her
mother's car.*

*You must still wonder what happened. And for that—
and so much more—I owe you an apology. The last time
I saw you was right after Janice and her mother had
sped off down the road. I had returned to the restaurant.
I was standing outside the window, watching you and
Kevin at the table, set for dinner. He was eating. You were
not. Neither of you knew that his mother and sister were
already gone, along with our money. Or so I believed,
my mind seizing as to how to tell you, Maggie. And what
would happen after I did.*

*Losing the money, I knew, would never make you give
up on Alaska. You might be worried, even furious that
I had showed Janice where our jar was and left it with
her—as desperate as I was to kiss up to her mother, to
buy her her White Russian. But you would come up with
another plan: We could work off our dinner by washing
dishes! We could find somebody to give us a ride to the
border! We could save up over the winter and start the
homestead the following summer. At some point, you might
even forgive me. Or try to.*

*Kevin, however, had changed everything. There was
nothing you could do—no cherries you could choke down,
no motel room where you could let him hide, no feasible*

way to swoop him up and take him with us. Nor could you leave him there, Maggie. Not alone. You would grate his cheese. You would make sure he ate his salad. You would be the grown-up at the table, until the someone more grown-up arrived to take over.

I knew who those grown-ups were, Maggie. Gib had made sure of it. And I was sick with fear outside that restaurant. I was shaking with it, just as I had been in the kitchen. I couldn't move. I couldn't go inside. Even if it wasn't me they were going to take away. Even if I had figured out, long ago, that no one in Carmel was ever taken away. No one was even ever called.

I told myself that if you spotted me out there, numb with cold, weepy with need, bits of gold and dirt ground in my hands, I would beg you to help me, beg you to take me back to Rochester with you, to let me be in the family Christmas picture, to let me rake leaves and make coffee cake with your mother. How selfish, however humiliating I might sound, you would do it. You would choose me over Kevin. You would take me home, as if I belonged there with you.

It wasn't an accident that you didn't see me. You didn't look up. You leaned in over Kevin, putting your arm around him, showing him how to twirl his long gluey noodles onto his fork with a spoon. He fumbled and bit his lip in concentration. You showed him one more time.

Though I knew I was soon to regret it, I left you on the Alcan that night, just as Gib predicted. Save for one thing. You had Kevin, and he had you. Neither of you were alone.

* * *

*The story of my walk up the last two hundred miles of
Canada, Cheryl tells me, is well documented. But I will
say that at that time, the highway was far less traveled.
I walked mostly in very early morning, before the truck
drivers woke up and pulled off the shoulder. Whenever I
heard an approaching vehicle, I ducked into the woods. I
was a woman without a pack or friend or money. Save for
the five dollars I had taken from the jar. Once that was
gone, I ate everything you had taught me to eat: puffballs,
lichen, berries, salmon too exhausted from spawning to
dart away from my hands.*

*At Champagne and Haines Junction, I salvaged food
from roadhouse dumpsters. Then took the first turn-off
from the Alcan, unable to finish the highway without you.
From there, I moved south toward Haines and crossed
back into the country at Pleasant Camp.*

*Remember how you made us store our birth certificates
and driver's licenses in our bras, just in case? Thank
god. You can't imagine how filthy I was, how swollen
and infected from bug bites. The look on that customs
officer's face. But what could he say? I was American. I
could prove it. He waved me through and from there, I let
myself hitch. The last ride, a truck driver for an appliance
company, invited me to tag along on the ferry to Skagway.
And even then, once we disembarked, I could not stop
walking. I headed over the mountain to tidal flats, to the
banks of a river where I slept under a bridge by the water.*

That was Dyea. At the time, the only sign of human settlement in the town was a hodgepodge of family members who had owned the hardware store in Skagway for almost a century, their forefathers having realized that selling long underwear and dog bread to stampeders was far more profitable than panning for gold.

Dorothy, the matriarch, offered me use of a platform tent with a barrel stove in exchange for garden work and looking after her broken-down horse. I fished for extra food. I ran a trapline for extra cash. I dug my knife into every promising branch or log I came across but could not manage to carve anything more than a confusion of slashes. When winter came and I didn't leave—where else was there for me to go?—Dorothy offered me a job at the store, two days a week.

My third summer in Alaska, the rain never stopped. Dorothy hired a carpenter to fix the barn and needed my tent for the season. I relocated to a campsite by the creek where I lay in my bag at night and tried not to think about Whitehorse or Carmel or, to my horrible confusion, my mother. Why couldn't I stop thinking about my mother? Why did I let myself imagine her trying to find me, tracking me down through Canada, showing up on the bank where I had pitched camp?

That deep in the alders, the mosquitoes moved in, a relentless, black, greedy frosting on my face. After a few weeks, I had trouble breathing. I had to get up and start walking through the woods until the sun rose, just to keep my heart from dying. That is what it felt like—cinders in the hole in my lung where I needed a breath.

Only the trees and the few, fleeting hours of summer darkness helped. Weeks went by without my sleeping. By July, I had this loose, whispery sense that something was hiding under the bark of a birch. I could see it almost. I took out my knife and hacked away the trunk down to the soft live wood. There was a turning in the grain. I cut away anything that wasn't it, believing for the longest time that I was carving you. What emerged, instead, was Janice. She did not look as she had when I had last seen her—hanging out the window of the car, yelling at me to hurry, to run faster. All that was gone, so much so she almost had no expression. Her eyes were shut. Had you asked me, at the time, I would have said that she looked peaceful. She looked asleep. Afterward, I went back to my tarp and passed out for days.

For the next three months, I did the same thing over and over—relief washing through me each time her face appeared under my furious slashes, each time exhausted by the end. Until the last one, the 121st, a number that meant nothing except for the sense of calm I felt when it was done, so much so that I did not need to collapse. I made a fire. I ate a can of beans. I hiked back to my camp.

Years later, when all the Janices were discovered by the larger world, I was told that with the paleness of the wood and the eventual death of the trees and the sheer number of girls' faces and the graffiti the high school kids in town had carved into those faces, the clumsy love initials and phone numbers for where to get a blow job, the result was unsettling.

As it should have been. After Whitehorse and even before Whitehorse, I was unsettled. I was not right. This

*is a condition that many people experience after arriving
in Alaska. Nothing here is fixed, nothing is any better.
Where is there left to go, except out of your mind?*

* * *

*At our age, it's natural to think about the past. The truth
is, Maggie, I never wanted to marry. Or to have a family.
That I have built my days on work, on feeding the dogs and
feeding the fire, eating long-expired cans of sardines for
dinner has allowed me, without any glimmer of intuition,
to arrive at a life that is mine. Every morning, I creak out
of bed and roll directly into the great endless task of making
something true—for lack of a better word, something without
need for applause or showmanship. At night I collapse
with the fear of knowing I have not gotten any closer to
succeeding. Nor will I ever. And it's that steadfast, endless
failure that lets me sleep—if only to wake up and try again.*

*Still, there are times when I wish I had written you
sooner, if only to tell you that the great love of my life was our
friendship. That I trusted you. That I miss you even now.*

* * *

*A few years after my last Janice, the cruise ships plying
their way up the Inside Passage began to dock at the*

Skagway harbor. A gallery owner from London named Omar Safar disembarked for a day excursion down the Taiya River, during which his guide—a young college kid from Oklahoma who was later to invent the famed Southeast spruce-tip IPA—pulled over just past the bridge to show him "a cool, creepy, secret locals-only spot."

That afternoon, Safar bought the land on which all the Janice birches stood. That night, he showed up at my campsite. Though the resulting molds and installations led to years of financial stability for me, I must tell you— and only you, Maggie—I have always been ashamed of Janice 121. *What seemed to move so many people was the dreamy refusal of her expression, her location in a remote, forgotten forest, the assumption that she had been drowned. Or strangled. Or raped. Or roofied. Or just plain killed.*

Why the world seems to find a dead girl in the woods both so upsetting and so reassuring is too obvious to discuss. And yet, whether I understood it while I was working on those faces, it was just that kind of lurid melodrama I was encouraging. I could have carved Janice urging me to hurry. Or bossing around her brother at the table. Or looking up at you, dazzled. Instead I carved all the loud, needy girl out of her, no doubt wishing that I could do the same to myself.

I wish I could explain the relief, the release I felt when I took my chain saw last year—a new electric model purchased at the Skagway hardware store—and cut them all down. Only to be sued by the consortium of private collectors who had paid for their preservation.

* * *

About that apology I have yet to give you: It begins with so much regret. I wish I had stayed in the dining room with you when Janice ran outside. I wish I had stayed by the mother's car when I didn't find her inside. Through the window, lit up like the drive-in theater we used to go to in Ithaca—wasn't it named Lakes?—I saw you standing by our table, while the owner of the restaurant dug through our packs.

For years, I wondered if you ever told him that Janice had taken our money. You couldn't have. How else could the mother have been allowed to slip outside? You were the one who tried to walk off without paying for dinner. You were the one the owner wanted to punish. What did he care if she went to check on her daughter, out there alone in the dark?

All this, of course, is conjecture. I will never know what happened. At the time, I could not afford to think of anything but how to find Janice and our jar. I looked under cars, under trucks, in the brush along the sides of the parking lot. No Janice. I ran across the highway to the Sunoco, then up the shoulder, then into the bushes on the side of the road. But the alders were too thick, the rain massing the branches into a wall of leaves. I tore through them. I begged Janice to come out—out loud, in case she could hear me. I screamed that if she didn't come out, I was going to kill her with my bare hands. Then I promised I would help her. Or give her half. Why wouldn't she just listen and come out?

Eventually I wandered back to the road. And finally stopped. She wasn't there. She wasn't anywhere. I had lost our money. I had ruined Alaska for you and rid myself of the one beautiful thing Eileen had ever done.

I was five hundred feet away from the restaurant when the Cutlass came roaring out from behind the building, no headlights, mud kicking up. Even that late, even in the rain, the sky was lit up and white. I could see the mother clearly at the wheel, driving toward me. I stood there on the shoulder, wondering if I could jump in front of the car. Or grab a rock and throw it at the windshield. But time doesn't work that way. There just wasn't enough of it. I saw her see me as she passed—her face panicked, her eye enormous, raw, blackened with blood.

Out of nowhere, she swerved and pulled over to the shoulder. Then stayed there, engine running. What was I supposed to do? Yank her out? She was a hundred yards ahead of me. I started running. But it was Janice who leaned out the window, Janice who was yelling at me. "You can do it," she said. "Run faster."

Maybe they were going to let me in. Or give me back the money. I kept going. Just as I was almost to the car, Janice threw something to me. I reached out but I wasn't ready, and whatever it was hit the ground and broke at my feet. The mother floored it off the shoulder, her lights flashing on, the puddle at my feet glittering. Janice was still hanging out the window screaming. "Give it to Kevin, okay? It's his. I didn't let him have it. I didn't give him his turn!"

And they were gone. It took me longer than it should have to realize that Kevin was still back in the restaurant, *that they had left him behind, that the puddle at my feet was for him. I bent down. I scooped up the gravel and gold with my hands. It felt as if somebody else was doing this, somebody else with dead fingers.*

* * *

For years, for decades even, I have thought about that gold. How it got under my nails and in my hair and teeth. How it clung to my skin as I limped out of Canada, no matter how many times I tried to scrub it with moss and creek water. Right after the success of Janice 121, *I bought a whole flat of similar flake from souvenir suppliers, hundreds of tubes of it, capped with cork.*

   Cheryl packed them up and shipped them to Venice for the Biennale, where I built a full-scale, functional water slide infected with beaver droppings (Fever Fountain, 2009). *When I failed to use the gold there, I had Cheryl ship it all to the Whitney for a monthlong installation during which I grew mushrooms inside cuts I sliced open in my own skin* (Bloom, 2015). *There, too, I failed to use it.* Janice 121 *was already a decade behind me. I was in the full height of my influence. I could do anything in terms of the world, galleries, museums—except carve. I was too afraid to carve. If only because I knew, with certitude, what a cheap, sensational hack I had always been. Hiding behind a drugstore razor and spore samples dug out from rotting stumps.*

All these years later, it was your piece that saved me, Maggie. At last. Over a thousand tubes of gold went into making Kevin Eating Spaghetti, *and though you are not identifiable in the wax and wood, you are there. Look at his face, the belief in it, the daydream in it, as if he were suspended forever in that moment when the two of you were at the table together, before either of you discovered what had happened, before that dinner had to end. He is looking at you, Maggie, listening to you tell him what was waiting at the end of the highway, that beautiful fairy tale you spun me as we lay in our bunks late at night: a little cabin, a tuft of woodsmoke, a garden where the sun never went down and the cabbages grew as fat and tall as bean stalks planted from a sack of magic seeds.*

Love,
Danielle

5. Maureen: Whitehorse, Yukon, to Whitehorse, Yukon

PEOPLE DO NOT SEE ME. That's okay. I take their orders and get the food out fast and pay attention. Tables walk off. Tips are last minute—a handful of Canadian change dumped before the border. The occasional twenty, American, from a pipeline driver. One time: a guitar pick. This is roadside service 478 kilometers from the Alaskan Port of Entry. Everybody is almost to that land of million-dollar salmon catches, oil dividend checks, and the last so-called frontier. Who would want to stop for a bowl of cut-rate Bolognese?

An elderly couple with bladder issues. A driver with the pill shakes. A mom with a fist-shaped puffy on one eye the color of a pickled egg. That particular Canada Day in July 1975, I was working yet another mid, lunch to closing at two a.m. The little girl at table eight was eating butter chips straight from the saucer, stripping off the wax paper and piling slices into her mouth. Her mom with the busted eye drank a full half-pitcher of Chablis before I even got the ticket in for the garlic bread. Then ordered the lobster tails, the most expensive dish on the menu, despite the freezer-burn.

I asked if she was sure—already concerned about who was covering the bill and why two hitchers were at the table. Hitchers didn't exactly flock to Pasta & Chops. They stuck to the Softee stand or a hot dog on the turnoff, beef jerky from a bag. The one with the smile smelled as if she'd crossed the entire continent in the same ragg wool socks. Still, she did thank me for filling up her water glass. Twice.

Her hitcher friend with the buck knife felt no such need. In the whole gamut of open-carry that goes in any wilderness establishment, a buck knife at the table is the equivalent of a pair of drugstore sunglasses. Hitcher friend wanted the linguini, but only if the clams were fresh.

Relief blew through me. A rich girl at the table. "Sure," I said. This being the Yukon, I had powdered milk, powdered Tang, canned peas, jarred sauce, wilted, week-old iceberg. Tonight's special, if she was curious, was a T-bone. Fourteen dollars. Cooked hard enough to bounce off the plate. Did she still want that linguini?

She wanted the lasagna. But not too much cheese.

Right, I said. Salad bar comes with it. Serve yourself.

She asked if she could give her salad bar to Maggie. Maggie liked iceberg.

Maggie, I gathered, was the one with a smile. Okay, I said, but don't get show-off about it.

The boy wanted plain spaghetti, no sauce, no ketchup. He had organized his utensils exactly straight and exactly the same millimeter of distance apart. At that time, there was no such thing as special or spectrum or emotionally different, but I had had two kids on my own and relied heavily on the kindness of daycare workers. Showing up late for pickup, week after week after week, meant I had to listen to the broken-souled supervisor at Sunshine Village bemoan how hard it had become to run a decent facility. Especially with one boy in the 4Ts who only ate white food and couldn't stand the feel of pants except for sweatpants and had today, out of nowhere, whacked a happy toddler on the side of her head with a wood block because "she had skipped too loud near his ears."

White-food boys aren't that hard to serve as a waitress once you realize that what they mean by white food really means: no butter, no olive oil, no dressing, but sometimes a side of ketchup. This one was no different. Kevin, the mom called him. He looked forlorn somehow and kept asking her for extra breadsticks. He also had a backhand bruise across his cheek.

At that moment, my thought was that a dad or stepdad had gone after Kevin and his mom. The family was on the lam. They had picked up the hitchers to save on gas. You make up those kinds of stories waiting tables at the ass end of the Alcan. It's not like anybody is about to tell you their official résumé of hopes and disappointments.

* * *

I KNEW BETTER THAN TO not ring up the lobster or leave a six-top seated with five potential walk-offs unattended, but I was tired. My daughter had lice from Sunshine Village, and because she had lice, my son could not sleep with her on the mattress and had to sleep with me on the foldout couch, where he flipped around all night, kicking me in the stomach, over and over.

Waitresses at Pasta & Chops are not allowed to sit during a shift. Except on a toilet in a locked stall, where, as I discovered, I had also gotten my period. Rust-colored blood had soaked through my pantyhose and from there left a sizable stain on the back of my tunic. I still had six hours of a mid to get through. On Canada Day. While my kids were at home with the retired lady from upstairs, watching TV instead of the fireworks.

I peeled off the hose. Then the tunic. The bathroom sink was out by the mirrors and there was no lock on the door to the hallway. The only way to rinse off the stains without a customer walking in on me naked was to hold that door shut with my foot. While, at the same time reaching all the way over the counter to the faucets.

Just as I decided to risk it, the door banged open. A pair of sneakered feet went thudding past. I knew the brand—Zips, the knock-off kind for kids. *Thunk* went the stall door. *Slish* went the lock. No pee sounds. No poop sounds. Nothing but hard, little panting breaths.

My thinking was skip it. Except that a girl alone in a washroom, upset, was hard for me to ignore. There were times, driving up the Alcan in '67, when I wished somebody would have checked in on me. And I was nineteen, in deep, dopey love with my boyfriend— let's not give him a name, he doesn't deserve one—a philosophy major who convinced me to drop out our sophomore year at Ohio State to work the cannery season in Alaska. His plan being for us to earn enough to extricate ourselves from the system and join a transcendental commune in Wasilla.

Halfway through Canada, I began to realize I was too closed-minded and midwestern for his utopian ideals, most of which involved me sleeping with any fresh all-natural camper who pitched a tent beside us or his sleeping with that camper or my sleeping with the camper and her boyfriend. Or all of us sleeping together. Throwing off the shackles of society, including his draft notice.

The day he took off, I was napping in our tent, worn out from the night before when I had tried to prove to him that I could be six weeks along and still keep up with him and a brunette he had met selling tabs at the campsite convenience store. When I woke up, everything was gone—the two of them, the van, the food, even the bug spray—leaving me, a girl from Port Clinton, on her own in the wilds of Yukon. I walked along the side of the highway until I saw a restaurant. I was pretty, I was young, I wasn't showing. Dimitri hired me, no papers, before I even made it to the hostess stand.

The very first thing I did was excuse myself to the bathroom— still American enough not to use the word *washroom*—and bawl my face off.

Eight years and two kids later, I was less than respectful about leaning over the divider to check up on a little lost somebody with a pair of discount sneakers. Though I was quiet about it. Not for a minute did it occur to me that I would find the white-food boy from table eight down on the tile, huddled in the corner. Right as I was about to tell him that the men's was across the hall, he pulled something out from under his shirt. A jar. Folgers. No lid.

Jesus, I thought. What kind of kid sneaks off with instant coffee? It wasn't even the kitchen brand. We stocked Nescafé, plus tea for the Canadians. He crammed his hand inside and pulled out a wad of cash. If I hadn't been holding on to the divider, I might have slipped off the toilet lid.

He started mumbling numbers to himself, numbers that made no sense in terms of counting up the total. Serial numbers, it sounded like. Over and over. He never noticed me, up there hanging over, not even when the fire door crashed shut.

The fire door at Pasta & Chops was down the hall from the washrooms. Legally speaking, it needed to be closed at all times or we got fined. But the busboys duct-taped the locking mechanism so it would swing open with a kick when they had garbage bags in both hands.

The walls at the restaurant were so thin, built Yukon-style from odds-and-ends lumber, beefed up with plaster mixed with flour and god knows what else, that when the metal door hit the frame, the crash ricocheted through the entire back of the building.

Normally, I didn't pay it any mind. But all that money had sharpened my attention. Somebody from the back lot was heading up the hall toward us. Maybe somebody who wanted all that money back. I crouched down. The washroom door flew open. Flip-flops slapped across the floor.

"Kevin!" said a girl. "Open up."

The girl had a bossy, nasally voice, one I recognized from when she had announced, "Ravioli, please. With extra meat sauce," as if proving to the two glamorous hitchers at the table that she was old enough to handle red food. Unlike her brother.

"I know you've got the money," she said. "Don't be a freak."

Kevin didn't answer. Or unlock the door. He let out a little grunt. She slid under. I stayed crouched. Unlike Kevin, the sister might look up. "Let's go," she said. "Mom said."

"Not only you gets the gold," he said.

"Kevin," she said. "Just because Maggie didn't tell on you doesn't mean she won't."

The divider shook suddenly. There were sounds of a scuffle. The jar hit the floor, bits of glass and bills exploding all over. I looked down. A fresh, crisp one-hundred was lying on the tile in front of me. American.

Bills that big weren't exactly exotic on the Alcan. Not in 1975, the heyday of the pipeline, the last hurrah of the Teamsters. Every night, ordinary guys with jeans and greasy company caps flipped open their wallets with a kind of jacked-up, terrified amazement blazing across their faces: They had money! They had to spend it! Now! On anything! Before it blew away!

The few times I had found a tip of that size, laid out under a highball glass or a saltshaker, I was careful to shove it away as if it was a single. But Dimitri, our owner, always sniffed me out and met me at the bus station. "Uniform rental," he said, blocking my exit, emptying my pockets. Or one time: my bra. The last time: my mouth.

Lying down there on the tile, that one hundred seemed to glow at me, bright as a coin at the bottom of a fountain. I knew what I was going to do, but before I even moved, a truck came roaring around the building, the wind it blew off snaking in through the window. The one-hundred fluttered over, revealing more of them underneath it, lots more, all stuck to each other the way that happens when money is fresh from the bank.

An entire laundry list of everything I had never been able to give my kids snapped through me: bean bags, tap lessons, walkie-talkies, the human-sized Barbie head for practicing hairdos, four-packs of fresh pork chops that I could cook myself on the stove, instead of bringing them home as cold, fatty leftovers from a ticket mix-up in the kitchen.

I jumped off that toilet and right as I was about to snatch up that stack of bills, another set of hands shot under the divider and got to them first. I grabbed the hands by the wrists. There was no face to them, no name, no voice that I could hear over the voice in my mind saying no, no, no, not this time. The wrists were smaller than mine, sticks. All I had to do was bang them on the underside of the metal divider, hard, right on the veins and bone, until the hands let go.

It was only her fingernails that brought me to my senses—chewed, worried down to the cuticles. All of a sudden I saw the smooth curve of her knuckles—and saw my own, clutched around her wrists, swollen and cracked from wiping down tables, winters without gloves. It wasn't as if the gloves ever left my mind. They remained there, vividly—leather gloves with wool liners, gloves thin and buttery enough to keep on when you had to deal with a car key—but so did the girl on the other side of the divider. She was ten. Eleven at most.

"Janice!" Kevin was yelling, as he maybe had been doing all along.

But I heard him finally. And I let go.

Janice slid out, running out of the washroom, losing a flip-flop in the process. I leaned the side of my head against the stall wall, so as not to bang it off. Leather gloves. Pork chops. Tickets home to Cleveland. The fire door crashed shut and that was that. I looked down at my lasagna stomach, trying to imagine running down the hallway naked and bleeding, my hands full of glass and money. To do what? Hide in the alders? If you break a girl's wrists and they catch up to you, money or no money, they take your kids. I stood up, picked up my tunic.

Over on Kevin's side—nothing but quiet little breaths.

"Honey," I said. "You better go. Your mom is waiting."

The breaths continued. Just faster.

"There's a back door, down the hall," I said. "Nobody's going to tell."

"Your job," he said, "is to bring me my spaghetti."

I sat down on the toilet. My tunic, the struggle with the zipper in back too much to confront. I started with my pantyhose, jamming in one leg, rolling it up to one knee. Jamming in the other leg, rolling it up to the knee. At which point the fire door crashed shut. I closed my eyes, praying for a busboy, a truck driver, some backlot girl high out of her mind looking to wash up, anybody, really, other than the mom coming down the hall.

That's who it was, of course—jingling with her bracelets, her splashy turquoise rings. "Who's in here?" she said—the question not so much a question as a warning.

I could see the look in her one good eye from the table, ordering those lobster tails, daring me to call her on it. I hadn't called her on it. And I wasn't about to throw down with her now. "Me," I said, "I'm here. And your boy. He's in the other stall."

"Kevin?" she said, as if I had ceased to exist—and maybe I had. He said nothing. But she slid under, careful of the glass. "You did good, honey," she said, picking up an overlooked bill.

"I want my spaghetti," he said.

"We'll get it later," she said. "Janice is out back. We have to go."

"I want my spaghetti," he said.

"Kevin," she said. "There's lots of spaghetti at the next place. And pudding."

Once again, the divider began to shake. But this time, I got up on the toilet, just in case. Already suspecting. Down below, Kevin was holding on to the plumbing pipes under the flusher—his whole body stiff and clenched, the way toddlers get when you try to force them into a stroller and they turn into a wall of muscle. The mom was holding him by the ankles, trying to pull him off. "Kevin," she said. "That friend of Maggie's knows. She's going to come back."

He hardened up somehow. And twisted.

"You don't want us to go to jail, do you?"

"I want—" he gritted out. "Not to go anymore."

"Please," she said. "You can have the gold. I promise."

The week before I had done something that had no doubt led to the episode with Janice and her wrists. My daughter had had lice again and couldn't go to Sunshine Village and wouldn't sit still, not even when I dumped the thick, brown, gas-smelling shampoo on her head with her ponytail still in. On and on she went, laying into me, telling me she hated my guts, no wonder her dad had left us for the other waitress when she was a baby.

Instead of reasoning with her, instead of telling her that her dad leaving us was my idea, I kicked him out, I grabbed the sewing scissors and snipped off her entire ponytail, sawing through the thickest part just under the elastic holder.

That was why she wanted the big Barbie head so badly. Because she didn't have any hair of her own to practice braids. Because Mom had got too tired and cut hers off. Or so she told the retired lady upstairs, who all of a sudden stopped charging me.

You want to think you're a good person. But everybody everywhere thinks they are a good person until that day comes when you're holding the scissors or the Folgers jar or the legs of your little bratty son, trying to yank him off the pipes, telling him to get his butt in the car, you can't take it. "We can't stay here," said the mom. "I mean it."

The marks on his face made sense all of a sudden, a kind of perfect, terrible sense. "Hey," I said. She looked up and the look she gave me wasn't hate or even fear, just a kind of pleading for me to do something. Like help her pull him off. Or tell him to listen to her. Instead I said, "Let's all go wash up. In the sink. Splash some water."

She shook her head. And with her attention distracted, Kevin let out a kick. She was bent down low by his sneakers, one of them connected with her eye—her bad eye. She slapped her hand over it, but blood was leaking through her fingers. Still, not a sound came out of her. She just leaned over—rocking back and forth.

"Mom?" said Kevin.

"I'll get some ice," I said. "Wait here. I'll get some ice."

"Kevin," she said. Then kept saying it, over and over: Kevin, Kevin, Kevin. Like she was trying to memorize his name.

I pulled on my tunic and ran for the machine. Later I would think—why did I leave that washroom? Nobody does the worst thing in the world with somebody watching. Not even because they will stop you. Just because they will know.

* * *

THE ICE MACHINE AT PASTA & Chops was at the far bus station, on the other side of the dining room. Back at table eight, Dimitri had the thank-you hitcher cornered in a chair by the wall. All her clothes, hairbrushes, sleep bags were piled up around the empty packs. He had dug through them. Or she had. "Another walk-off," he said. "Where were you?"

"Washroom," I said, scooping ice from the machine into a bowl.

"I told you," said the hitcher, "my friend will get the money. She'll bring it back." She was kicking the chair beside her, like a kid on the bench by the secretary, waiting for the principal. Her name was Maggie—the Maggie that the mom had brought up, the Maggie who liked iceberg lettuce.

"Table six needs a water," he said, looming over me, reeking of Chivas and hostess mints. "And the lady at three says her veal came underdone."

I pushed past him with the bowl, grabbed a dishcloth.

"Keep an eye on her," he said, nodding to table eight.

I moved faster, unable to look at Maggie and her panic, telling her that Janice had her money. As if Janice wouldn't turn around and tell her—tell everybody—that I had tried to take it from her. A girl.

"Maureen," said Dimitri. "Jesus Christ." He had noticed the period stains, my unzipped tunic. He had either drunk enough to fire me or drunk too much to fire me. Before he could make up his mind, I was too far across the room for him to drag me back to the office.

* * *

SOME PART OF ME WAS hoping I had taken too long. The mom and Kevin would be gone by the time I got back. I would get the broom. I would clean up. I would pick up my tips and go home. But when I looked under the door, there were Kevin's shoes. Zips. I held out the bowl of ice. No one took it. "Kevin?" I said. "Are you alone in there?"

"You can't make me go," he said.

I think I knew right then—even before running to the fire door, telling myself that the mom would be out there, her and Janice. There was no one out there but the dumpster. I ran to the front of the house, to the parking lot. No mom. No Janice. Nobody in any car.

It took me a minute. And still I thought they had to be some-where inside. The noise of the dining room felt suddenly so loud, so bright. I heard the tinkle of silverware on plates. The talk, talk, talk of people at tables. The hiss of the soda gun, a crack of beery laughter. All of it far away, in a bubble. They weren't there.

The kitchen, the storeroom, the men's—all of it was pointless, but I checked them all, all the same. Only then did I go back to the ladies'. It was quiet, so quiet I could hear my own breath. I didn't say anything to Kevin. I didn't know what to say. I realized that I still had the bowl of ice, that I'd had it this whole time. I set it down on the counter, along with the dishcloth. I picked up Janice's flip-flop— dusty white-and-blue rubber—then placed it by the bowl of ice.

At the door to Kevin's stall, I told mysef to man up, slide under. But I knew if I got too near the floor, I was going to stay on the floor. Glass or no glass. I knocked. I told myself not to cry, though that was impossible. And I did cry a little, promising him a nickel for the gumball machine. Then an ice cream. Vanilla. Two scoops.

It was better, maybe, that he stayed in the stall. Silent. Holding on to the pipes. It gave me time to pull my voice together, to pull my mind together, to remember what to say: His spaghetti was ready. No sauce, no butter, no ketchup.

The lock *slish*ed open and he walked out at last, so proud-looking. As if he had won.

I told him I had a job for him. It was a big job. I needed his help. He had to help me with my zipper. And he did help me, working it up past the middle of my back, telling me that I really should just tell somebody when I needed the next size up. That's what his friend Carol said when his feet didn't fit into his sneakers.

I said, I would do that. That was good advice. I said he didn't have to hold my hand if he didn't want to. But I was having a rough day. I had lost my job maybe. And if I hadn't, maybe this time I should finally quit.

It was Kevin, not me, who led us out of the washroom, all the way to table eight. Dimitri was nowhere to be seen. Maggie was still waiting by their packs, rolling up clothes, stuffing them inside. She stopped when she saw us, asking if I had seen her friend. Or if they really arrested people in Canada for not paying. They didn't, did they?

I set my face to waitress: I was busy. I had tables. Kevin sat down at his place. I served him his spaghetti. I served her her alfredo. Then I went into the kitchen and filled a saucepan with milk, ignoring the line cooks yelling at me to get out of their stations, testing a drop on my wrist before pouring it into coffee mugs.

In the office, Dimitri was watching me through the open door. He had the Mounties on the line. But it was Canada Day, all of Whitehorse calling in about blown-off hands from firecrackers, drunken family smackdowns, the usual holiday excitement.

His bottle of Chivas was out on the desk, like always. He looked up at me—so hopeful, like always. As if I was going to sit down with my mugs and tell him that I had come to my senses, he liked kids, he was responsible, we could finally go on a date after my shift.

The idea, for the first time in my life, felt almost comforting. I could not afford comforting. I pushed past it, back to the table. I set down the milks for Maggie and Kevin. I freshened up their water glasses. Then just to not stop moving, not for a second, I served up all the other orders: the lasagna, the ravioli with extra meat sauce, the lobster tails, the garlic bread. Putting them in the middle of the table, the way you do at Thanksgiving.

There was nothing left to do. Except sit down at that table like I belonged there. Kevin was halfway through his spaghetti—not asking about his mother and sister, maybe knowing already or maybe just turned off inside, the way that happens to babies when you take them to weddings and they fold up and pretend to sleep.

Maggie pushed away her alfredo. It was cold, the so-called cream sauce hardening into cement. She ignored her salad, the milk I brought her. She didn't thank me and I didn't blame her. I wasn't hungry either. It just felt like I should eat. And not say what had happened, not make it real until the Mounties came. They knew what to say. Or who to call.

I pulled the nearest plate toward me. Lasagna, not too much cheese.

"That's Danielle's," said Maggie.

"Danielle?" I said.

"My friend," she said. "She's coming back."

I didn't think I was crying. But it felt like I was. "You could go outside and look," I said. "The Mounties aren't coming. Not for hours. If you want to take your pack."

She studied her place mat. Her empty water glass.

"At the Sunoco," I said. "There's always some long hauler who needs the company to keep him awake on the drive."

"Watch," said Kevin, twisting up his spaghetti onto his fork.

Maggie smiled. But not really. She was looking out the window. It was steamed up, pink with neon from the sign overhead. A boom rattled through the restaurant, shaking the glasses. There was another one, then another, the pale, wet sky lighting up with a burst of pale, wet, watery color. The fireworks had started—the way they did every year, before everybody fell asleep on their picnic blankets, waiting for it to finally get dark enough to see their bright, flowery light.

Diners ran outside to watch. But not Maggie. Not me. Not Kevin. We stayed at the table. We knew what was out there already—gravel, trees, a highway that led all the way to Alaska, provided you kept going until you reached the very end.

SLIDE AND GLIDE

MY WIFE, MERYL, WAS HAVING an affair. All through our prep for the pear-and-Gorgonzola salad, she kept trying to tell me about it—turning suddenly toward me at the cutting board, her face a blur of panic and determination. Only to turn just as suddenly away.

Our friends were due at the house in twenty minutes. She dumped the pine nuts into the blender, then a bunch of parsley. As she reached for the garlic, she looked up at me as if for the last time, which could have been my imagination, but probably wasn't.

A whoosh went through me, the way it does when your ski catches ice and skitters out from under you. I had a jug of corn oil in my hands and steadied myself by studying the happy yellow corncob on the label.

"How could I forget olive oil?" said Meryl. "And the basil?"

I looked at her. She had gone to the store last week and stayed there for six hours. The bag she had brought back was mostly milk and bananas.

Into the blender went the corn oil—thin, industrial-colored—one cup, two cups, three, double what the recipe called for. And still I poured.

"Stop," said Meryl when I reached the lip of the pitcher. She broke off from my eyes, reached for the puree button. I grabbed her wrist. The doorbell rang in the background. Neither of us flinched.

"What if we got out of here?" I said. There was something hoarse and horrible in my voice, something that snuffed out the charming, disastrous husband I had been for most of our marriage, and all I could do was hope she would ignore it.

"The cabin!" I said, the idea coming to me as if it had been there all along. "We've never been out there in the winter."

"I don't know," she said, slowly, so slowly I wondered if my brain was still syrupy from the weed I'd smoked that afternoon. I imagined a jovial tone and tried to infuse it through my next sentence. "We should all go! Me, you, Jack, Conner! Everybody!"

There was a long, quiet stretch, before she tilted her head. Then asked, "How long would we be gone?" The sorrow in her voice bled through me, and despite the fury sparking inside my mind, as it had been for the past few weeks, growing harder and clearer, despite the doorbell's insistent second ring, I understood that I would not grab her other wrist and shake the truth out of her. His name. How he had brought the groceries for her to give them extra time together. How she had looked down at his anorexic bag and known that she would never leave a store without a bunch of Swiss chard or dried mango or the rest of the items on the list on our fridge, how she had known that I knew this about her.

And yet.

I hit the puree button. "A few days!" I said, over the crunch and spin of metal, the pesto silkening into liquid. "A few days at the cabin will be good for us—as a family."

* * *

THERE WERE SIX OF US at the table. To my right sat Paulie, my best friend since seventh grade. He was a broad, bearded guy, a pediatric dentist, who, no matter what the season, smelled of woodsmoke and fluoride rinse. Every summer, he and his wife, Ginny, marched their four daughters up the peaks of the Wrangells and camped out for six weeks.

"You're a brave woman," he said to Meryl when I mentioned the trip to the cabin. "I don't do kids in the bush under ten."

The jambalaya went around, followed by a bowl of pasta and the corn-oil-parsley-pesto glop. All of which Meryl let pass by, in favor of a fast, very full glass of Cab.

Janice, who was married to Neil, my other best friend from seventh grade, worried about the ski to the cabin. Cross-country with a toddler was . . . well . . . exhausting.

"We'll use a sled," I said. "Conner can sit there. I'll pull him. Lots of people do it."

"You got a KinderSleigh?" said Janice.

Meryl glanced at me, her face disbelieving but also so heart-breakingly and openly hopeful that I had a Norwegian KinderSleigh, to the tune of three grand, hidden in some closet of our crappy split-level that still needed a new deck. She knew me so well . . . and still. I knew her so well . . . and still. Were these twin snowflakes of delusion the only reason we were even married—believing that one amazing day, either she or I would finally do something so unlike ourselves that we would finally make the other happy?

"Well," I said. "I still have Blackie's harness."

"Crappy Blackie!" said Ginny. "I miss that dog."

Laughs all around, I poured a glass of white and tried to keep the injured look off my face. Giving up Blackie was still a sore point for me, despite his many digestive issues and his habit of chewing on the kids' fingers. I had brought him home as a surprise, thinking—however stupidly—a puppy might help us.

The whole table chimed in with suggestions about the kind of sled I should use: A Flexible Flyer. A cafeteria tray! A lid from the garbage can! More laughs, even from Meryl.

"First off," I said. "I'd never put my son on a Flexible Flyer. They're too heavy and he can't sit on hard, bare wood that long. Second, I was going to use—"

"A plastic saucer," said Neil, quietly. "Light. Not unstable."

I could have hugged him. He and Janice lived down the street, in a log palace with one too many antler chandeliers. But of all of us, he was a master outdoorsman. Two summers ago, he had disassembled his helicopter, shipped it from Anchorage to Tunisia, reassembled it, and flew around the desert, hunting wild boar. Meryl thinks he is a nutcase. I think she grew up in Wisconsin not Alaska, and mostly, that's the end of the discussion.

"I thought I'd test out waxes on the bottom," I said.

"I'd go old-school with a saucer," said Neil. "Soap it."

A kind of golden quiet ensued, during which I believed that he, Paulie, and I were all thinking the same thing, how our dads used to haul us all out to the wilderness in rickety Super Cubs and rusted-out campers, leading us down rivers in some leaky raft borrowed from a guy at work.

Meryl looked up. "What if Jack won't listen?"

For a moment, there was only the sound of forks on plates as our friends looked at each other, presumably remembering the phase right after Meryl's ex-husband had just left the state, when Jack used to punch himself—hard, on the side of his head—anytime we asked him to brush his teeth or put on pants.

"It's ten miles," said Paulie, jumping in. "Flat ice, start to finish."

"The kid can slide and glide," said Neil. "Can't he?"

"Anybody can slide and glide," I said.

"It's just . . ." said Meryl, out of nowhere. Her face was overtaken by a rush of sadness again, so deep and fast-moving, it almost looked like grief. About what? I wondered. Jack and his meltdowns? Me? Spending time with me? Us in general? Then I got it. It was that kind of affair, when even the briefest separation makes your heart feel suctioned out of your chest.

"I don't know," she said. "About a trip right now."

I pinched out a candle, stared at the smoke black on my fingers. The silence festered and spread down the table. Janice looked at Neil, who looked at Paulie, who looked at me. "Jack will be fine," he said. "You guys should go ahead."

* * *

ENDING UP THE LEAST SUCCESSFUL of all your friends does have its advantages. Paulie lent us his sat phone. Neil offered to fly us out in his Beaver. Ginny dropped off a high-tech snowsuit for a ten-year-old that worked in temps down to forty below. It was purple, but a version that Jack called girl-purple. She tossed it onto the pile in the garage while I put on some herbal tea. When she sat down, she was frowning. Only slightly. She had a soft, round look that people mistook for plumpness until they saw her swing an eighty-pound pack onto her back. "You've got a lot of gear out there," she said.

"My real problem is that Jack will quit," I said. "Meryl was right. He'll bite. He'll lie down halfway and kick off his skis."

"Where is Meryl?" said Ginny.

I shrugged. "Showing a house?"

"Bobby," she said. "Can't you get a job?"

"I have one," I said. "Almost." The job was a freelance gig

designing brochures for the state tourist board. I was supposed to follow up with a conference call on Monday, which wasn't going to happen while we were eight hundred miles away from civilization.

"There's something you need to know," she said. "But don't get mad at me."

Panic zipped down my spine; my mouth went dry. How was finding out who Meryl was fucking—in love with, whatever she was doing—going to help me now? I started picking through all the gear on the floor of the garage, the sleeping-bag pads, the camp stove. Ginny got a funny look on her face. "Ten miles is too far," she said. "Especially for Jack."

"We're going—"

"I know you're going—"

"Then help me."

She picked up the camp stove, fiddled with the latch. "Jelly beans," she said, finally. "Give Jack a handful every few clicks. The sugar high will keep him from whining—at least for a while."

"I always saw you as a purist. Trail mix without the chocolate chips."

She smiled—but her voice caught and, for a minute, I thought she might cry. "I have teenagers," she said. "Montessori and wooden blocks are a long, long way behind me."

I thought for a minute what Meryl had been like before we'd had Conner, back when she used to send Jack to his dad's for the weekend and we stayed up all night drinking red wine and singing TV theme songs I picked out on the banjo. Her favorite was *Laverne & Shirley*. I loved the way she danced with her back to me, and the secret blond streaks that only seemed to show when she was sleeping. When she laughed, it felt like tiny jingle bells breaking out all over my skin.

I had thought I could make her laugh like that all the time—
and maybe she had thought that too. Now she was stuck paying our
mortgage and pleading with Jack's principal and hauling Conner to
daycare, so that I would have time to send out my résumé and get a
job with healthcare for Jack's therapy. We were in a credit-card free
fall, not to mention the five grand Neil lent us last spring.

And yet, the day of the dinner party had not been unlike many
other days this winter. I had spent my résumé-sending time defrost-
ing moose sausage for the jambalaya, then cruising over to Kincaid
to skate-ski the long loop. Just past the halfway point, a group of
high school kids whizzed past me at speeds so effortless and super-
natural it seemed a little disconcerting to find a group of them just
standing around like regular human beings behind a tree. They
motioned me over, held out some kind of e-joint. I improvised
an inhale, clumsily, wishing for my old wooden one-hitter back at
home and reserved only, as I had promised Meryl, for weekends.

The kids were, without exception, boys. Boys in snowflake hats
with skinny long bodies, boys flushed with sweat and heat, smelling
faintly of just-eaten oranges and perfumed vapor. I wasn't joking
when I told them that I wanted my boys to grow up and be like
them when they were older.

They laughed, not unkindly. Then warned me that two hits got
you pretty toasted.

It had been a long day, a longer year. I did five.

Just for the record: Though Ginny said that jelly beans were
cheaper than power gels and did not melt in your pocket, Meryl
was never, ever going to let me give Jack candy. He had what the
school called an environmental sensitivity problem—a condition
that both the doctor and the therapist believed video games and re-
fined sugar exacerbated. My opinion was that Jack loved his mother

and did not like me, and this was not such a problem, as long as we weren't out in the wilderness, on a trip that I had cooked up to save our marriage while high on Matanuska Thunder Fuck, grown from "choice heirloom seed."

I groaned—out loud, a real live groan, the first of my midlife.

Ginny didn't seem to notice. "Do you remember when we used to sit around and talk about ourselves?" she said. "There were whole decades when I considered myself pretty interesting: how I felt about things, who I wanted to be."

"All I talked about was girls," I said. "Women, I mean. How to get them to like me."

"Love." She smiled, still a little sad. "I remember that too."

When she slid on her coat, I noticed the tip of the scar on her wrist. She had fallen into a crevasse a few years ago and on the way down had bashed against an ice formation that ripped open her arm—wrist to elbow—right through her jacket. Paulie had eventually managed to haul her out, but there had been a while when she had hung in the void by her harness, listening to the blood drizzle out of her.

It takes a certain kind of strength not to look down at a bottomless fissure in the frozen earth. Ginny, Paulie said, had looked up the whole time, up to where he and the girls were calling to her, waiting for the rope to move, waiting for them to save her. That to me was love, or maybe something more than love—trust.

*   *   *

AN HOUR BEFORE OUR FOUR a.m. start, I woke up from a dream that had something to do with Ginny and Meryl and snow that began to fall like soft, quiet pieces of cloud. I sat up but didn't turn on the light. To my surprise, Meryl wasn't sleeping either. She was staring at the ceiling. "Did you ever run away?" she said. "You know, as a kid?"

"Jack's not going to run away," I said. "But he might set fire to the house."

"I ran away," she said. "My idea of running away was to go out to the garage and sit there miserable, smoking my mother's menthols."

I waited for a minute, understanding that, under no circumstance, should I say I ran away all the time, or that running away was fun—right up until the point it suddenly wasn't. The way a trip to the dentist was, when he stopped letting you play with the model jaw and whipped out the drill. I rolled over to face her. I went right into a story, the old winsome kind I used to ply her with on dates. I did not know where it was going; it was a memory, how back when I was a kid—maybe six, maybe seven—all the happiness in the world could be found at JCPenney's.

This was back in the 1970s. My dad, like all the dads in the neighborhood, worked six weeks on, six weeks off on the slope for the pipeline. By week five of his being gone, my sister and I were fighting over ownership of the crack of the couch. Desperate, exhausted, Mom would drive us both downtown, where the retail options in Anchorage at the time consisted mostly of Nude Model Studios and Arctic Fur Showrooms.

And yet, there stood JCPenney's—a glamorous land of discount gold and slip-and-slide linoleum. Once past the handbags, my sister looked at me. And I looked at her. And we broke free, leaving Mom trying on Isotoner gloves at a counter. There were games we played in that vast, rambling store—hiding toasters in the dryers in Appliances, stealing credit-card carbons from the trash cans.

On the day we split up, we'd had some kind of argument. My sister flounced off. Though I wanted to follow her, I remained in Moderne Fashions. For a while I did the usual—spinning a rack of blouses until they blurred into a gauzy polyester fog. But alone, nothing felt the same. The store grew vaster and shinier and more professional. I stuck my thumb in my mouth and slipped inside a rack of pants.

The pants were wool, impenetrable. Overhead, the glass circle on the rack funneled down a dusty beam of light. A broken hanger poked out from a corner. It was thick and clear with a diamond pattern cut into the plastic. When I held it up, little slivered reflections jitterbugged all over the darkness—a blizzard of tiny, electric flickers.

Hours passed or years or minutes, I couldn't tell which.

"Hours?" said Meryl out of nowhere, but right there beside me in the bed. "Your poor mother."

"Yeah," I said. The alarm went off on my phone—a musical meltdown on electronic glockenspiel. There was no way really to ignore it.

* * *

PORT ALSWORTH IS ONLY A few fishing lodges, a church, and a school. In the summer, commercial hangar hands show up when a plane sets down on the landing strip, plus the occasional fishing guide. That morning, that early, there was nobody. Nothing. Not even a dog. Neil helped us dump our stuff by the side of the Beaver and took off. He had a meeting back in town with his twin girls' Suzuki violin teacher.

I looked at the pile of gear, and the sharp, low mountains ghosting up behind us—pale as chunks of moon and pocked by patches of rock. The air smelled of fuel and gravel from the village pit. The thermometer on the hangar read fifteen below.

A few lights glowed in the half-dark through the trees. My idea was to hustle us away from the idea of heat and the advice of our fellow man, and hit the ice as fast as we could. Meryl and I made three trips from the runway to the dock, carrying the skis and packs, the sled, and Conner, who bounced on my shoulders, the crotch of his diaper so snug around my neck, I almost wished for a hot, cozy poop to fill it up. Except that I would have to strip off my gloves to change him.

By the time I came back, Jack had sat down on somebody's snow machine by the side of the runway. He lifted up his arms, as if for me to pick him up too, and I was tempted to, just to save the daylight that a fight would cost us. Then I shook my head. I started back with the last load. "Follow the trail," I said, immediately realizing this was an unfortunate move, because the first thing Jack did was wander off the trail on purpose and get stuck in a drift—the deep, heavy kind that built up over a winter of consistent snow loads one on top of another. His thrashing did not help. I dug as fast as I could. He started crying, mad-crying from what I could see through the yellow plastic of his goggles. "Mittens are for babies," he said, as soon as he was out.

I sighed. I thought of the stickers in my pack—two skateboarder guys, one Army helicopter—that I had brought along to slap on the snowsuit when he had a fit over the girl-purple. But, as so often happens, Jack had found the one thing I had no plan for. He wanted gloves with fingers all of a sudden. He wanted my gloves. And when I explained how mittens kept your hands warmer, how my gloves were too big for him, he wanted to go home. "I miss Blackie," he said—with a cheap, victorious smile.

Just for the record: Jack had not liked Blackie. Blackie jumped on him. Blackie crapped on his pillow. That was why I had had to give Blackie away before we even got to get him paper trained.

Right now was when, at any other time in our lives, my voice would go tight and flat, and I would tell Jack there was no going home, home was a ninety-minute flight away through Lake Clark Pass or a ten-day hike over every kind of uncrossable mountain during which he would bite it on the first ascent. Only to have Meryl come up, give me an angry stare, and say to me, "Maybe this is too much, maybe we *should* go home." Or say to him, gently, "You're just going to have to listen to Bobby, honey. Say your anger mantra. Don't give in to fear and rage."

Either of which would only inspire Jack to start with the terrible grunting noises that he had taken up after punching himself on the side of his head had lost its appeal—those huffing, chuffing, ragged noises that felt as if he was taking a cheese grater to your soul and just shredding, shredding off the humanity. A sound made all the more unbearable when you wondered, as I had over and over, if these ragged animal sounds might just be Jack's way of saying what he knew was true but was too young to have the vocabulary to express: I had made love to his mother in the staff-only parking lot behind his daycare. I was why his toddler car seat had been unbuckled and knocked to the floor. I was why his mother was always late to pickup, and why his father had blown off child support. I was the dark mushroom in his little seven-year-old life, the black mold in his mind, spreading out.

But not today. Today, I reached into my inside pocket and handed him a wad of gummy worms. His eyes went big and blinky. He looked down at the brightly colored tangle glistening jewel-like in the center of his palm. "Eat it before it freezes," I said.

He nodded, too stunned to argue.

I headed down to the ice, listening for the swish-swish-swish of his snowsuit to make sure that he was following. At the dock, I strapped Conner onto the saucer, wedged a sleeping bag behind him as a backrest, held them both in place with double bungee cords. I took off my snow boots, put on my ski boots. Quickly.

Meryl had her skis on already. "Toe," she said to Jack. "Toe."

I bent down and jammed his boot tip into the binding and set it. On the way up, I lifted his face mask and stuck a hunk of Kit Kat between his lips. Little Roman candles went off in his eyes. He giggled. I stuck a finger over my mouth. "Don't tell your mother," I said.

We did a pinkie promise with our thumbs, due to his mittens. Then kicked off, shuffling across the tiny bay that led to the big open stretch of Lake Clark. It was hard, hot work, the heat gusting up from the neck of my jacket, the sweat freezing anyplace it was exposed to air. As we rounded past the ranger cabins and turned a hard left away from the national park, the sun broke through—the whole world a dazzle of ice and blue and light.

We caught a rhythm, all of us: slide, glide, slide, glide, Meryl in the lead, me bringing up the rear, slowed by the sled. The air tasted the way it does only in deep winter, each breath a sharp mineral shock of oxygen.

Every half hour or so we stopped for water, and Meryl brought out a granola bar, beef jerky, raisins. I would watch her fuss these into both boys' mouths then, while she was busy checking Conner's diaper or temperature, I'd snap a Twix in half and watch Jack snuffle it down, his brown spit freezing in a ring around his lips. Ginny had been right about the jelly beans. Chocolate melted in your pocket. By the fourth or fifth stop, I had chocolate on my gloves, Jack had chocolate in his hair. We tried to wipe it off, but Meryl caught us.

Before she could yell, I stuffed a drippy hunk of Butterfinger in her mouth.

"This is—" she said, chewing. "Not even food."

"It's a candy bar," said Jack, in a tone usually reserved for introducing God.

She looked at him and me—and surrendered, saying only "Don't let Conner see, okay?" At the next break, I snuck her a handful of Goobers and that was that. She always loved movie candy.

* * *

BY THE TIME WE PASSED Mitch Carmichael's island, we were flying. Mitch Carmichael was related to the famous Carmichael family who had brought the first cellphone service to Alaska. He spent the weekends out here in the summer. The snow had flattened all the willows and alders around his private runway, allowing us to see the whole log spectacle from the ice: the houses and guesthouses and the barns, the long narrow building that I had heard had a lap pool inside, filled with heated glacial water. Smoke drifted up the caretaker's chimney.

From out of nowhere, a black horse came blowing down the length of the island like a piece of living cinder, his breath trailing white behind him.

He stopped. He reared up and pawed the air and screamed.

It was magnificent. And not quite real. And I was glad I hadn't seen it alone—with the ice creaking underneath us, stretching so far in the distance, you understood why explorers believed there might just be an edge to the earth. I looked at Meryl and she smiled and squeezed my arm, Jack standing beside her, his eyes round as planets under his goggles.

Village rumor had it that Mitch was turning this part of the country into a suburb, that soon the lake and shore would look like town, complete with subdivisions and grass lawns—and maybe those rumors were true. But for once, I was not torn up about it. I was not thinking how I hadn't ended up like Mitch, or even Neil; how I didn't own even a cabin and still had to rent us one from the old Dena'ina family who owned most of the far shoreline. I was too busy watching Jack study his bootlace with the kind of wonder that laces have when you don't know how to tie them, while Meryl inched up the mask on Conner's sleeping face, so tenderly that a memory of my own mother floated through me—the way she used to brush her fingers over the back of my neck when she passed by me doing homework at the dining room table. And at that moment, I didn't want my own cabin. I didn't want anything—or to be anywhere else. I was there with my family, the world a white, crackled eggshell with us in the cup of it.

Then Jack pitched a snowball at my back and I threw one at him. At that moment, as so often happens in Alaska, the clouds should have swept in and a blizzard set in. Only it didn't. The sun kept on, gilding the mountains at the edges, softening the snow under our skis. We went for a few more clicks, singing "The Wheels on the Bus" for Conner and "Yellow Submarine" for Jack. An hour or so later, we arrived at the beach with daylight to spare.

We kicked out of our skis and headed up. From the beach to the cabin was no more than fifty feet, but with the deep snow you couldn't tell what was path and what was alders. Finally, I ended up breaking a trail alone, using my body weight and a lot of struggling and stamping. All the windows and doors on the deck were boarded up with plywood and bear nails sticking pointed end out. The hammer I had left in the plastic tub under the eave was still there, and I started clawing off the nails that held the plywood over the doorframe. Jack came up behind me. "I could help," he said.

"Sure you could," I said, trying to think of something he could do without bashing open a thumb.

Meryl came struggling up the stairs, Conner in her arms. He was crying. "Didn't you hear us?" she said.

"I heard you," Jack said.

"Me too," I said—but not as believably.

We both stood up a little straighter. Meryl shrugged Conner a few inches up her hip. "He won't take water, he's not cold. What if he's got a fever?" I stripped off my glove liners and felt his forehead, which felt warm, but we all were warm, we had been busting hump for six hours.

"Maybe he's mad," said Jack.

"About what?" snapped Meryl. She began to pace around. Conner's crying built, insistent, and getting stronger, then weaker, then stronger again. The sweat on my neck grew clammy. The light was fading, the temperature dropping. I began to get tense; we all did. Conner never cried. He was the kind of kid who just scooted around, pulling things off the table and laughing when they boinked on the floor. I started ripping at the nails around the edges of the plywood, trying not to remember if nail heads broke off at twenty below. "Stand back," I said to Jack, more sharply than I planned.

He looked slapped. Conner wailed, harder and harder. "Jack," I said. "Jack, I'm sorry." I reached in my pocket. The chocolate was gone, and we were down to the sack of jelly beans. I held out a handful. He shrugged—done with sugar, apparently.

"Just get the door open," said Meryl. "I think I have a thermometer in the pack."

"I'm trying," I said.

"You said I could help," said Jack. "I can hold the hammer." I gave a terrific pull and the bear door came crashing down, a few nails flying, exposing the other door, the beat-up one that dated back to the guy in the 1950s who had built the place for trapping. We stumbled inside. The room was dark, the table and the stove frosted over. I threw kindling, starter, logs into the stove, moving faster and faster as Conner cried and raged and cried. Meryl tried to give him a raisin. No. No. No. Which with his lisp came out sounding like Wo. Wo. Wo. Though perhaps that was what he was trying to express. Some kind of existential toddler despair.

"What's wrong with him?" she said.

"How should I know?" I said. But I checked his nose for frostbite—none—then pulled on a headlamp and went back for the packs, Jack following behind me in the narrow cone of light. By the time we were all inside, the stove had taken hold. And Meryl had fired up the lantern and put a pot of snow on the stove to melt. Conner was lying on the ground now, sobbing and kicking his feet.

There was nothing we could do but step around him. It was as if his crying had set loose little rats in our brains, the kind that scrabble around, chewing off the ends of your thoughts. Jack began to suck his thumb. Meryl kept finding and losing the same pot holder. I grabbed a canned chicken in the pantry and dumped it in the pot of melted snow with a bouillon cube and some carrots we had packed in. A layer of gray fat scum pooled along the surface, but the smell velveted through the room—salty and rich.

I stabbed a chunk of meat with a fork, held it under Conner's nose. He sat up, opened his mouth—and sucked it down, still gulping. He took another and another. The quiet that followed was golden harp music. "You did it," said Meryl, all the love in her voice suddenly back again.

I wanted to feel victorious—but couldn't find the energy. My body was falling down ahead of my mind.

The cabin was basically a low room with a slanted ceiling and a loft at one end. To reach the loft, you had to climb up an eight-foot ladder. Conner couldn't sleep up there, without falling down the ladder or the hole in the floor where the ladder rested. Jack refused to spend the night in a dark, spooky corner all alone. We all collapsed in the big bed downstairs together.

Two hours later, when I woke up, I felt Meryl's hand on me. My mind was slow and clumsy with dreaming, but I felt the warmth of her fingers, her hands. Things moved so quickly, I was already out of my boxers and had her silk long underwear down around her feet. The kids were sleeping like kittens on either side of us. I shifted with my hip, right up behind her—and I could have just slid in. I almost did. The feel of her narrow back, her liquid white skin, ran up against the dazzled look that passed between us watching that black horse as the most perfect moment I'd had in my adult life.

Jack sat up. "I can't sleep," he said. "Can you sleep?"

"Yes," I said. "I'm sleeping great." I patted the bed, for him to put his head back down, but with the kind of dark urgency that always makes dogs and kids do the opposite of what you ask. He leaned over me. Meryl went rigid. Conner sighed and began fingering her breast—the way he does sometimes, as if still nursing in his dreams. I lay there. I tried not to feel my stiffness, the little hot cleft of wetness I was already half-nudged into.

I wriggled back into my boxers. Then grabbed two sleeping bags, busted up the ladder, and went back for Jack. He didn't want to go. "Fine," I said. "I'll take Conner." On the ride up to the loft, Conner shook off his sleepiness and seemed to think it was pretty awesome being able to touch the roof with his hand. He ran like a drunk firecracker from one end to the other, laughing. "Come on up, Jack," I said. "I can't come down."

"Bobby," said Meryl, "let's not do this."

But to my surprise, Jack poked his head up through the ladder hole. I was lying with Conner on the sleeping bags. "I like ladders," he said. "You could get me a ladder at our house."

"I could!" I said. "Nobody move." I shot down and grabbed a glass of water, a pillow. And my jacket with the bag of jelly beans still in the pocket. I climbed back up the ladder. By now both boys were fully awake and Jack had to pee. Conner and I drank the water. Jack whizzed in the glass, splashing only a little. "Don't eat yellow snow," he told me.

"Don't drink yellow water," I said. Then I told him slowly, calmly, that I needed him to do a big responsible job. He had to cuddle up with his little brother for five minutes. I would time him. He could not, under any circumstances, let his brother near the ladder hole. "You said you wanted to help," I said. I held up the bag of jelly beans. "You can eat them all," I said. "The whole time I'm gone—and then I'll be back."

"Okay," he said. He took the bag. He dumped it on the floor and began moving the pieces of candy around like little cars or robots, making scarily accurate machine-gun noises. This was the kind of game Conner loved, one that let him sit and worship his brother with his eyes, saying in his lispy voice, "My turn now, Wack? My turn?"

I climbed back down, skipping the last two rungs. All we had was five minutes. All we needed was five minutes. Meryl was on her side, her face not alive with desire, but not set against me either. My woody was gone. I spit in my hand and brought it back to life. I leaned behind her. I kissed her on the back of her neck, her shoulders, and all the way down the way she liked—and for a minute she rubbed against me, her ass wiggling into me, and we were there, I was there. Until I pushed myself up on my elbow and caught her hair and somehow yanked it across the bed when I slipped.

"Ouch," she said. "Jesus. Can't you just stop?"

The expression on her face. I took a minute, the kind of minute you need to take when you realize you are feeling one thing and the other person is feeling something so very, very different than you are—despite that other person's body beside you.

"Mommy?" said Conner. He was at the hole. I leapt out of bed and up the ladder and led him back to the bags. Jack was flicking the jelly beans across the room as if they were marbles.

"You were supposed to watch Conner," I said.

"I was," said Jack.

I hunched low and made my way over. A jelly bean hit my foot. It was a red one. It tasted like all jelly beans—a mouthful of sugar sawdust. I ate another and lay down. Conner came over and tried to sit on my chest. His diaper was wet.

"Here," I said. "Try one."

He made his wrinkle face.

"No, not the green," I said. "Try a red. All the cool kids eat red."

Another wrinkle face.

"He's sick of jelly beans," said Jack—in an absentminded way, still working on how to flick one bean into another with enough force for it to spin off across the floor. "Uncle Paulie gave him the whole bag last time and he ate all the black ones and threw up."

I stopped—all of me, my heart, my body. So did Jack. He looked at me. It was dark in the loft and hard to see the fine details of another person's face, but I knew the expression. His mouth was working around, trying to find a way to unsay what he'd said. "Uncle Paulie sure eats a lot of jelly beans," I said, in casual stepdad voice, nonchalant.

Jack's face collapsed.

"It's okay," I said. "It'll all be okay."

He whispered, "Does this mean we don't get the Xbox?"

Somewhere under my skin, my face looked like his. When he lay down on the sleeping bag in a tight little ball, weeping so quietly, so profoundly, I hoped that his grief really was about the Xbox and not everything else that he probably, somehow, had figured out.

Conner went over to him and started patting his head. "Don't be wad, Wack. Don't be wad."

I felt very strange. I think what I was supposed to do was go down and ask Meryl if she had enjoyed fucking Paulie while our kids ate Ginny's candy and played her teenager daughter's video games. But the loft wasn't soundproof. She had probably heard us already. I heard a shuffling sound, as if she were packing or just picking stuff up and putting it down, not knowing what to do. Jack had his face in his hands.

"Everybody messes up," I said. My voice was breaking, but I knew better than to stop talking. "Do you want to hear about the time that I messed up?"

He nodded.

And I told him about me hiding inside the rack of pants at JCPenney, as if it were a cozy bedtime story. I told him how the salesladies and store detectives were searching the store for me, and how I didn't hear them and didn't notice and didn't come out. Until my mom found me. Because moms knew where you were. They could smell you.

"Did you lose all your privileges?" Jack said, Conner already passed out beside him.

"Yes," I said. "I lost all my privileges." And with that, the sobbing began—silent and racking, my only noise a ragged intake of breath. Jack still had his face in his hands; I could not see if he heard me or if he'd fallen asleep. I stood on the ladder, my head still poking out the hole, thinking of the grown-up part of the story I had omitted for him, though maybe I shouldn't have. Maybe he was the one person who might have understood it.

My mother had been a young mother at the time, and when she raked open the hangers on the rack, I saw her face and shrank away—ready for a yell, a panicked slap. But she paused. Her face softened, and she stepped inside and sat down next to me, cross-legged in the darkness. Neither of us spoke. The quiet was the quiet of children alone with a toy they don't mind sharing and I was surprised she knew not to ruin it.

I smiled, then held up the crystal hanger and made the little flickering lights bounce off the dark. She gasped with delight—the real kind that almost sounds like fear.

Outside, the salespeople and detectives were still calling my name. I could hear them now. She could hear them too, but we stayed there together, my mother with a finger over her lips until I knew, the way you know about grown-ups when you are little, even if they won't tell you, that she didn't want to leave either. Not now, not ever. Not to go back to our car or our street or our house. And I felt rich and special to know this—that my mother was unhappy, even if I didn't know why and couldn't fix it.

It was only when we heard my sister's voice calling, and my mother didn't move and didn't move, that I began to get scared. My sister sounded as if she were crying. My mother smiled at me, her face white, smooth, almost serene. "Bobby!" my sister was calling, "Bobby!"

I looked at my mother. I took her hand—and led us out.

I was six years old at the time, maybe seven. I was forty-nine now, but with the same helpless feeling deadening through my body. Meryl was pacing below. I was standing on the ladder. I waited, listening, as if there was anywhere else to go but down.

VALLEY OF THE MOON

MY SISTER IS IN TOWN and wants to meet. I pick Suite 100 for its wide selection of French varietals and its convenient location on the B55 People Mover. The People Mover pulls up late as usual. The seats are filled, the aisles blocked with crutches, broken sacks of clothing, and for the first time, a dog.

It's a big dog, with a big craggy head resting like a boulder of teeth on the mat. How it got past the bus driver, I have no idea. The girl holding on to him is not blind but seems to have achieved a dazzling chemical distance from the rest of our fellow passengers. Despite her painful-looking dreads, she leans against the window, bewitched by the starless purple sky and the bright palaces of commerce that line Diamond Boulevard.

I sit down next to her, just to be closer to the dog. He is the mottled color of tortoiseshell. A strand of frothy drool dangles from his lower lip. The girl nods off and a few stops later, rests her head on my shoulder. She smells of poop and woodsmoke and sticky raspberry brandy. I breathe through my mouth and try to straighten up a little, to keep her head from lolling back and whiplashing her awake.

Her eyelids flutter. The whites are ragged with broken red.

Fred Meyer's slides by. Then Alaskan Reindeer Sausage Factory. Las Margaritas with its thatched roof and neon FAJITAS!

FAJITAS! sign. The girl smiles faintly through an opioid-flavored dream. The dog pants on my ankles. I sneak a pet on his head. A gust of diesel heat blows down the aisle. Then a silver gum wrapper.

October is a snowless month in Anchorage, but colder than anyone ever expects. People use the People Mover as a floating motel until service ends at nine p.m., which I did not know until I lost my license for a wet and reckless the previous summer. This was a lucky turn of events, Dad says, considering the current proclivity of local judiciaries to declare cases such as mine as DUIs with mandated jail time. His opinion: a wet and reckless in 2014 just isn't what it used to be back in the real days of Alaska when guys used to cruise down Northern Lights Boulevard with a twelve-pack in their cab, tossing beers to promising young ladies at stoplights.

Most of my lucky turn of events, however, was fabricated by his rabidly diligent lawyers. I don't mind not having a car, not really. There is something almost cozy about being driven where you need to go, with no other responsibility except to hold up a girl's head and push the button to get off. I would not mind staying on the People Mover tonight. It is almost tempting. I'm a little afraid of my sister. At the old shut-down Borders I look in my purse, but there is no money—I'm not allowed money—only Mom's Amex. I stick it in the girl's pocket. Maybe she will find it and use it to buy herself dinner. And a bag of kibble.

* * *

SUITE 100 IS LOCATED IN a boxy, low-rise complex next to a vision clinic and a podiatrist practice. The windows are tinted and the entrance is a hallway lined with rent-a-plants and a framed listing of professional tenants. I click past all this—pleased as always by the official sound of my heels on the tile—and pull open the door. Other than the missing treasure chest and the receptionist's desk, the decor of the wine bar still looks like the dentist's office it formerly was: a muted assortment of chairs and tables, inoffensive lighting. A few men wait at the bar peering into voluminous glasses of cabernet, as though an ancient *Highlights* crossword might surface from the depths.

On a hook by the hostess hangs a key attached to an awkward hunk of driftwood—presumably meant to keep you from misplacing it on the journey to the restroom. The hostess is missing and the tables mostly are empty, save for a few women with tasteful sunsets of eye shadow over each eye. They sit by the fireplace, bronzed in the clingy light. At least one is familiar to me: High school? Cotillion? Girl Scouts? Katie? Kirsten? Carleen? There is something familiar about her spray-on tan, her charm bracelet, her hesitant way of crossing her legs.

The most reassuring part of dropping out of the Anchorage elite is that you no longer have to remember who is who or the last time you forgot it. You can just smile and nod slightly, as if you are on your way to pick up your free bouquet of flowers on the other side of the room. This is my method, and tonight is easier than most. I am swaddled, head to heels, in creamy beige cashmere, stolen from my stepmother's latest Neiman Marcus mail-order shipment.

Jamie waves me over. She has taken an expansive leather booth for six or more all for herself. She does this everywhere we meet, but this time she has a reason. She is pregnant, indisputably so, overflowing onto the table.

"Don't get up," I say and slide in next to her. She smells of cocoa butter and the faintest whiff of morning sickness. I can't help it; I reach for her stomach. It is so warm, so firm. As if on command, a dense lump of baby heaves up under her skin, the size and shape of a tiny head. I follow it with my hand and meet my sister's hand and when all three of us are stacked up like this—me, Jamie, baby—the whole world seems to go quiet, beautiful, glazed with the kind of understanding we used to have, back when we could look at each other and know, without a word or a peek into each other's cupped fingers, that we had both chosen identical butterscotch candies from the bowl on the bank lady's desk.

"You are amazing," I say. "You're going to be a mom."

"I'm already a mom," says Jamie, which is true but slightly painful. Her three-year-old daughter, Jude, lives with her and her wife, Flora, in Portland, Oregon. I have never met them or seen their blue bungalow covered in wild sea roses, except on Instagram. Jamie refuses to bring her family up to Anchorage and I can't leave Mom by herself more than a few hours.

We let go hands, and Jamie begins to cry. Her tears are loose, silent, runny. They go on for a while. She doesn't even rub them off with her napkin. According to my memory, which is not always the most reliable, Jamie doesn't cry in front of other people. She also doesn't eat pineapple, sleep on her stomach, or talk to Mom, except in the presence of Dad. And even then, she won't look at her.

"I can come back," says the waitress. She is older than us, with a faint white scar down her cheek that I like to think is from a tabby cat who did not mean to scratch her, but that is so clean, so precise on its edges it implies only a knife. My sister and I had a babysitter with a similar scar on her face. Her name was Fern. When I think of Fern, I think of Mom. When I think of Mom, I worry that she is trying to do something ambitious. Like trying to make popcorn on the stove instead of the microwave. We have an agreement about this, but it's not as if I'm exactly stringent about rules.

"A bottle of Stag's Leap. Nineteen ninety-seven," says my sister, still crying. "The Cask 23."

The waitress glances at her baby bump. "We have tests in the restroom. Free of charge." This is the most recent idea of a local city councilman, who retrofitted the tampon machines in local bars to dispense two-minute pregnancy sticks. A record-setting number of babies are born in our state with fetal alcohol syndrome. Drunk women are supposed to go into a stall, pee, and if a plus sign pops up, stop drinking.

There are potent mysteries in this logic. Such as: what women do when panicked. I am not the genius in our family—Dad and Jamie vie for that—but I do have a terrible feeling that if you were to graph the number of Jäger shots against the number of positive pee sticks on the bathroom floor, you might end up with a data set of rapidly escalating birth defects.

"The wine is for her," my sister says, pointing at me. "I'm not drinking."

I look at her—again, confused. My sister never lets me drink, and besides, my license has a Do-Not-Serve line through it. One of the unavoidable downsides of a wet and reckless.

Over by the fireplace: laughter, more laughter. The waitress glances at the Sunsets, as I name the group with the eye shadow. The woman next to the woman whose name I can't remember mouths silently to the waitress: *crab cakes.* Then holds up her empty glass. *Merlot.*

"Anything else?" says the waitress to my sister.

"Just the bottle." She blows her nose. "And why the fuck not? A dozen oysters."

* * *

A FEW THINGS FOR THE record that might explain how the night unfolds: The first one took place long ago, when our mother did not drink except at parties and left the house regularly for groceries and trips to stores and offices and other grown-up places. Even then, however, she pulled Jamie and me from school for "snuggle days," during which we never changed out of nightgowns and read picture books in bed. *The Velveteen Rabbit* mostly. Or *Sylvester and the Magic Pebble*.

Mom was a loving, wonderful parent, even when she started disappearing in the afternoons. She hired a girl named Fern to babysit us. Fern was nineteen and soft in a plump, bewildered way as if she expected you to throw a can of soda at her. She had the scar on her face, plus braces and limp, feathery hair that smelled of hot oil treatments—a ritual she completed each week with a magical little vial that she warmed up in the microwave.

That summer, Fern also had a boyfriend named Buck, who worked at the strip mall carnival in the back lot of Fred Meyer's. The strip mall carnival had been on our radar for most of our lives. Out it sprang each July—suddenly there on the asphalt like a little toothpick city against the mass of the mountains, each teetering, aging ride pierced with tatters of falling screams.

Of course, we were dying to go. Dying! Fern wouldn't let us. We fought her and crushed her and hopped in the back of Buck's eagle-hooded car for an afternoon of all-free rides and all-free games, the last of which was when Buck tried to take me into a Porta Potti and show me how to wipe his dick. I was seven. Jamie was thirteen. Jamie banged on the door, yelling she was going to puke on his boots, she was going to call the troopers. When he opened up, she grabbed my hand and ran with me to the popcorn cart, where we hid until we heard Fern calling for us.

"Guys?" she said in her helpless voice. "Come on, you guys. I'm going to tell your mom on you."

She didn't tell. We didn't either. Instead Jamie made Fern make us sloppy joes every night for dinner and give us home perms in the guest bathroom. By the end of the summer, Buck was arrested for aggravated assault and rape. His victim was a sixty-five-year-old Native lady walking home from a picnic. Six months later, when Fern tried to steal Mom's Mikimoto pearls to pay for Buck's bail and bungled the effort, Mom fired her, then arranged a job for her as a receptionist at our father's office. Then paid for computer classes so Dad wouldn't fire her either.

"Imagine," Mom told us. "Being so alone in this world." She smiled as if a sad, old-fashioned song had just come on the radio and only she could hear it.

At the time, Dad may have applauded her efforts. No one in our family was ever denied the opportunity to self-improve. Like most people in Alaska, we had come from dirt and sorry circumstance, as he described it. Even our house was constantly being gutted and redone, with all new carpet or crown molding. He still lives there with our stepmother, though even I can hardly recognize it under the stonework and marble and acres of fastidiously painted white decking that, in the winter when Diamond Lake freezes, makes it look like a cruise ship doing a deep final dive into the Arctic sea.

A shiny flotsam of airplanes and speedboats and snow machines washes up by Dad's dock, depending on the season. The old family Beaver changes from skis to floats and back to skis. It is an enormous plane painted the same electric green as the tractor Dad drove as a boy growing up on a dirt-floor farm in Minnesota. He bought it to fly Jamie and me out to the wilderness to fish and hunt and not turn into spoiled lake kids. To reinforce the message, he drew up homemade contracts we both had to sign: I will go to college, learn to fly, shoot a caribou, and vote in every election. Signed, Jamie (age eleven) and Becca (age six).

The order in which we were to accomplish all this was at our discretion.

Dad is an orthopedic surgeon, but only when he's not starting corporations and shell companies in the Caribbean. He brought the first MRI to Anchorage and developed what many in the town call a medical monopoly, which includes various surgery robots and DNA centrifuges and other then-visionary diagnostic devices. He housed them in a for-profit clinic, where the majority of patients proceeded to pay their bills using an in-state subsidiary of a larger out-of-state HMO on whose board he silently serves. Some of this success was accomplished while he was sober—but not much.

Or so I've heard. I am too young to remember the details of parties that neighbors and various strangers bring up, still dumbfounded and nostalgic about the night in the backyard with Danny Bob: the time Danny Bob sculpted a king salmon out of ice using an electric turkey-carving knife, the time he drew a drill bit for ACL reconstruction on a cocktail napkin that would go on to be patented and render all other models obsolete, the time he shot his compound bow off the roof of the house and hit a watermelon in a canoe floating in the middle of Diamond Lake.

Then there was the glacier bear, about which these people always say, "Did Danny Bob ever get that blue bear back?"

Mom has the bear, as of a week ago. Dad showed up at the door and gave it to her. She was so happy to see him and made a huge, sloppy fuss about my putting it in the living room, by the window.

She asked him to stay for dinner, which at our house means take-out Siam Cuisine, a handful of Klonopin, and a vodka-blueberry smoothie. He was very kind about declining and very kind about the rotting piles of newspapers, which Mom stacks up and uses to cut out paper snowflakes. They are very worried-looking snow-flakes. And there are a lot of them.

Dad picked one up and looked at me through intricate, shaky slits. Then said in a tender voice, which took me by surprise, "It wasn't all shit and shenanigans, sweetheart. At the end of the day, we managed to end up with you."

I stood there, letting all the little quiet bubbles of happiness fizz through me, but also wishing in a secret, terrible way that Jamie had been there to hear him say this.

I'm still not sure how memory works. Sometimes I can remember the silky rush of Mom's dress as she walked by and the bright electric bits that sparkled off her, between the pantyhose and fabric. I can remember looking at Jamie to see if she had seen these magical fireworks and confirming by the bright brown gasp in her eyes that she had. I can remember sitting on Dad's lap as he flew us in the Beaver, and his pointing to the sky ahead and telling me to pick a cloud, any cloud—and my believing, at this time, that they were his to give.

No one can ever understand the particulars of another person's loneliness, but it still seems so confusing that it was Dad's best friend that Mom fell for. Jamie says this happened the summer with Buck and the carnival, which explains why Mom was never around. She was across the lake at Will Bartlett's "getting her rocks off," as Jamie describes it.

According to Jamie—and Jamie is the only person who will tell me about what happened—everything came out at Dad's annual Christmas-in-July party. I do not remember everyone leaving or Dad banging Mom's head over and over against the edge of the mahogany credenza or Mom dragging herself and me and Jamie through the kitchen and down into the crawl space to hide. I do remember the smell, though. Most of the newish houses on Diamond Lake are built on stilts in case of flooding. Once you have spent a few hours squatting in dank, cakey, salmon-smelling clay, your mother's hand over your mouth to keep you quiet, you can't walk across a living room—even one lined in glossy white Italian stone—without feeling at least somewhat disconcerted about what lurks underneath.

* * *

A FEW DAYS LATER, MOM loaded up Dad's cream-colored Coupe DeVille and drove us down the unpaved Alcan to British Columbia. Two thousand two hundred miles of potholes and radio static and great lush Canadian trees rushed by, as Jamie and I lay in the backseat—bickering and a little afraid. Mom refused to wear sunglasses and walked right into whatever little roadside store we happened upon with her bashed-in eyes like two burned-out lightbulbs in the center of her face.

Mom is a delicate, overly patient woman who speaks as if she is reading a good-night book while asking you to take out the garbage or go see if a man is hiding in the bushes at the end of the drive, her voice rising up at the end of every sentence the way kindergarten teachers' do when they're about to turn the page. Not once has she ever yelled at us. But there was a flinty, fearsome resolve she displayed during those two long weeks that I have never forgotten and never seen since. She had a plan and the plan was not what we expected from a woman who had never been outside of Alaska, except for a honeymoon to Hawaii and the tiny factory town in Ohio where she had been raised.

The plan, she told us at the steering wheel, was Montreal. They spoke French there, she said. She had always wanted to learn French. It was the language of diplomacy. And art. And culture. Jamie, to my surprise, was all for it. She wanted to see a ballet. A real one with toe shoes. Like in the movies.

We spent six hours in the suburbs of Montreal, before Mom turned the Coupe DeVille around and drove us straight back to Alaska. My sister was the one who walked into our house and found it stripped empty, save for Dad's blue bear. Everything we had owned was gone and so were most of the walls and appliances. Upstairs, she found our soon-to-be stepmother—Fern—with some tile and wallpaper catalogues.

I was asleep in the car, but I can picture it from what Jamie later described in lavish detail. Fern's disco shorts. Her bangle bracelets. Her plastic slip-on heels. She had dropped the weight and gotten highlights and now spoke in an airy tone, addressing everyone as bunny. For example: "You poor bunny, sit down and let me get you a glass of Evian."

Meanwhile, our mother was having a nervous breakdown in the driveway, from which she was never to fully recover. I say all of this only because this is where my memory fizzles out and I feel terrible for Jamie and need to recognize some of the hardships she endured. It was Jamie who drove Mom to the hospital and forced Dad to buy the crappy rancher next door for the three of us to live in after Mom was released. It was Jamie who made Dad sign a homemade contract that somehow held up in court, stipulating that he pay for a working vehicle for Mom, plus heat and electric, as well as any living expenses Mom might incur as long as she provided itemized receipts.

Jamie was fifteen by then. Nobody knew it but me, but she still had the ballet tickets. She hid them in her jewelry box. Under the lining in the back of the top compartment. Les Grands Ballets. Orchestre. L33, M33, S36.

Even now, I wonder which one of us would have had to sit alone.

* * *

AS IT STANDS, MOM AND I still live in that rancher. Jamie moved out a few weeks after we got settled and, without a word to either of us, moved in with Dad and Fern. For the next few years, she was either running around in a bikini with Fern across all that new white decking or racing down to the dock to jump in the Beaver with Dad and whatever captain of industry he was flying out to the wilderness to fish and cut another deal by the campfire. There were no parties. But sometimes Fern or Dad invited me over to dinner, where a chef named Ernesta made all the food—sushi hand rolls mostly. Afterward, Jamie took me upstairs to her room and told me all the old stories, over and over, plus new ones: how Fern had spent sixty thousand dollars on an opal necklace, how she drank pineapple juice to make her twat taste better, how she didn't let Dad near any booze and he went along with it, because it turned out, "Dad was a total fucking pushover" when it came to women.

The whole time, Jamie was brushing her hair and throwing clothes at me to try on—sweaters and sequins and leg warmers. "You should move in," she said. "We could share a room."

I went home to Mom. Those were the years when we were reading all the James Herriot novels about his veterinary practice in the English countryside. Or playing Boggle. Mom only drank the little bottles of vodka then, and only three or four at a sitting. She just didn't like to leave the house very much. And it wasn't that hard for me to buy what we needed or just sneak over and take it out of Dad and Fern's cabinets.

Meanwhile, Jamie got her degree at MIT and her pilot's license. Then her PhD in biomedical engineering. She shot a bighorn sheep with Dad in Arizona and got her nose touched up with Fern in Argentina. On a random research trip to Portland, she fell in love with a kindergarten teacher named Flora. She stayed there and invented a smart-foam pad you insert in the bottoms of running shoes, which reduces your chance of knee injury by 40 percent. Despite the offers from Adidas and Nike, she produced the insert herself and it is now sold around the world, in every pharmacy and big box store on the planet. Ten percent of her profits, she donates to abused women shelters.

*   *   *

AS SOON AS THE OYSTERS arrive, Jamie wipes her face, leans over, and tells me that my snuggle days with Mom are over. I don't know what she's talking about exactly, but the oysters look like what oysters always look like—hunks of dead lung on a shell.

I look at the water glass, the little bubble of fabric where the tablecloth has bunched up. The wine is not here. Where is the wine? Jamie gives me a patronizing smile. "Miss," she says to the waitress. "My sister needs her bottle. Right now."

Off the waitress whisks, as people so often do around her, suddenly electrified with the desire to serve. "Have an oyster," says Jamie. "They're a delicacy."

"I need to check on Mom," I say but don't leave.

"Look," she says. "You're in trouble. Do you understand that yet?"

The idea has occurred to me. I am not the best with email or voicemail or mail-mail or meter readers or people that come to the door and ring the bell.

"I've been telling you this day would come," says Jamie. "Dad and Fern are overextended. He's aging and made some risky moves that didn't pan out. She's spending the way she always has and won't listen. Last year, I offered to take over Mom's mortgage, plus both your expenses. But the more I thought about it . . ." Her voice slows, silkens. "I just feel that the situation isn't healthy. Not for you. Or Mom."

She stops. She looks down at an oyster but doesn't eat it. She loves oysters. For a minute, I think she's trying to prove to me how disciplined she is—unlike my slovenly, wet and reckless self—then I remember that pregnant people can't eat shellfish.

"And so," she says, "I came to a decision. I will continue to pay for the house. I will get Mom a professional caretaker. Under the condition that you move out—and get a job."

I eat an oyster. I eat another one. They taste like what oysters taste like: chilled death. I eat another. I wonder what Mom would do, but I know what she would do, make a vodka-blueberry smoothie and forget to put the top on the blender and tell me I'm her "magical baby girl" for cleaning the splatter off the ceiling.

Taking care of Mom, as much as I love her, is a lot of work.

Down in Portland, Jamie's life is one long farmers' market, with her and Flora and Jude running around in matching sneakers and licking Popsicles. They throw sticks for their golden retriever. They grow kale in their backyard. I see it all on the Instagram, when Flora posts the pictures.

What this makes me hope is that one day all this happiness will make Jamie happy. Last year, she tried to start proceedings to put Mom in some kind of facility. I didn't know that a social worker could deem you unfit for wanting to stay in your own home, cut snowflakes, and drink vodka-blueberry smoothies, but as it turns out, if you are an agoraphobic alcoholic with a caretaker who occasionally takes your antianxiety meds and drives into a Papa John's pizzeria one night, the state can mandate certain at-home visits. It has been six months since Mom and I finally got rid of Miss Caroline and her preprinted self-care checklists.

I look down at my hands. They are shaking. "Where is Flora?" I say. "Why didn't Flora come?"

"She's busy transitioning Jude into a toddler bed."

I swallow the last of my oyster. The wine comes. The poor waitress doesn't even know how to present it and improvises with a few flourishes and some clumsy drama involving a napkin. Due to the vintage, it has to breathe in a carafe for twenty minutes, during which I watch the dense velvety liquid behind the swoop of glass—along with the reflection of my stunned, stupefied face. "I thought Dad and you don't talk anymore," I finally say.

"We don't. We negotiate."

"I know how to negotiate," I say.

"Great. I'm open. We're at the table. What do you want?"

This takes me a minute. I want so many things. "A dog?" I say.

"Go get one," says Jamie. "You're not really the fuck-up in this situation. You'll see. Once we get you away from Mom and her more-helpless-than-thou power trip." On she goes: Mom is the problem. Mom let the world run over her and dragged me under with her. When was the last time I showered the shit off her when she messed herself? Last night? Tonight?

Though this last situation happens more regularly than I'd prefer, it's not as if Mom does it on purpose. She always cries. She
always tells me to just go ahead and leave her like Jamie did.

The only thing I know how to do when my sister is talking like
this is to go into the little home movie I have in my mind of her cutting oranges on a beach. So much of my memories are gone but not
this one: Jamie has a little knife. Dad is downriver fishing. Mom is
lying on a blanket reading a book. Jamie takes the slice of orange and
peels off all the white stringy yuck and feeds it to me—with the tips of
her fingers. "You be the baby eagle," she says. "And I'll be the eagle."

Even then, I thought, I want to be the eagle. But at the time,
I thought the game was only going to last for the afternoon. And
besides, she wanted to be the eagle so bad.

The Cab, of course, is not ready. I sit up all the same and pour
myself a glass—that first sip glittering through me like melted ruby
slippers. I take it with me when I leave the table. Jamie is still talking. I may be passive, as she says. And self-harming, as she says.
And willfully loving to those who cannot love, as she says.

But I am not beyond self-defense.

Over at the bar, the men perk up—aware all too quickly that a
woman under forty is headed their way, clutching booze. They are
useless to me, unrelated to Jamie and what might upset her. I swerve
over to the Sunsets. As I suspected, I do actually know them.

"Becca," says the one I noticed when I entered. She smells
like every scented candle in the world. The whole delicious gamut:
toasted almond to Zanzibar.

"I meant to come over earlier." I gesture vaguely, as if sweep-
ing aside the pesky crumbs of time. We clink glasses. A name sizzles
through me, as sometimes happens: Kirsten. Kristen. I mumble out
some version of the two.

And her friends? Stacey, Michelle, and Dina. Which, like Mark, John, and Dave, are really all the same name. All four are plastered on wine by the glass—a purchasing habit that incenses Jamie. Not just because it costs double, but because women have to stop lying to themselves about their desire to get drunk and just order a bottle.

"So you're still in town," says Kristen.

"Only when I'm tipsy," I say.

She laughs.

I laugh.

"I heard that," she says, in a kind voice. "Is there anything I can do?"

It is true that my arrest—but not the settlement with Papa John's—made the papers. But something else lumps in the back of my mind, a crude and reptilian understanding that makes more sense as soon as Kristen looks over at Jamie.

Jamie looks down at the oysters. Because—of course as I must have known without really knowing—they were sweethearts way back when, hanging out upstairs on her white canopy bed in Dad's all-white house, supposedly studying for a Mathtastic match.

Kristen raises her glass. Jamie nods and saunters over—as only she can do while eight months pregnant. "Are you hitting on my baby sister?" she says. Cool as mountain stream.

"I heard you were in town," say Kristen. "Jerry and I wanted to have you over." She looks at me. "We'd love to have you too. I mean it's silly, you and me living so close by and us not getting together."

I nod, listen, weep internally for her as she continues: Jerry and her live across the lake from me and Mom. Jerry and her have two girls. Jerry and her have a chocolate Lab. Jerry loves double espressos with foam. Jerry is doing so well at Exxon. In public relations.

"Wow," says Jamie. "Public relations."

Luckily, one of the drunk, lonely guys at the bar comes over. "Hey, ladies," he says, thickly. "Calamari?" He is holding a half-finished basket. I am so anxious for Kristen, who is so obviously still hung up on my sister, so anxious about my sister and whether or not she is about to do something cruel or kind or terrible to her. Or to me. Or worse, cheat on sweet, absent Flora back at home transitioning their toddler into a toddler bed, that I grab hold of a calamari and pop it in my mouth.

All five glossily highlighted female heads turn toward me—horrified. I have accepted something from Drunk and Lonely and because of that the odds are that Drunk and Lonely will now think that he and I are destined to leave the wine bar together. I try to spit the piece out. But it is too late. Drunk and Lonely has friends—a table full of them—and they cheer him on.

"Thatta a girl," says Drunk and Lonely. He puts his arm around me. He gives me a nice big squeeze, heavy on the shoulder.

I look at my sister. She looks away.

"Excuse me," says Stacey. "Not to be rude, but my husband is in the state legislature."

"We're all just getting along," he says. "We're eating some seafood." He sniffs my glass. "We're having a nice glass of old-vine Cab."

Everybody knows—with all the fear and familiarity of women in a bar alone in Alaska—where this is going. Drunk and Lonely's friends start moving over to our table so they can try to meet all of us and we can all just get along.

The waitress shows up to try and help. "Is everybody comfortable?" she says to our table, glancing at our neighbors. "How about a crème brûlée on the house? Five spoons?"

"One more bottle of whatever she's drinking," says the guy, and lets his finger brush across my nipple.

"Are you sure?" says the waitress. "It's quite pricey."

"I can cover it."

"It's two seventy-five."

He smiles, recovers. "Why not?" he says. "Worth the investment."

It is time to leave. And it is time not to make a scene. We all laugh. Then Michelle and Dina go off to pee and never come back. A few minutes pass, during which Stacey orders a round of shots and pretends to get a call on her cell—then she goes out in the hall to pick it up. We all toss back our shots, whereupon Kristen recognizes an old friend who is really a random busboy who walks her out. I eat another calamari. And another.

Jamie looks a little bewildered now that we are alone with the guy. And his table of friends. I am not exactly sure what to do about her. She needs to get up on her swollen feet and find some excuse to leave. Except that maybe she has been in Portland for a little too long and forgotten about the sexual assault situation in our hometown, which clocks in as the second highest in the nation—and not in a roofied and raped kind of way, a bash-the-girl-and-drag-her-into-the-woods-behind-the-strip-mall kind of way.

"Please," I say to her. "If you're going to puke, don't do it on my cashmere."

"Oh," she says. "Right! I'm morning sick." And lumbers out of there.

"I think—" I say.

"If you're going to run off," says Drunk and Lonely. "Run off. You don't have to be so mean about it." His face is hurt, puzzled.

"I'm not mean," I say. "Do you think I'm mean?"

"Yes," he says—in a voice so thick with hate, you can feel the spit beneath it.

I get up.

He gets up.

"Hang on, buddy," says the bartender. "Let's settle up for that bottle before we rush out."

* * *

WE HAVE ABOUT THREE MINUTES to make a plan. None of the Sunsets drove. As it turns out, Stacey's husband really is a state legislator and drops the three of them off on Fridays and picks them up at midnight. Jamie took a taxi from the hotel; her rental car won't be dropped off until tomorrow morning. And Ubers in Anchorage are mostly driven by what's known as GDIs—goddamn independents—who do not snap to when requested to show up at restaurants.

"It's not even nine o'clock," says Michelle. "We should go back in and enjoy our evening."

"We could go downtown," says Kristen, looking at Jamie. "The Captain Cook is open." The Captain Cook is a bar. And a hotel. With the obvious hotel rooms upstairs.

"Can't somebody call us a taxi?" says Jamie.

I am feeling a little anxious. So are Stacey, Michelle, and Dina by the looks of how they are scanning the parking lot—which is dark and full of landscaping bushes and too far from an intersection. If Drunk and Lonely and his band of merry friends show up, it's going to get tense and ugly pretty fast. "We can always take the People Mover," I say.

Laughter all around. Understandable. There are about four

People Movers in the whole city. And in their world, who doesn't own a car?

"I love the bus," says Jamie, suddenly. "Why not?" The Sunsets giddy up, her and Kristen bringing up the rear. It goes without saying my sister was student government president and general king of school and that everybody saw her on the cover of *Wired*.

* * *

THE BUS LUNGES UP. IT'S empty. Save for the driver and the dog. The dog is tied to the last seat and has managed to slink underneath it, leaving only his whippet tail exposed. This is maybe why the driver has not noticed him. Either that or the driver is too afraid of getting bit. I sit next to the poor guy and try to hide him with my legs.

Dina, Stacey, Michelle come down the aisle.

"A doggie!" says Dina.

I put a finger over my mouth.

"Got it," she says and winks.

There is a whine of machinery. The driver is lowering the handicap ramp for Jamie, who apparently looks too pregnant to mount the steps. Kristen helps her down the aisle to our seats, which is when my sister whips open her maternity jacket and pulls out the carafe of Cab.

"Party bus," says Michelle.

Around the wine goes. Around it goes again.

Kristen turns it down. "I guess you know about Jerry," she says, but mostly to Jamie. The other Sunsets circle around. Hugs. Toasts. Jerry is selfish. Jerry is a fucker. Jerry is having an affair with a woman who runs a natural food store. She is ten years older than Kristen, which should make it better but only makes it more humiliating.

"Well," says Jamie. "My wife kicked me out of the house last week."

We all swivel our heads, even the dog.

Jamie waddles over, takes a glug off the carafe. It happens so quickly, it's almost as if she forgot she is pregnant. Then she takes another glug. Then she starts to cry. Loudly. "She says I stifle her. She says I'm overbearing."

"I just don't know," says Stacey, the wife of the state legislator, "if I'm okay with this."

"You guys are so . . . so American," I say—me, whose one trip out of the country was our six-hour stay in Montreal. "It's perfectly fine for a pregnant woman to have wine."

They all look at me.

"It's red," I say, "an antioxidant."

"I'm out of here," says Stacey. She waves at the driver as if he is the chauffeur. And with a small, exquisite smile he ignores her. She sits back down, punches into her phone for a taxi and there is nothing but fluorescent, rattled silence until the next stop. The door heaves open, Stacey flounces toward it, Michelle and Dina follow. Then Dina hurries back. She kneels down in front of me and hands me a card. Darn Yarns, it says.

Her store, apparently.

"If you need a job," she says, "call me. My mom always told me how your mom made her all that caribou stew when she got cancer."

I must look confused. She brushes the bangs out of my face and says, "I was in seventh grade. You were still pretty much of a baby."

"Of course," says Jamie, "love on my sister. Like everybody else."

There is so much I could say to this, but why bother? My sister is a jerk. My sister is a bag of toxic vagina. The bus lurches off. Kristen and Jamie start whispering. And I lean on the window making breath fog on the glass, until the empty carafe rolls down the aisle and hits the fare counter. The bus pulls over. The driver leans down and toes the carafe. "Off," he says. "Use the back exit and don't try to pretend you're passed out."

The dog looks at me. I don't have a knife and I don't know knots, I tell him with my eyes. My sister strides over and undoes the rope with the assurance of a person who has tied up a lot of turbo floatplanes and speedboats in her life. "Well," she says. "You got what you wanted at least."

She hands him over. He looks up at me. He has a quizzical, uncooperative look to him. This is not the dog I wanted. I wanted a golden retriever or one of those fluffy, pillow-sized dogs that sleep in your lap while you watch TV until three in the morning, Mom rambling beside you about a totally unrelated episode from *Falcon Crest* circa 1989. But that is my problem, isn't it? I didn't ask for what I wanted. Because I don't know what I want—except not to leave Mom alone or do anything Jamie wants me to do—and so I asked in the general category of what I thought I could get.

The doors fold open and we step into the night. It is foggy. Something in the trees smells like lighter fluid and swamp. A park service sign looms by a parking bollard.

"Holy fuck," says Jamie.

"Oh," I say. "This is perfect."

"Valley of the Moon!" says Kristen, with an awe that endears her to me for the rest of our lives. Valley of the Moon being a playground that every kindergarten teacher in town takes her class to on field trips, which for me transcended even the joy of visiting the downtown art museum (where we got to carve a bar of Ivory soap into a sculpture of a guy in a kayak) or the mile-long walk to a Quik Stop (where we all got a free pack of Twizzlers).

I can almost taste the tipsy, wrecked half-planet made of metal bars we used to climb up to reign as Lord of the Universe. Or the creaky spinning wheel where we lay down—our friends running, gathering speed, jumping on at the last minute, the sky whizzing by in a puffy, peaceful vomit of clouds.

Best of all was the rocket-ship slide, which required a climb up a rusty ladder so high you wanted to climb back down but couldn't—not with everyone watching—followed by a headfirst dive into the dark of the endless metal tunnel, at the end of which erupted a series of painful screws, followed by a pile-on of kids trying to block your high-speed exit.

And yet, when Jamie, Kristen, and I break out of the trees that shelter the entrance, we find that everything has been replaced. There is still a planet, a spinning wheel, and a rocket-ship slide. But they are the plastic versions of the old equipment—all with the soft, molded feel of crayons. The moonlight makes them glow a little. Dully.

A fresh round of gloppy fog rolls in from the trees. "I can't believe it," says Kristen. "We used to get high here in high school."

"I'm doing the rocket ship," says Jamie.

"Are you sure that's a good idea?" says Kristen. "With your size?"

"I'm fine. Pregnant women can go down a slide." Up Jamie goes, slowly on the plastic steps, as if accentuating the loss of our rusty ladder. Kristen jumps around in the grass, doing spritely dance moves. A leap. A twist. A split.

"Didn't you used to be a ballerina?" I say.

"I wish," she says. "Gymnast."

Jamie is now sitting at the top of the slide. She waves. Kristen cartwheels through the grass. Handspring. Roundoff. She waves to the crowd, accepts an invisible medal.

"Becca?" says Jamie.

"I'm not going down," I say. "This is Fern's cashmere I'm wearing. I may need to sell it."

"No," she says. "It's just—can you come a little closer?"

I come over. I look up. She has her hands gripped on either side of the guardrails. "I'm—" she says. "It's pretty high up here."

I remember, in a dim, possibly erroneous way, she is afraid of heights. "Just come back down the steps," I say. "You have a baby inside you."

"I know," she says.

"I can't catch you. I have the dog. And you're too big."

"I know you can't—"

"Then come down—"

"It'll make me feel better," she says. "If you're there, at the bottom. Just in case." Up at the top of the not-so-high slide, her face is clenched, pale, needy-looking even.

This is a story she will later tell us both, I realize. Her story will be funny and self-lacerating and so horrifically precise about our love and fury for each other and that whole diseased seesaw we can't stop daring the other to get off first. At the end, Jamie will have either shot out of the slide, landing on me and the dog and knocking us both over in the mud. Or whizzed off the end, after I stepped back, allowing her and her unborn child to land on her fragile, forty-four-year-old tailbone.

There is another story, though. I have almost told it to her every day of my life but haven't. Even now I am unsure as to why.

Back in Montreal, at the hotel Mom checked us into, we had to leave the Coupe DeVille in a parking lot in the basement and go to the theater on a train that ran underground. It was called a metro. *Metro*, I remember saying to myself. *Metro*.

We went down some stairs and through a metal bar that spun around. Then we stood on a long cement platform, with a bunch of other people. Some of them were kids. My sister and Mom stood together, Jamie hanging on Mom's shoulder. This was how Jamie was back then. Always trying to get Mom's attention. Always playing with her necklace or the mole on her chin as if it were a little brown diamond, always the first to find her keys when she lost them, the first to say you're the best mom in the world.

I was younger, slower, dumb to the race we were in. Most of the time I was dawdling off in a corner, unintentionally forgotten. A few feet down from my spot by the column, a woman with long dark hair and two shopping bags waited beside me. Both bags were made of brown paper and filled with what looked like little balls of tissue paper, as if she were moving and had decided to pack up all her glasses and fancy, breakable things and take them with her.

On the top of the bag closest to me, a sliver of shiny red showed through a gap in the tissue. Everything in me longed to reach in and touch it. If only to know if it was a Valentine as I suspected. Or a bit of chocolate foil. Or something else, something mysterious and Canadian.

The cement under my feet began to rumble. The woman moved closer to the yellow line. I had never been on a subway or a train. I moved closer too. She moved another step closer. Me too. Our toes were right on the edge, which is how you got on a subway, I thought. You want to be the first one. You had to be right next to the train to get on.

The headlights roared in.

When I looked back, Mom had her hands over Jamie's face and Jamie was screaming and everyone was screaming. Except for Mom. She was staring at me. Her eyes were huge green bruise holes. When she came over, she walked dreamily, slowly, as if underwater. I didn't know where her purse was and I don't think she knew where it was either or where the Kleenex were inside it, but all the pieces of tissue paper from the woman's bag were floating by us. Mom plucked one from the air and wiped the blood and sticky other stuff off my cheeks.

Then we went back up the long dark stairs and back to the hotel and got back in the car and drove straight back home. Mom saying the whole time we were all okay. We would figure it out. We would put me in a hot bath and go to school and do our homework. Jamie was crying. "I can't believe you," she said. "I can't believe you're taking us back. Not to him." She chanted this over and over all through the vast plains, the lakes, the forests, the cities, the gas stations, the truck stops—that whole endless foreign country speeding by us in the windows.

I was in the backseat, pulling little threads off the edge of my jeans. Mom kept pulling over and shaking me by my shoulders saying, "Are you all right? Are you hungry? Do you want a hot chocolate? We can stop for hot chocolate if you want." I was fine. I was tired. I leaned against Jamie, who had just begun not to talk to Mom or to talk to her as if she were a ghost with bad breath.

I was seven years old. I knew nothing, except that I was not upset the way Mom and Jamie were upset and never would be. They had seen the part on the platform that I didn't see or didn't remember. And I had seen what they were too busy and far away to see—how peaceful the woman looked, how happy even as a train thundered in and she jumped into the lights with both her bags, the bags exploding into hot white flowers of tissue and shattered glass, as if we might be at the ballet already where Mom and Jamie had told me beautiful, tiny ladies leapt into the air while snow fell and music played, and we all clapped to be polite and show them that we recognized how hard they had worked, how strong they were, how much we wanted them to stay in the air above us and never come down. Bravo, I was told to say. Even if I never got the chance to say it.

OUR FAMILY FORTUNE-TELLER

THE SIGN IN MY WINDOW says "Card Reader." It is small, fuzzy, and lit up in a shade of 1960s pawnshop neon that implies my lack of card-reading expertise as well as a dwindling interest in the so-called future of my business. Still, people knock on my door and come inside. And come back. And ask me for the kind of giveaway they receive at espresso drive-throughs: one free session for every ten.

Nothing, it seems, is more trustworthy than irrelevance.

Except to a landlord. Today, mine is waiting for me at the end of our driveway. I hobble toward her, my knees swollen into fat, black spiders of bone on nerve. She is new to the property. She does not know about my arthritis and she struggles with her own discomforts. By the time I arrive, breast milk is leaking through her puffy down jacket. Her daughter grabs at the stains, balls them up with her baby fingers, and sucks on the wet warm fabric.

The three of us stare up at my home of the past four decades. It stands on the far edge of her two-acre lot, behind a clump of wizened spruces. Even considering the few remaining meth houses on our street, the last of the Latvian dating services, and the one remaining classic isolationist cabin—bedecked with rooftop garlands of barbed wire—my backyard shack is fantastical. Tar paper flaps off the façade, full-grown alders sprout from the foundation. Anytime I flush the toilet, the front door bangs open and hits the wires dribbling off the eaves, releasing a lively shower of blue sparks.

"It's quite cozy," I say, "inside."

My landlords sighs. I hobble in a little nearer. She smells of crisp white vinegar, soft brown shit, and the bulk rotting apples that she stores in the Arctic entry of her much larger, almost renovated house across the driveway from mine. It is astonishing what she has accomplished in just six months of hammering and sheetrocking, often with her daughter strapped to her chest in a sling.

Now that the weather is too cold for home improvement, she whizzes through her kitchen, pureeing and baking and fermenting blueberry mead in casks she bought off the internet. In the yard, her just-washed clothes dry in rows of frozen cloth dolls, clipped by their shoulders to the line. To my mind you can't help but admire her work ethic, the new-to-Alaska idealism that radiates off her like a vapor of vitamin C.

Her name is Violet. Her daughter's name is Michael—the idea being, I think, to give the baby an edge with the boys to come in school. Not that Michael needs it. She clamps her legs around Violet's midsection, gives me an appraising stare. Her eyes are the color of winter. She rarely blinks.

"The thing about the sign is," says Violet. "It's obvious. It's a lot."

"Agreed," I say, "though not so obvious as LUCKY ORIENTAL GIRL MASSAGE."

This was the sign in front of her house, until the previous landlord—a paranoid hydroponic pot dealer named Reggie—cut it down and left it in the backyard to rot. My eleven years living next to Reggie were long ones, mostly due to his fear of DEA drones and radioactive mosquitoes, both of which he believed had been released throughout Alaska by ex-members of the KGB.

Imagine my relief when he retired to Wasilla to play video games, selling the property to Violet and her husband, Daniel. They laughed when they discovered the sign, then hung it over their couch. Until they decided it was racist and dragged it off to the Anchorage dump. LUCKY ORIENTAL GIRL MASSAGE was painted, not neon, and a quieter kind of advertisement than CARD READER. Though equally misleading. None of the girls who lived here were lucky. Or Asian.

"All I'm saying," says Violet. "Is that you have your profession, we respect that. We'd never undermine your income. But we maybe can't sustain a lot of traffic coming in and out—a lot of people. You can see people, of course. But not stranger-in-a-car people. Not with a baby in the house." She hitches Michael up on her hip. "You understand, I hope?"

I lean into Michael, drink in her baby musk, so faintly discernible under her mother's herbal diaper potions. "You should come by for a session."

"She can't talk," says Violet. "Though she does have lots of deep thoughts." She nuzzles Michael's neck. "Don't you, Michael?"

"I meant you," I say. "Babies and I don't communicate." Which is true, even if I expressed it incorrectly. Children are a silent mystery to me, as are dead people and anyone outside a twenty-five-foot radius of my person.

Everyone else I know the way clairs have known nonclairs for centuries. That is to say, with an intimacy that nonclairs both long for and fear, depending on the moment.

"Are we good with no sign?" says Violet. "Can Daniel come by after work to help you take it down?"

"I thought he was staying late," I say. And give her a minute to think about his staying late. "Can't you put Michael in front of the

TV? A quick session can be quite . . ." I search for a word in her vocabulary. "Refreshing."

Violet smiles at me—a firm, kind no. On the way up the driveway, she stops to fiddle with the lid on my trash can. It doesn't fit. She knew it wouldn't but still enjoys the pleasure of confirming such small, reliable irritations. She will buy me a new one tomorrow, she decides. With a moose-proof latch.

* * *

BACK AT MY WINDOW, I try to lift CARD READER off the sill. The sign is too big, the tubes too hot and sticky with frizzled bits of dead insects. I could unplug the cord, but the plug is hidden behind a bookcase that is too heavy for me to pull out from the wall, unless I remove all the books, then move the bookcase, then unplug the cord, then move the bookcase back and put all the books back.

My whole body throbs at this idea.

The two white towels I drape over the neon smother the legibility of the words, but still allow its dusky orange glow to seep through. Perhaps Violet will think of this as comforting, like holiday lights left up a few weeks into February. Though I do suspect that my clients will feel slightly betrayed. The sign has been up since before my arrival in the early 1970s, when my predecessor, an Armenian clair, worked on the property.

At the time, the services it advertised were a rarity in Anchorage, and the reason, people say, why Lucky Oriental Girl Massage became so successful. The city was overwhelmed with lonely, overpaid men working on the pipeline; escort shops outnumbered schools and supermarkets. CARD READER'S neon lent the establishment a certain cachet.

In our present era, new clients use real estate as an excuse to knock on my door, claiming they are browsing nearby houses. The area, they say, is on the up-and-up. Spenard a family neighborhood? Who would have thought it? They are too polite to ask if I have ever witnessed a Spenard Divorce on the property—"Spenard Divorce" being a distasteful local expression that refers to the formerly rampant executions of drunk wives by their drunk husbands in nearby homes and bars, usually by a shotgun blast to the face. They wonder if I've ever thought of selling. Then they say, as if the idea had never occurred to them until that second, "Are you open for a . . . ?"

I point to the sign.

". . . reading?" they say.

"Reading," I suppose, is the closest word. But by "reading," I think what the clients mean is seeing, believing as they seem to, that a clair watches prerecorded episodes of their lives inside her head.

If only this were so, as I can't afford cable and, with my swollen knuckles, can hardly punch the buttons on the DVD remote. Imagine the friends and admirers I would have, if I had such visions. "You put your car keys in the refrigerator!" I would announce at the end of our sessions. "Don't trust that co-worker who brings in all those pumpkin muffins!"

The word "voyant" was only added to the word "clair" in the eighteenth century. Clear seer, the combined terms translate as—a word invented, I believe, to distract the public from our true abilities. We do not see any differently from nonclairs. We are not soothsayers, mediums, or mystics. We do not hallucinate, speak in tongues, or hear voices.

All we do is know—in flashes of exhausting clarity—the thoughts muddled inside another person's mind, especially those thoughts too upsetting to fully consider.

Children have traces of this ability. As do the mentally ill. Adults have residual vestiges they resist. Take Violet. My lack of healthcare, my lack of children or friends who might take care of me—she knows all this, though I've never told her. And yet she is going to try to evict me—which she also knows and can't admit to herself at this particular moment. The Card Reader sign is just the start. She has spent the past six months fussing away her irritation about my clients parking in the driveway with imaginary anxiety regarding her paint chip selections and sourdough starter.

"Our family fortune-teller," she calls me on the phone to her friends. She says this with affection that, in the moment, she almost believes. As in: "Our family fortune-teller gave my daughter a Cheeto!" Then she laughs, with even more affection.

What she doesn't know is that rubbing a crunchy extruded corn puff against your gums is soothing to teething babies. I learned this not through my abilities as a clair—as I said, I am shut out of Michael's mind and that of any child—but through King Charles, my former employer, who bought bag after bag of these electric-orange snacks for the younger escorts when their wisdom teeth came in.

Despite his swashbuckling, frontier charisma, King Charles had a sensitive nature. He behaved with empathy and even understanding about my isolation. He bought me every book on my shelves—biographies, cookbooks, mysteries, self-help manuals, historical novels about the rise of the Roman Empire or the fall of Japan—and sat at my feet while I read to him aloud, staring up at my face as if to commit it to memory along with the chapters that he often recited back to me, sentence by sentence.

It took me longer than it should have to understand he was illiterate. That I fell in love with him, that I ruined it, that he paid me in poker chips or clothes with the price tags pinned to the shoulders should not in any way diminish his achievements. He managed his escorts—and me—with an understanding that bordered on genius. No one needs a clair more than a woman who has serviced a party of ten drunk Teamsters with a fetish for empty beer bottles. And no one needs an escort more than a clair, sitting alone in her backyard shack, exhausted by the darkness of other people's thoughts.

Escorts, in my experience, are some of the most hopeful people on this earth. The real house they will live in one day, the Shetland pony they will own, the mothers and stepfathers and uncles who will beg them for their forgiveness when they finally go back home for a visit—they don't just think all this, they believe it, so much so that it coats their fragile minds with a layer of ironclad fairy tale that comforted even me.

How I miss them, even now—their junkie lapses in conversation, their unexpected presents: chocolates, charm bracelets, tiny pink and blue glass animals purchased from the Avon lady once a month. Unicorns and seals, mostly, some of which still stand on the top of my dresser and shoot a faint dazzling circus of color over the ceiling when the sun comes through the window. "Tell me more," they used to say. "Tell me about the time when I almost won that dishwasher for my mom in the radio contest."

* * *

LONG AGO, I LEARNED THAT a clair can't tell her clients that she's going out of business. They will just show up and try to convince you otherwise. Considering the conflicts to come with Violet over the "stranger-in-a-car people" in our driveway—I have only one option.

Every client comes with a list of questions they forget as soon as they arrive. There is only one real question they need answered. The question is never what they think it is and the answer they already know. And yet, during that last agonizing minute of a session when they ask this question, it always surprises us both.

Whether they come back—or not—depends on how I respond.

After my meeting with Violet in the driveway, I begin to answer it incorrectly. On purpose. I tell the hairdresser he really does want to move in with his partner and buy a condo that he can't quite afford. I tell the college dropout her father will support her need to pursue pottery. Off they go into the world to make the most regrettable decisions in their lives, never to return.

It is tiring, however, fighting your professional ethics. When my best, oldest client shows up for her weekly session, I give up on driving her away. She is middle-aged, the mother of two teenagers. She has wonderful taste in nail polish and this week has picked a fanciful powder blue that conflicts intensely with everything else about her: her ironed hair, her pointy features, her incapacity to smile.

"I'll sit here," she announces, swiftly pulling out a chair. She glances at my bed. The quilt is filthy. She can smell the dust from here. "If you don't want mites," she says, "you really need to change your pillow every other season."

"You're right," I say, as I almost always do. The response calms her. She knows she has a problem with telling others what to do and how to do it, but she is unable to stop herself, especially when her job requires that she do exactly that. My best, oldest client is the CFO of a small, local corporation that peddles opiates to people with imaginary back problems through a chain of legal "pain-management" clinics. She is excellent at her tax strategy and increasing profits, but often finds herself in heated conflicts.

In her mind, people don't like her because she refuses to dumb down, which led to a vicious fight at the neighborhood book club with Candace Mackie over the genius or not-genius of Stephen King. In my mind, her need for authority undermines her ability to make friends. Both of us agree that the landing strip she constructed on Diamond Lake last winter—to help her husband land his plane more safely on the ice—did not help her situation. The bright, orange cones were butt-ugly and ruined everyone's view.

While I chop onions, she tells me I really should consider a mandoline. They are easier than a knife and just as sharp.

I look down at the counter, my gnarled grip. "Todd's confused again," I say.

She puts her face in her hands. Not to look at me. Clients never want to look at me. As we both know, her son, Todd, has a gun problem. And a girl problem. He got kicked out of Diamond Lake High for scratching the word "slut" with his key on the girl's car. Then kicked out of the fundamentalist academy he attended—due to the sizable donation that my best, oldest client made—after he threatened the school librarian with a fork.

When my best, oldest client would not kick him out of the house, her husband threatened to leave her and take their daughter. This led her to give Todd twenty thousand dollars in emergency money and house him in a condo she owns through a shell company.

The boy is now nineteen. He has a trunk under his bed with a significant amount of automatic weaponry inside, as well as a smartphone he keeps duct-taped to the back side of the tank of the toilet, which he uses to harass the girl via texts, as well as to comment on a Reddit thread called IncelMetalheadMindmeld that attracts both fans of Motörhead and young lost boys who think that girls will never sleep with them because girls are fucked-up cunts. Or Jewish.

My best, oldest client is heartbroken about this. She knows who her son really is: the little boy who picked fireweed on his way home from school to give to her, the boy who used to lie in bed at night, describing the cabin he was going to build when he grew up, a cabin with bunk beds and a swimming pool. On a mountain. She could live there too one day. As long it was only her and him.

"If you don't want to cry," she tells me, "you have to rinse off the knife with warm water. Lighting matches doesn't work." She then advises me to cut the onion crosswise and lengthwise, so the whole bulb will fall into little precut pieces.

I do as she suggests, which she also likes. Not enough people in her life listen to her, she thinks. Not even her own husband, an anesthesiologist whose medical license allows them to lawfully operate their clinics. Even though the idea for the business was hers. Including the app they have created for home delivery.

My hips begin to ache from standing. And my tailbone. I chop more slowly. Despite her lucrative success in pain management, she doesn't seem to notice the way I hold on to the other chair for support, waiting for her to think about her son again.

She studies the table, tapping her nails, considering if she should still keep coming here. I am expensive. I am probably some kind of highly skilled fraud.

My best, oldest client is not the first to have this thought. How I know what my clients know always happens too quickly to believe. They long for some struggle on my part, some pageantry. For a few years, I tried to placate them with tea leaves and tarot—both techniques I could not seem to execute without laughing. Toward the end, I even stooped to macramé, hinting that the disastrous tangled knots I created were somehow products of their inner lives. Then King Charles gave me a biography of Sigmund Freud. The famed doctor cooked for his patients, I discovered, and served them elaborate, multicourse meals. Doing so, he claimed, inspired deeper levels of intimacy. The same holds true with my clients—even if the meals I usually prepare for them are canned ravioli, sloppy joe sauce on noodles.

The onions came from a mesh bag of vegetables that Violet left by my door. Fresh food in the winter this far north still arrives by plane or barge. It is excruciatingly expensive. In addition, Violet shops at the one gourmet grocery store in town, run by a Japanese family that stocks the seafood tanks with edible purple urchins. She feels bad about these urchins and also bad about the nonorganic potatoes she gave me, which like all root veggies just *sit* in a ground-water bath of pesticide. She is worried about my ability to care for myself in general—and whatever advantage my sorry physical state provides her in our owner-tenant conflict, you cannot fault her logic.

I know all this because she is not puttering around in her own house, twenty-five feet away, but right outside my window, shovel-ing snow. Two feet of heavy drifts have built up over my walkway. Somebody is going to slip, she worries. And possibly sue.

Onions, I tell myself. And toss the transparent bits into the pan, waving off the fumes. At this moment, my best, oldest client thinks that I am a cold unfeeling bitch and that I do not care about her or her son. "You keep looking over at that woman," she says. "Can you ask her to hold off until we're finished?"

"She's anxious about her marriage," I say. "Outdoor work helps her. When's the last time you got any sleep?"

My best, oldest client sits up straighter. But even her thoughts are ragged and exhausted. She lent her son her hybrid SUV, then followed him around town in a rental Kia. His first stop was Target for duct tape and contractor bags. His next was various pull-outs along Seward Highway, where he got out and looked around as if judging which one was most desolate. His last was the girl's house—the girl whose car he keyed and who he threatened in front of the principal—where he parked across the street and watched the windows even after the lights went off.

I tell her what I know: She knows she should call the girl's parents. I tell her what she knows: She doesn't want to get Todd in trouble. And what evidence does she really have? You're allowed to buy duct tape if you want. And park on a street where you don't live.

The smell of hot, buttery onion is seductive, and I drift off for a minute. I had forgotten this smell. It is the smell of families, of lamplight, the hour left before the children playing on the dining room rug must come to the table. The effect on me is swift and surprising: My family. My mother. My childhood. The child I didn't have.

She was a girl, I like to think.

Even now I wonder if she had been born, would she have inherited my clair abilities? Would she have had my red hair, my skin that seems to freckle even in the dark? Would she have slept with me in my bed, the way that Michael does with Violet?

King Charles gave me a small velvet bag of pills to end the pregancy, which I did. To do otherwise was inadvisable, considering his draconian punishment policies, but not impossible. He had a violent allergy to bees, a fear of water. Both conditions I was aware of and yet didn't use to protect her. I have never met another clair, but if I did, I think she would tell me that I was never afraid of King Charles hurting me or limiting my freedom, only worried that if I didn't do as he asked, he might stop loving me.

Even though I knew—far better than he—that he had already stopped loving me.

This is the thing about being a clair that I learned far too late, mostly because there was no one to explain it to me: Clairs can't ever love nonclairs. When this happens, all we want to know is what our beloved knows. Other clients turn suddenly boring. Food is boring. Sleep a waste. Our one impulse is to stay as close to that nonclair as possible, siphoning off his or her every thought—all of which, no matter how dull or pedestrian, glitter through us like bits of tiny, frozen brilliance.

More upsetting is our need to share what we discover. At night, I lay beside King Charles, unpacking every gorgeous facet of his flaws, every exquisite detail of his personality, explaining his own mind to him, proving that I understood him the way no one ever had—a connection that humans supposedly long for but, in reality, do not like. At all.

By the end of our intimacy, he not only loathed me, he loathed everything about himself that I had dissected and glorified: his need to joke about his childhood in Atmore, Alabama, his fear of spiders, his reliance on his lucky gold-nugget belt buckle as a talisman against bank tellers and bail bondsmen and anyone else who might ask him to fill out paperwork.

Deluded by my affections, one night I even offered to teach him how to read and write, which was also the only time he ever hit me with that belt buckle. My mouth healed, after a while. I learned how to chew with my back molars. I forgave him and begged him to accept my forgiveness, but he knew better. He realized what I didn't. Love, even self-love, requires some degree of mystery.

* * *

SNOW BEGINS TO FALL, LAYERING the branches of trees outside my windows. My best, oldest client looks out the window at Violet, shoveling, and wonders why she can't be more like her: fresh, energetic, with a baby in a snowsuit.

There is no way to help her with this, except to set the table with my least cracked plates. And a stub end of a candle. She has been such a devoted, reliable client, for so many years. Ever since King Charles died and the mayor's citywide sanitation movement closed down all the escort establishments in Anchorage, she and other mothers like her have been my one economic constant.

I should despise them, I often tell myself. They have what I most wanted and threw away. But mothers seem to need me more than any other kind of client. They pay the most and struggle the most and never, ever cancel a session. Nothing, I have noticed, makes you long to be wrong about what you know to be true more than your own children.

Unlike violent offenders—quite a few of which have slunk into my shack—a mother is not there to be who she is in secret. She is there to find out who she is and who she might have been and who she almost was and if the pasty, angry, frowny face in the mirror is really her or maybe just some fucked-up version of how she sees herself?

This is a question I never can fully address, hidden as it is under a thick, tangled layer of thoughts about her husband or ex-husbands, her kids or stepkids, her father, her mother, her childhood friend, her boss, her neighbor, the waitress who served her unmelted nachos at Las Margaritas, the babysitter, the teacher, the tutor, the soccer coach, the lice lady, the camp counselor, her work friends, her doctor, her breast doctor, her ob-gyn, the sad lady at the checkout at Carrs, the fish who is so lonely, he perks up even when she doesn't shake the fish-food can, the dinner-party mother who for some reason doesn't invite her to dinner parties, the PTA mother who does invite her but only to ask her to run the school benefit, the therapist who should not be her friend but is. Just not real friend. Because she costs two hundred dollars an hour and doesn't take insurance.

Granted, I minister to a segment of the population that hands down cashmere sweaters, as well as manages a lobotomy's worth of household employees. But I have, on the occasion, taken on a pro bono mother without such financial resources and found that the mental load on them—and me—was the same, if not more excruciating, because the broke, single mom living in her car had to rely on a lot more people just to survive. All without the ability to pay them.

Sometimes I think all this churning insight and worry has spread from these women's minds into my own and, from there, into my joints—leaving me hunched and unable to run away from them. Especially when they show up at my door, seeking confirmation that they have failed or they are to blame. Once again.

What can I say? I know only what they know. Which is, yes, you are accomplished and behaved heroically about your daughter's math quiz, but about the 5.8 earthquake that hit Anchorage this morning and knocked your Chagall lithograph off the mantel . . . it's all your fault for the following reasons: (1) You did not use the heavy-duty picture-hanging kit even though you knew better; (2) Your son, Todd, left the poker leaning against the fireplace, pointy end up, a gesture you said nothing about because you didn't want him to get mad, start trashing furniture, and leave; (3) You were asleep when the earthquake hit when you really should have been up, sending emails about your daughter's school benefit in the living room, where you could have caught the Chagall before it fell directly onto the poker.

Here is a detail you will never tell anyone other than me and illustrates exactly why I have such affection for you, my best, oldest client, despite my envy and repulsion: You bought that lithograph knowing that Chagall made thousands of such lithographs and that this one—of a happy, plump green woman holding her little child under a half-moon—was no more than a horrifically overpriced poster. Still, it was yours. It was the one thing you would take with you if your husband finally divorced you over Todd. And now it has a ragged, ash-flecked hole in the center as if someone had punched it in the heart. Right below the moon.

* * *

WARM GLAZED ONIONS, IT SEEMS, can revive even the depressed and discouraged. My best, oldest client seems as astonished as myself by the buttery, crunchy slop on her plate, none of which, fortunately, conflicts with her Paleo Diet. It has been years since I have eaten real food—decades. We sit at the table. We spoon and smile, chew and smile.

"Delicious," she says. "Next time, you might consider a little salt."

"You're right," I say.

My best, oldest client smiles. It's not that she doesn't know that I always give her the same answer or that it shouldn't make it her feel good—but it does make her feel good.

If only that feeling would last. Tomorrow, my best, oldest client is going to start reorganizing two of the pain-management clinics into nonprofit status, which will allow the clinic to circumvent yet more taxes and inflate her husband's salary to 90 percent of the revenues. Then search the internet once again for an art restorer, specializing in Chagall lithographs. And buy a Glock.

The girl that her son, Todd, is fixated on—and "fixated" is the word my best, oldest client always uses—is named Annie. Annie is a cross-country skier. Annie is training for the Olympics. Annie is black and the first real athlete of color to dominate Nordic trials in the history of the sport. Everybody loves Annie. And nobody loves her son. Except my best, oldest client.

I tell her I can't wait to see her next week. I will think about that mandoline. And the new pillows. She gathers up her purse. Then turns to me and says, "He would never hurt me, would he?"

The last question. The Glock. My heart withers. Neither of us knows the answer—and this is why the last question with any client is so tricky. Your response means everything and nothing, nor will it save them unless they take some kind of action in their lives. "From what I have read," I say, "if you keep a gun in the house for self-protection, you usually end up shooting someone in your own family by mistake."

* * *

THE SNOW THAT VIOLET SHOVELED has left a winter's worth of ice exposed. She doesn't believe in salt or chemicals and sprinkled sawdust down my walkway. Three fresh inches fell over the sawdust—then melted, then refroze—leaving a slick white coating flecked with wood bits. I can try to pick my way down to check my mailbox, but if I slip, I'll throw my hands out to stop my fall and break my wrists. This is not a prediction. It is a reality that every woman over fifty living in a northern climate knows merely as a matter of survival.

Through the window, the spruces lean against the bluish sky like weary, old stragglers. Somewhere in that stand of trees lies the back-yard grave of the clair who I replaced on the property. She was Armenian, King Charles told me, and an excellent dancer, her life ended by knife wounds from a jealous client. Even now I wish I could have met her. There are still so many questions that I have: Why can't I know my own mind, the way I know my clients'? What if I met another clair? Would I know her thoughts? Would she know mine? Could I care about her without her feeling repulsed and overwhelmed?

It is a kind of self-punishment, probably, to fantasize about a life with another person. I have been alone for most of my life. My mother sold me to King Charles after a single meeting at a gas station in downtown Dearborn, Michigan. I loved her the way I loved him, perhaps even more so. As a young child, I followed her from room to room, touching her hair, stealing the sash of her bathrobe, explaining to her why my father had left us, why she didn't love me, and why it didn't matter, not really. I would not eat or go to the bathroom unless she came with me. At night, I slept under her bed, and in the morning, I recounted her dreams.

Her dreams, I believe, were my greatest violation. Every dream, no matter how beautiful or terrifying, always sounds foolish when you describe it to someone else. And in her case, she didn't even choose to describe it. I chose for her—a willful, besotted child.

* * *

THERE IS AN UPTICK IN visits from my best, oldest client. Todd rented a chain saw at Home Depot and never returned it. Todd got into an altercation at a dispensary parking lot. My best, oldest client is now my only client, but she comes every day.

Her Audi infuriates Violet. Not only is it an SUV that just hogs up space on the driveway, it's also simply a more tasteful Mercedes. If you spend that much money on a car, Violet believes, you need to spend a little more time volunteering at the food pantry. Violet drives a Subaru, which she knows is less expensive and better in the snow. But what really makes her upset is that despite her best efforts, she lusts after that stupid, gas-guzzling Audi. That panoramic sunroof. That gleamy forest green.

She glances over at it while collecting eggs from the hutch, veering closer to me than I prefer. Her thoughts swarm through me like fresh, dark snowflakes. My shack, she has just begun to think, would make an ideal guest cottage. Daniel could help with renovations, maybe while she visited her family in Minnesota next summer. Besides, she tells herself, the place can't be safe to live in at this point. Mold. Asbestos.

I unplug the Card Reader sign. And lock the door. And yet my best, oldest client turns up that afternoon. Todd has been arrested. This time for real, not just a summons and deferred time for community service. Her fear, her rage come at me in waves from the other side of my door. She knocks and knocks and knocks. She looks in the window. I cannot make it under the bed to hide. Not in time.

"Are you there?" she yells through the glass, staring right at me.

I creak up, hobble over, and let her in. She sits at the table. Her nails are brown this week. A glossy chocolate brown. But for the first time since I have known her, she is missing lipstick. Her eyes are bloodshot and the skin around her nose is papery and chafed.

"He didn't do it," she says.

Todd, as we both now know, is facing a charge of possession of narcotics with intent to distribute. Someone phoned in an anonymous tip. The troopers searched his condo and in addition to finding two hundred patches of fentanyl in his oven, they discovered a perfectly legal cache of automatic weapons, a perfectly legal backpack filled with a perfectly legal roll of duct tape, contractor bags, and a hacksaw, as well as a perfectly legal diary with graphic drawings that illustrated—perfectly—what he planned on doing to an unidentified female.

I rummage through the mesh bag of vegetables and find something that looks like a potato crossed with a root. A parsnip. I put the pot filled with water on the hot plate.

"Be careful of that cord," says my best, oldest client. "If you get it wet, it will short out your electricity."

"You're right," I say. "I forgot."

She does not bask in the pleasure of my response. She is too terrified, too angry, too betrayed. It was her husband, she knows, who phoned the police and who placed the two hundred patches of fentanyl in Todd's oven. Two hundred patches are a felony charge. If convicted, Todd will spend the next ten years in prison.

The water bubbles. I watch the parsnip bob along in the boiling water.

"He thinks he is protecting me," she says. What she will not say is that she still loves her husband. She has always loved him. It is just that he doesn't need her the way Todd does and, sadly, some part of her wonders if her husband is less concerned with the safety of his family and that girl Annie and more concerned with his lifestyle. His freedom. "Todd eats up all the energy," he said last year, during their fight over whether or not to send Todd to a wilderness school in Utah. "Todd craps on every goddamn bit of happiness we have."

The irony of her husband's actions seems to escape her. Through his pain clinics, her husband peddles opioids to half of Anchorage, many of these so called patients my former clients—mothers with achy backs or blown knees, mothers who are his neighbors on Diamond Lake and nod off in the afternoons, allowing their teenage kids to sneak a few pills for their parties on the weekends. Until finally those mothers wake up and discover that because their kids can't go to his pain clinic to satisfy their addiction, they are snorting heroin off the marble counter of the guest bath.

Or so I used to hear from my other clients, one of whom came to me through my best, oldest client's book club and who arrived after having taken an eighty-milligram Oxy. The slow, swoopy blandness of her thoughts did require some acclimation: She liked my hair. She wanted to touch it. She wanted to touch the Card Reader sign. It was so warm, so orange. A little campfire made of fuzzy, fuzzy neon.

Even more disorienting was her euphoria—and how it seemed to infect me, so much so I forgot Violet, I forgot my arthritis, I forgot to cook. Nor did she need me to. Everything for the length of that session was wondrous, painless, honeyed with chemical bliss. For weeks afterward, I waited for her to come back, just to taste her thoughts again—in all their gauzy vapidity. But she never returned. Perhaps because I didn't help her. Perhaps because she was bewitched by something far more powerful than my abilities.

"You sit down," says my best, oldest client, taking my spoon from my hand as if she has just noticed I have trouble standing. But she hasn't. She is just too upset to sit there, watching. She needs to do something. Anything. Though she tries not to take over, she does know significantly more about cooking than I do. Just as she knows how to prove what her husband did to his only son—and to her.

It was my best, oldest client who set up all seven of her husband's pain clinics, including the security systems, compliant with federal regulations. All she has to do is sit down and watch a few hundred hours of video until she finds the footage where he removes a few extra patches from the pharmacy distributor each day.

What is unfathomable to her—even maddening—is that her husband knows she has the pass codes for the cameras. He knows she is not stupid and will arrive at this conclusion. And yet he did it anyway, as if he believed she would choose him over Todd.

"Believed?" I say. "Or hoped?"

She stirs away at the pot.

"There is a difference," I say.

She looks at me and sighs. "You should have peeled the parsnip first." As she knows all too well, a parsnip is not a potato. You roast, not boil, them. And why does it feel, she wonders, as if I am on her husband's side? She realizes what she must do: report him, divorce him, and liquidate as many assets as possible for Todd's bond before her husband realizes what she has done. She doesn't know how much bond costs. Or a lawyer. It is a Saturday. There is nothing to do but wait until Monday. She is not very good at waiting. She will go home and pack up her ruined Chagall and send it to the restorer in New York. In a double box, just in case.

She stabs the parsnip with a fork and cuts it into two equal pieces—one for me, one for her. Both halves look wrinkled and grotesque, somehow medieval. Neither of us eats. "Isn't there something wrong with you if you don't love your own child?" she says.

The last question. And, sadly, she thinks she is talking about her husband.

"You have a daughter too," I say. "I wonder who she would choose: Todd or her father?" My best, oldest client looks at me with the kind of hate that always bubbles through the last few sessions with a client before she decides to never return.

She picks up her purse. She smooths down her sensible, colorless sweater. She whisks out the door, shaking with realization and fury—and slips.

* * *

THE BREAK IS DEEP IN the femur. My best, oldest client refuses pain medication—as any person familiar with opiates would—and screams every time the EMTs touch her. I would like to go out there and apologize or offer her a blanket, but Violet has the crisis handled. She is quite upset: Sirens are blaring all over her house; the ambulance knocked over her moose-proof trash cans; and Michael's sleep schedule is officially ruined.

Also, it is traumatic. The bone. Violet still feels a little sick. Only after my client is loaded into the ambulance does she show up on my doorstep. "Do you understand the jeopardy you have put us in?" she says. "Legally? That woman is going to sue."

"She has other problems," I say. "Is Michael napping?"

"I just think," she says, "that we should sit down and talk— openly—about what's going on. Maybe all three of us? With Daniel?"

"Let's have a session. How do turnips sound? I can mash them."

"I don't think you're listening. I'm not the bad guy here."

"No," I say. "You're really not."

"You like Daniel better," she says. "But it's him, not me, who wants to tear this place down. He needs a home office."

Her husband, Daniel, as she knows, does not want a home office, or to be at home at all.

"Just one session," I say. "It won't hurt." Though it will hurt, badly, and the pleasure I will take from this is disconcerting. Violet has already called Daniel six times today. My shack is more than twenty-five feet from her house, constructed there by King Charles expressly to keep me ignorant of his thoughts, the exact distance marked by the birch sapling he planted. And yet all day long she wanders through the yard with her phone closer and closer, her mind tearing me out of a nap or crossword puzzle. First she calls Daniel to tell him that Michael said an actual word, "Papa." A lie. Then to tell him that Michael bumped her forehead. True, but an injury that went down with ice. Then to tell him they are having squash casserole for dinner or vegan sushi. After which she stops calling because she knows it is demeaning. Daniel never picks up. And never comes home before two in the morning.

We can go through all this episode by episode. Or I can just say, the way I decide to finally say, "It's not that Daniel is afraid to be a father and having an affair. It's that you wish you had married that woodworker from college."

Her mouth opens slowly. The last question, how I dread it every time. Even this one.

But a cry interrupts us: Michael's voice from the monitor in Violet's pocket. Off Violet goes up the icy walkway to her house. Furious, but vindicated. She never could quite believe I didn't have internet. And now she is sure that I not only have it somewhere in my shack, but also know how to use it. Fucking Insta. Jesus Christ.

*　*　*

AT LAST, I AM AT the bottom of Violet's bag. Beets. I try to make them for myself. They are too tough, too slippery for me to grab hold of. I bite into one as though it were an apple, hit a rotten molar, spit out the bloody mouthful in the sink.

How I long for a can—the soft, salty slop, the jerky progress of the opener as it trundles around the lid. Violet isn't the first to try to woo me with fresh, nutritious foods. Confined as I was to Lucky Oriental Girl Massage, I never got to see the Russian Jack River, where King

Charles fished every summer. Or the crowds of Alaskans that gathered on its banks. But during the brief time he adored me, he showed up on the doorstep in the evenings with king salmon after king salmon— presenting each one the way some men might present flowers, lifting them up by the gill cover until his arm shook from the weight.

King Charles, I began to call him—a name soon adopted by all the escorts on the property. Though flattered by his gifts, I was also twenty years old with a full-time job and a hot plate for a kitchen. I did not know how to cook a fifty-pound fish, or what to do with the head, the entrails, that glittering eye. My idea of a vegetable was duck sauce or ketchup. My idea of love was to keep the person you loved from getting upset—and sending you away.

I threw his salmon into the dumpster behind the nearby Paradise Inn. Never realizing I was too valuable for King Charles to ever send away. After our intimacy ended, the girl he found to replace me in his affections was a nonclair, a Latvian. He kept her in the main house, too far from my shack for me to know anything about her, save for what I glimpsed through the kitchen window—the tilt of her head as she opened up the freezer, the easy, graceful way she leaned against the refrigerator door.

As the years passed, I retreated deeper and deeper into my room, lying in my moldy bed, staring at the wall where in my mind, I saw so clearly their happiness together as if I had acquired new abilities, the very abilities that clients want clairs to have. The children they would have, their marriage, their old age spent on the property—I envisioned it all, too isolated and ignorant to understand that these were the kinds of meaningless daydreams that everyone has when the future they have built their lives on has disintegrated.

Around this time, my joints had just begun to swell, my fingers to curl. King Charles sent out older escorts with my meals and jugs of drinking water. One fall afternoon, however, right before he died, he appeared in the backyard, standing beside the birch that by then had grown into a tree. I opened my door, but he came no closer than the twenty-five feet. What did he want? To say good-bye? To let me know that however slightly, he still loved me? To know, all I had to do was walk toward him. But I didn't. I stayed in my doorway. The look in his eyes was the same as the look in mine—ailing, bewildered, clouded with regret.

Eventually, he returned to the house. Two weeks later, when he collapsed in his bathroom due to a pulmonary embolism, it turned out that he had named his Latvian the legal heir to his business. She evicted the remaining escorts, sold the entire property to the hydro-ponic pot dealer, and ran off with a bouncer from Exotic Escapes, our neighboring competitor.

*　*　*

I HAVE A RADIO. BLAND, official fuzz from NPR informs me of Obama-care, Social Security, the new Section 8 housing the city is building. I do not know how to do any of this: what forms you fill out, what web-site will prove you were alive before you blew off the edge of the world into human vapor. I am fifty-six, and no official trace of me exists.

The beet smiles up at me on the counter, the dark, meaty red of candied liver. My hand beside it is a ragged claw with knuckles. I will beg Violet, I realize. Just let me stay here, Violet. I will be help-ful. I will be quiet as dirt.

There is a knock. I hobble over to the door and, for the first time in years, do not know anything about who is behind it. Except that it is not my best, oldest client in a cast, leaning on crutches. It's a girl, wearing fantastically form-fitting leggings, a high-riding shirt, and a splash of belly button. Why teenagers in Alaska dress as if they live in California I will never know. Literally. However old they may appear to be, they are still young enough to resist my abilities.

Under the girl's arm is a framed, dreamy picture of a woman and a baby. The woman and her breasts overflow from her open gown. She is green, the baby is white, its hands outstretched. Above them dangles a dark half-moon. Below them, where a rosebush blooms, the glass lying over the picture is broken. Jagged cracks radiating out from a hole in the woman's leg. My best, oldest client's Chagall. My best, oldest client's daughter. "Does your mother know you're here?" I say.

"Aren't you supposed to know that?" says the girl. She leans the lithograph against the wall, glances over at the beet massacre on the counter.

"I'm sorry," I say. "But I don't take artwork as payment."

"Todd stole all my babysitting money," she says. "Last week when he came over."

"I don't work with children either," I say. "Especially not my clients' children."

"I'm not a child," she says. Underneath all her makeup and arrogance, something loosens in her expression, something needy and possibly even desperate. What does she want to know? Though I have no way to help her, I sit down at the table, take a breath, and improvise: Todd hogs up all the attention? Todd did something to her? He hurt her? Physically?

Her face crumples. "I knew it," she says, wiping tears off her face. "You're total bullshit."

"Look," I say. "You're too young. I only work with grown-ups."

"You don't even like my mom," she says. "You think she's a drug dealer."

I shrug. Because, yes, I do think her mother is a drug dealer.

"You think you're the first one to kiss up to her?" she says. "You're just like everybody else: You let her boss you around. You keep telling her that Todd loves her. Just so one day you can ask for a script. Or maybe just a sample pack, under the table."

The idea has never occurred to me—not fully. But it's also not unfamiliar, as if it has been there all along, smudged at the back of my brain. The mindless, blissful thoughts of my book club client. The agony that shoots down from my tailbone into my heels. Yes, I would like an Oxy. I would like a big, fat handful of Oxy, followed by another handful of Vicodin, capped off with a nightly drip of ever-flowing morphine. But how does she know this?

I sit down at the table. I try not to look at her—and it occurs to me that this is how my clients behave around me. As if a lack of eye contact might protect them.

On the girl goes: I do not tell her mom that she is a bully. I do not tell her mom that she is a bitch. Or that it is partly her fault Todd acts the way he does—just to fuck with her, trick her, and laugh behind her back. "You want her to think she can fix him," she says. "You want her weepy, coming over all the time so you can say: *I'm old, my bones hurt, I need a little something, just to think straight and help you with your precious headcase son.*

I tell myself that my best, oldest client bosses her daughter around. And this is how the girl knows how my best, oldest client treats me. Just because a young girl may understand my motivations does not mean she has my abilities. Still the idea that she might be clair sirens through me—terrible and beguiling.

All my life, I have longed to meet another of my kind.

It is almost a relief when she stops speaking and wanders through my shack, rearranging the glass animals on my dresser, adjusting my pillow until the dust makes her cough. She is like her mother, unable to sit still. At last she finds her way to the counter and picks up the knife. "I thought you'd be different," she says. "Like powerful. And wise."

Her arm comes down, the blade slicing swiftly through the beet. "Not just some broken-down old lady," she says. "Sitting around in the dark, thinking about how you have nobody." Slice, slice, slice. The knife moves so quickly, the beet seems to evaporate into a pile of whisper-thin red circles.

"Please," I say. "Stop."

But she goes on: Her brother is a royal asshole. She knows I have almost told her mother this a thousand times, but maybe I don't understand royal assholes. Maybe I was one of the women who never figured out that when a guy doesn't love you, it's because he wants to fuck somebody else. Not to end up with you and another little royal asshole.

End of beet. I laugh, lightly, but even I can feel the wince behind it. Some part of me reminds myself that my life is not that unique, that this is why she can name my losses with such accuracy. Some other part of me wobbles on the words "royal asshole." What a clever leap it is from King Charles. If she is a clair, she is so much wiser, so much better at disguising it to protect herself. Her mother did not sell her. Her mother did not sleep in her car to get away from her.

"You can stay here," I said. "If you feel lonely and don't want to go home."

The girl looks up, sets the knife slowly down on the counter. Her expression curious, but not confused. With a swoosh of frozen air, the door bangs open. It is Violet. She has Michael with her, clinging to her hip. It occurs to me what a disadvantage I am in, to be in range of three people and know only one of their thoughts: Violet's.

Violet has really had it this time. That goddamn woman with her goddamn Audi has side-swiped the Subaru. Violet has already called the police and the insurance company. She blames the entire episode not just on the entitled parking that has gone on since she bought this house but on me. She will find me someplace else to live. She will help me move even. But I have to leave. Possibly by the end of the week.

She is so furious, so livid, really that it takes her a minute to see the girl sitting at the counter instead of the mother with the broken leg. Wait, she thinks. Who?

"She's not a client," I say. "She's my guest."

Violet shifts Michael up on her hip and studies the girl. Her braces. Her leggings that expose not just her lack of a thong but her need for somebody, anybody to notice she does not shave or wax.

I force myself upright, make my way over to the hot plate. I fill a pot with water, take out the powdered milk. The girl will get my favorite mug, the one with the daisy on the side. By now, if she is a clair, she must know that Violet pities her—a dangerous scenario with any teenager. But even more so with someone of my abilities.

"Hey," says Violet. "Maybe we should call your mom. And talk about what happened with her car. You know, calmly. Honestly. Zero drama."

"Nothing happened," says the girl. "I drive the Audi all the time."

"Okay," says Violet. "But there's my car too at stake. The broken side mirror?"

"Do what you want," says the girl, not with anger. "She won't pick up. Not if I call."

Violet thinks of how she has tried to phone her own mother back in Minnesota and tell her what is going on with Daniel. How her mother avoids the topic. How her voice goes tight and bright and midwestern. "It's easy to be married when you're happy," her mother says. "But nobody's ever happy all the time." All of a sudden the doorbell rings or she feels the need to share her cousin Ginger's recipe for mayonnaise-less chicken salad.

"Well," she says to the girl. "I'm sure she's just busy. Moms do get busy."

"I'm fine," says the girl. "It's not like I'm in jail like my brother."

Violet tilts her head, smiles. Inside, however, she is worried. Very worried. This girl is at risk. This girl needs her parents. "You're supergood at veggie prep," she says. "YouTube?"

"TikTok," says the girl. "I cook all the time. My dad eats out, and my mom doesn't eat—not really."

Violet wonders if she made a mistake by calling the police. She left her phone in the kitchen. She could always call them back and explain it was a mistake. She can claim the dents on the car as her fault for running into a mailbox.

"Go ahead," I say. "Or the troopers will make you press charges."

Violet blinks, then looks at me. Wait, she thinks. I didn't—

Just as Michael gurgles. It is a deep, soulful gurgle, the sound of a baby who has been adored for all of her short, plump, wholesome life. Violet nuzzles her. Then tells herself that one day Michael will be this girl's age—but that she will be different from her, different from Violet too. Michael will be listened to. Michael will be respected. She will be strong and independent, not because she was forced to be, but because she was taught to be. She will never need to show up and pay for answers from some lying, manipulative— Violet wants to use the word "bitch" but as a feminist, she can't, it's an awful word, a man's word. There is a long, dizzy silence in her thoughts. Then there it is: "crone." A lying, manipulative crone.

Hate rolls through me—bleak and unrelenting.

I can't say anything, but I beg the girl in my mind to tell Violet everything she knows about her: That Violet was not forced to be strong and independent. She was not listened to, yes. She was not respected, yes. But she did not learn from any of it. Underneath her frosting of self-improvement, she is weak and clingy and afraid—so afraid that instead of confronting Daniel about why he never comes home, she sent her old woodworking boyfriend a suggestive text.

All afternoon, while feeding the chickens and shoveling more snow, she has worried that he will not text her back. And worried that he will text her back, because she doesn't really know how to sext or have an affair over FaceTime or whatever, because she is too old and never goes to see music anymore and just sits home with Michael. Waiting for Daniel to call back or come home.

The girl is picking at her nail. She has no reason to protect me. But can't she understand what I can teach her? How long I've waited to find another clair? How lonely she will be too one day if she doesn't find another of her kind?

I shuffle over to the counter and try to take her hand—my fingers bent and distorted, hers long and slim and tipped with the same brown polish her mother wore on her last visit. "Please," I say. "Help."

The girl pulls away. The look on her face obvious: disgust. I stumble backward and sit down on the bed. I am weeping, the tears runny and rheumy in my throat.

"Hey now," says Violet—not to the girl, to me. She feels terrible. "Maybe I should make us some tea."

"Don't let her suck you in," says the girl.

Violet straightens up, adjusts Michael. "Young lady," she says, just the way her own mother did. "Have some respect."

The girl's face goes white. For a minute, I think she is finally going to go after Violet, to tell her about the woodworker, to send her fleeing out of here, sorry she ever barged in. But she doesn't. She looks down at the floor. A child. "I'm sorry," she says. Now she is crying.

"Oh dear," says Violet. She clucks. She actually clucks. She is her mother, and maybe that isn't so bad, maybe that is who she has been all along. "You're having a rough time, aren't you?"

"I'm fine," says the girl, still crying.

When Violet tries to rub her back, Michael reaches over and grabs a loose strand of the girl's hair. She pulls it. She laughs. The girl laughs too. "You could hold her," says Violet. "If you want to."

"What if I drop her?" says the girl.

Violet is also concerned about this. But if she wants to help this girl, she must earn her trust. "Don't be silly," she says and deposits her daughter into the girl's arms. "She likes you."

Michael looks up—and gurgles, as if on command.

The girl crinkles her face into goofy, exaggerated expressions: Oh no! Yum yum! Peekaboo! Michael laughs again and rubs her forehead against the girl's shoulder. The girl laughs and continues. I shut my eyes. All this means nothing. A clair can like a baby. Everybody likes babies. Except royal assholes.

"Hey," says Violet. Not to the girl. Or to Michael. To me. "I just made a banana bread. With almond flour. If you're not into gluten."

The girl *is* gluten free. Who isn't?

"Maybe you need a little time to yourself," says Violet. To me. She is worried. I don't look so good. I am underweight actually. That happens to old people.

Time to myself! I laugh and it sounds the way I want it to, like a crone, like a miserable, bitter, old crone. Violet feels just a little uncomfortable. Maybe I am losing it. She has always been judgmental about my situation, she realizes, and maybe even smug. She will work on this. She will invite me over for tea—soon—but now she just can't leave the girl here with me. Not in my condition.

Off she goes through the door. She will feel out slick patches on the ice. The girl and Michael will follow behind her, so that nobody slips. I turn over, my back to them. I stare at the wall, listening to the girl tickle Michael, snuggle Michael. I forgive you, I tell myself so the girl will know and I won't have to say it out loud. I love you. Please come back.

The door shuts. Then opens only a minute later, the girl rushing in without the baby.

She has come back! I sit up. I was not wrong. She is a clair! I am so happy I almost whimper. She leans over me close. She smells of bright, fruity shower gels and toothpaste. I take her hand. She lets me. Then she says, "Does my mom know? What I did to her Chagall?"

A branch bangs against the window. A load of snow tumbles off the eave. I sit there with her last question, and my extinguished hope. No clair would ever risk asking something so revealing, even from a fellow clair. Not because we don't long to be understood, but because we know the long, brutal cost of such understanding.

The lithograph leans against the wall where the girl left it. My eyes follow the curve of a crack in the glass up to the dark half-moon where a smudged angel that my best, oldest client has never noticed or mentioned is fleeing across the sky. What a fool I am—and have always been. I will never meet another clair. And I have no answer for the girl that isn't guesswork of the kind that caused her to mistrust me from the start.

The title of my best, oldest client's lithograph is *Mother and Child*. "You think it's Todd," I say to the girl. "In the picture. But it's you, your mother sees in her arms."

The girl looks away—almost disguising her pleased, young smile. I lie back down and face the wall, unable to watch her leave, listening only for the snap of the door, the tumble of tiny icicles off the gutters.

AN EXTRAVAGANZA IN TWO ACTS

TENT BUILDING BEGINS AT FIRST light. The thwack of mallets into half-split stakes. The clatter of poles off the pileup. The slap and suck of boots in mud, the spit and churn of wheelbarrows in mud, the hard, flat drizzle of piss and rain and honey buckets flung just outside a neighbor's door flaps. This morning in particular there is a leaden-sounding clunk, a curse on bearcat bitches, newbie pikers, the dripping *kunte* for brains who dropped a sandbag on the foreman's foot. Behind it all, the so-called creek thunders by, relentless as the rain-swollen river it is. A seagull calls. A meat cart shudders. Somewhere on the bluff above camp, a rifle shot splits open whatever natural quiet is left, the two halves dropping to the ground, out of which flies the scream of a rooster and the tin whistle of the new cannery.

And yet, it's Genevieve who wakes up Walter. Genevieve in her high mahogany bed. The noises that she makes are slick, unmistakable. He is careful not to breathe too loudly, not to stare anywhere but at the ceiling. That she would pleasure herself a few hours into their pretense of a marriage is hardly a surprise. So much so he has prepared himself: He will not look at her; he will not reach under his blanket. Or if he does, he will do it so slowly, so discreetly she will never realize.

Her technique, however, is almost disappointing. Not so much as an overblown sigh to provoke him, not so much as a grand-finale grunt of relief. Her timing seems almost medicinal in its efficiency. A slash of her hand, a rumple of kimono, and she is finished.

Hours pass, or maybe minutes. Smoke drifts through the tent, wet and acrid as the cook fires from which it escaped. Still Walter lies there on his Army-issue cot, under his Army-issue wool blanket. When he turns over—slowly, without a noise—Genevieve is on her side staring at the canvas wall. She seems unaware of him, almost as if she has forgotten he is there. The expression on her face, however, is so alien to everything he knows about her, so fragile and exposed, he almost feels as if he is spying on the daydream behind her eyes.

Outside the tent, a shovel clinks against gravel. A dog yelps and runs past the door flap. Genevieve glances over and meets his eyes. Years later, long after she has been dragged away by the men sent to fetch her, long after her tent is gone, the camp is gone, a town of fifteen thousand erected in its place, Walter will wonder if that moment was when he should have told her: He was lonely too, he had had his daydreams too, and his, like hers, were wistful and best left undiscussed—populated by people he had trusted in secret but never quite enough.

* * *

THE DAY BEFORE, WALTER AND Genevieve were still at an impasse. Once again. She would *not* be attending the Passion Play, she said, nor would she listen to Walter's reasoning. Even so, he continued in an undefeated voice: Mr. Carmichael, the director of the Engineering Commission, had arranged for the senior staff at Ship Creek camp to view the performance on a special platform erected high above the mud and crowds. After which, Mr. Carmichael's wife had invited them to a social at the Crescent Hotel, featuring lemon cake made from three real lemons, fresh from California and stamped with the date to prove it: June 2, 1915.

"Jesus and wives," said Genevieve. "All in one night!" She had her ruined foot propped on the desk chair and her petticoats whisked up. The foot was terrible, a childhood injury that had left everything below her ankle a lump of flesh and fluid, jammed into a half-laced work boot. She felt upward along her thigh, tied off, and inserted a brass syringe. "Medicinal," she said, the way she always did when he forgot not to watch.

Lately, he forgot too often not to watch. Blood bloomed inside the barrel, then vapored off with the liquid into her vein. Was it the rawness of the drug that so compelled him? Or was it Genevieve and her ability to stand around high and half-naked, as if bronzed by her own sweat? She had a kind of cool, marbleish glow, her auburn hair in disarray over her shoulders.

Walter glanced at the lantern behind her—drowned gnats in the ripe glass bulb. In the pecking order of the Engineering Commission, there were only three viable candidates for deputy chief of surveying. Having arrived only this week, three days into the search for a candidate, he was the least likely to be selected.

All of which Genevieve knew. Just as she also knew that his attending the Passion Play with a woman of her wealth and education would demonstrate to Mr. Carmichael that Walter was a reliable citizen of their tent city, the kind likely to build a wood-frame house with windows and donate to the school fund. The trick, however, was not to mention any of this to her. Especially not in a voice that sounded as though he were begging.

He leaned against the dresser behind him, ignoring the look

she flashed his way—one that seemed to register his sweat-soaked tweed, his overdone bowler, the lingering phantom stink of a childhood spent on a chicken farm in Augusta, Arkansas. The shit. The gizzards. The homemade soap like curls of graying death beneath his nails. He did not pick at a button. He breathed as if he were strolling down a distant sidewalk, in a foreign capital, a sprig of linden in his lapel. "Come," he said. "Or don't. I give up."

She smiled. She thunked her foot to the floor. "We leave the minute the Christ rises," she said. "Under one condition: I'm not your wife."

"My sister, then."

"Your daughter."

Walter shook his head. He was twenty-six years old; she thirty-four or forty-three depending on the strength of the closest lantern.

"If only you realized how willing people are to believe the impossible," she said. Then slid her hair up into a comb.

"That may be," he said. "But they're not idiots."

"No," she said. "Just hopeful."

"Can't you be my cousin?" he said. "Everybody has a cousin."

"You know what 'cousin' means to strangers," she said and blew a kiss at the ceiling. "I'll be what I am. Your charge."

Legally speaking he was, in fact, her guardian. An arrangement designed to humiliate them both. "You could be my fiancée," he said. "Then just break it off in a month or two, after I'm named deputy." He toed a piece of gravel along the groove of the plank floor, hoping she would not take him up on the latter part of the suggestion. Married men, in this particular railway camp, rose so much faster. The wives in the Engineering Commission liked other wives to have dinner with.

Genevieve laughed. It was slow and expensive-sounding, a

whorl of tortoiseshell. "Climbing is so tiring. Aren't you out of breath?"

"If you need a rest," he said, "we can always send you back to Wisconsin."

It took a minute for his threat to actualize on her face. And when it did, he knew he had gone too far. He wanted to take it back, but what other option had she left him? "So," she said, syringe in hand. "I'll be your family spinster. Your hoary, infirm aunt with the gimpy leg."

* * *

THE NIGHT OF THE PASSION Play, the air smelled of sweat and pea-nuts, pomade and burning spruce, plus the usual syrupy fog of fish guts and human waste. The Mercantile was low on axes, lime, and canvas. Puddles roiled with mosquitoes. Outhouses and bathhouses had overflowed.

In the summer of 1915, any man of any ability—or inability—could find work at Ship Creek camp. The latest rolls reported 1,740 men, 263 women, and 14 children. And it was only June. The post office was housed on a docked, leaky barge commandeered by the federal government. The stage for the Passion Play was located be-hind the tent for the Catholic Church—a raised plank platform, stag-gering out of the mud.

Thanks to the planning commission back in Washington, Ship Creek had not only laws against alcohol, firearms, narcotics, and prostitution, but also a highly organized grid of streets designed by federal engineers—none of whom had factored in the power of Alaskan tides. Twice a day, brackish inlet slop overran the river and washed through camp. Drop your hat and it vanished, sucked below the muck. Step off the walkways and your boot was gone too, along with your far more valuable sock.

There were rare weeks when sun broke through the cloud cover, the sky a sudden berserk of blue. The ground dried. Broken bottles and tree limbs surfaced. Clouds of fine gray silt blew over the tents, then settled, only to explode whenever a wagon passed or a fight broke out, the sediment baked into the men's clothing suddenly loosened in a cough of powdered earth.

Mostly, though, it rained. And rained. And rained. As it was doing now. A flat, bleak drizzle so regular in its timing, it seemed designed to rinse away the gathering crowd. Past the pool hall, Walter kept close to Genevieve's side, slowed only by the dramatic manner with which she swung out her foot. Look, she seemed to say, with each lurching step, look how terrible I am, how beautiful, how above you.

Boys in fish-smeared tatters stopped to openly gawk. A Dena'ina woman in a white-lady apron reached out to touch the brown crushed silk of her sleeve—an impulse Walter had also had, staring at the row of tiny mother-of-pearl buttons along her wrist.

Closer to the platform, people went so far as to widen them an aisle. In a world of dandy dancers, tent bitches, railroad humps, freight haulers, Army no-hows, Russian trappers, cannery pimps, café girls, and beleaguered, aging whores, how could a rich, middle-aged, crippled woman be considered remotely out of the ordinary?

Save for her attitude. And, perhaps, her ill-suited escort. Genevieve was taller than Walter, louder than Walter, richer and less afraid and more experienced about everything, including but not limited to absinthe, opera, foxhunting, lapdogs, Romance languages, and Greek mythology. All of which even a half-wit could see just in passing. And there were quite a few half-wits, by the look of the workmen at the edge of the stage. One tipped his hat at Genevieve, his smile bleary.

On the viewing platform, Mr. Carmichael waved Walter forward. One of the junior engineers rushed down to usher him and Genevieve up the steps. There was no time for introductions. Jesus and his disciples were already praying on the stage. Mr. Carmichael tipped his hat. Walter tipped his. Mrs. Carmichael nodded. Genevieve popped a peanut in her mouth. And chewed—not without a few well-orchestrated, open-mouthed crunches.

Walter glanced over at Mr. Carmichael. If appointed deputy, he would supervise the construction of a proper town on the bluff above the camp, complete with wooden houses, licensed businesses, and a functional drainage system, allowing Mr. Carmichael to occupy himself with the construction of the railway, and his Dena'ina mistress.

What an idiot Walter was, buying Genevieve peanuts. Her gloves were now stained with oil. And the crunching, the crackling of the bag. As gelatinous as society was in camp—slick with questionable pasts, wobbly with schemes for enrichment—there was an exoskeleton of propriety that the population seemed determined to keep in place. What else was there, really, to keep a few canvas tents at the north end of civilization from melting back into the tidal slop?

* * *

FOUR MONTHS AGO, WALTER HAD met Genevieve on the terrace of her family's beaux arts mansion in Milwaukee. She was loose and expansive on brandy Alexanders, smoking a cigar stolen from her previous guardian. Walter was occupied in a similar fashion, free finally from his roommate at Princeton, his roommate's father, the crystal snifters by the fireplace, the talk of the war overseas.

Never in his life had he imagined he would end up the house-guest of the founder of the Greater Wisconsin Steamworks. The nuances of the weekend—the cheeses so easily mistaken for tiny frosted tarts, the towels in the water closet that hung like delicate foreign undergarments—had been, at times, overwhelming. Touch the linen, he discovered, and you left a fingerprint behind in grime.

Still, there he was, on the terrace. The six years of mimicry to strip the country from his speech, invisible. The predawn hours of panicked study, justified. The late-night games of dining club poker now far more valuable than his degree. Cards, more than any other subject at Princeton, had proved essential. How else could Walter have funded his clothes, his books, those horrifying everyday expenditures that arose with each casual invitation to a collegiate picnic or a beer-soaked outing to town? Bored young men of means almost enjoyed being beaten by a young man of no means at all. Provided a game was occasionally thrown.

Their parents had a different opinion, which was why Walter had slipped away, avoiding the inevitable insinuations about his roommate's squandered allowance. A wall of boxwoods and climbing jasmine surrounded the spot where he was standing—not far from a tall, hunch-shouldered woman. She had a recklessness to her stance, not to mention the ability to stand alone in the dark without pretending to look up at the stars. Where had she been at dinner?

Tending to some elderly aunt, Walter suspected. Perhaps as a paid companion. Or an accompanist to a querulous soprano.

As she limped toward him with her misshapen foot, he had even felt a wisp of pity. On and on he had described his impending trip: the frontier, the ferries, the recently commissioned federal railroad, whose newly built towns he was hired to survey, construction of which would soon enable fast, efficient transport of resources across the Arctic and into barges bound for Seattle, San Francisco, and beyond. "One day," he said, "you may heat your bathtub water with Alaskan coal."

"Alaska?" she said.

"There'll be grizzlies," he said. "And Natives. Every kind of—" He paused, rejecting the word "danger" in favor of "challenge."

She clapped her hands. "I want to come!"

"You should come," he said. Then added, in a kindly, patronizing tone that he would cringe about for years to come, "I understand they're in desperate need of schoolteachers."

She laughed—a laugh so different from the pearlescent titters of the debutantes he had been seated beside at dinner. Brash. Flippant. Too loud.

Only the next morning, when her guardian, an elderly second cousin, called on him on the sunporch did Walter understand what he had set in motion. The speed with which the wealthy moved. The efficiency. Genevieve had taken his invitation to come to Alaska as an actual invitation. Her guardian bore powers of attorney, titles of transfer, and hints of previous, undiscussed scandals.

Genevieve, as it turned out, was his roommate's half sister from his roommate's father's first wife—the original heir to the Steamworks. She had done better on her travels to the Continent, he said, fussing with his vest button, "where people were . . . well . . . more Continental."

"Of course," Walter said, confused.

"I will add one thing," said her guardian. "Genevieve's excitements have worn the family down. If our arrangement doesn't work out, if you feel overwhelmed at any point, there are certain gentlemen we can send up to Alaska to relieve you. Genevieve will come home—and will stay home—under more supervised circumstances."

Walter tried to nod, even as oily discomfort pooled inside his mind: What men? What circumstances?

"Genevieve is aware of this condition," said the guardian. His grip was as limp as softened bacon fat, his handshake quick and binding. Leading Walter to realize that this exchange was a purchase as much as an agreement—and that, like Genevieve, he too had been bought.

But at such a price. The amount of money offered to him to oversee the finances and movements of his middle-aged charge was staggering. Immediately, he wired his parents the funds needed to pay off the farm. His mother refused the money, save for the seventy-five cents it cost her to telegraph him back the message: YE ARE FROM BENEATH STOP I AM FROM ABOVE STOP YE ARE OF THIS WORLD STOP I AM NOT OF THIS WORLD.

Nothing wriggled by her. Nothing ever had—not a wormy hen, not a late-night snake, and most especially not an inexplicable windfall from a son she had sent off on a train eight years ago and long suspected of ungodly arrogance.

* * *

ON THE TRAIN, WALTER AND Genevieve had separate compartments. On the ferry, separate berths. She was his aunt, his sister, the companion to his sister, who was ill with motion sickness and couldn't come out of the cabin. He was her brother, her nephew, her father's attorney bearing legal documents. Whatever their story, Genevieve passed it along—with the addition of a few conflicting half-truths—

through porters, maids, and valets, who in turn whispered that story to their employers while brushing their hair or turning down their sheets. Genevieve's one condition was that she wasn't his fucking wife. Walter's one condition was that he wasn't her fucking guardian. Mostly because he could not stop her from doing anything she wished whenever she felt the urge—unless he threatened to send her back to Milwaukee, the consequences of which would punish not just her but him.

Walter had developed a taste for goose-down pillows. And chilled crab cocktails. His threat had to be used judiciously, he soon realized, or it would wear thin. Such willpower had been taught to him early on, since he was a toddler. The year the laying hens had died, their meat poisoned by sickness, he had watched his mother watch him, waiting until he could hardly walk before slicing off a wisp of salt pork. Thin as a wafer. Rancid. She laid it on his tongue, got down on her knees, and begged: Get up, Son. Walk, Son. Live.

Who was he anymore, he wondered, as they rattled on through America and then Canada in first-class berths, him worrying, worrying, worrying that they would be found out. This feeling had been with him ever since he could remember: nagging at him before sleep, after school as he doggedly followed rules, listening, studying, imitating, hiding. Underneath his accomplishments, always, he was an X on the page in the Bible where his mother recorded his birth next to all the other dead X's, his father a drop too Choctaw to be white.

Genevieve, with her pale, glittering wealth, seemed to have squelched all these quandaries. She was prideful, deviant, indulgent—a spendthrift dragging around a family bank account and a dirt-dusted boy from Arkansas. There came a point in the trip, the lowest point, when he gave up and simply signed off on all her purchases. At every station or port of embarkation from St. Paul to Olympia, she ordered barrels of oysters, crates of whiskey, tapered candles, and laundered tablecloths. Plus otherworldly delights held aloft by Chinese coolies in lacquered wooden boxes or paraded down the aisles on chains. A monkey that farted songs on command. A parrot that plucked a pearl from your décolletage. All of which served as amuse-bouches at her intimate, in-compartment dinners with stevedores and stowaways, flexibly minded doctors and secretive lesser titans, waifs from steerage, coquettes seduced from the captain's table, laudanum-dazed heiresses, and, one time, an Argentinian spiritualist who claimed to see the dead children and ancient emperors you had once been in a past life.

Every morning, Genevieve shook these people out of her existence with the same nonchalance she used to free her hair from its combs. Then followed up with a gift that bedazzled each one into going away with gratitude, if not affection. A brooch. A pendant. A silver pocket watch with hand-enameled moons and stars. Even Walter had been sucked into her circle one evening, sampling from her brass syringe at her urging, the cocaine glittering through his veins and transforming him into a chattering, sweaty marionette who obsessed about his desire to become governor one day and escort his mother to an inaugural ball in Washington. In a carriage. With six white horses.

Nine hours later, he had woken up on her floor and tried to flee, stopping only to ask her if they had done anything, if *he* had done anything. As though, even drugged and ecstatic, she would have the slightest interest. He knew her tastes by then: the smooth-skinned women, the boyish girls, the raucous, foreign rarities of ill-defined sex.

She admired his directness, she said. But also felt the need to clarify. In the past, several of her guardians had assumed an openness about her, an openness which they had believed extended to themselves and their anatomy. She and Walter were allies of convenience. Nothing less. Nothing more. Nothing in between.

Walter, she added, did have a kind of ingénue charm.

At that moment, a moth fluttered through her compartment. Genevieve caught it, cupping her hand. Years later, Walter would realize that that was the moment his foolhardy fondness for Genevieve first began—watching as she tipped the moth out the window, holding it just so, allowing that lost bit of insect a moment to feel the wind before it was required to fly.

* * *

ACCORDING TO MR. CARMICHAEL, THE production of the Passion Play had been undertaken by the lone Catholic priest in camp, who, rumor had it, had felt compelled to compete with the lone Russian Orthodox priest, the lone Methodist pastor, and the nondenominational revivalist who lurked outside the pool hall trying to lay hands on slow-moving shoppers. The script was raw, basic, zero pageantry: the praying in the garden, the betrayal of Judas, the court of Pilate, the cross carried through the crowd, Jesus falling three times. Mary was played by the buxom Lithuanian wife of a railroad foreman, as wives in the Engineering Commission felt the production a little too Catholic to be associated with, the café girls were busy working, and whores were not allowed to volunteer.

The production seemed to move the crowd, especially in the final scene—Jesus lying on the stage, spent and bloody, Mary keening over him, her arms upraised. Perhaps it was the flat, gray clouds, the mountains in glacial blue relief behind her, but more than half the camp was weeping.

Genevieve sighed. Walter readied himself for her withering critical assessment. But Mrs. Carmichael commented first. "I wish," she said, "there had been music." She was far younger than Mr. Carmichael, dressed in modest Mercantile muslin. "It seemed a little . . . brutal."

"God *is* a brute," said Genevieve. "Imagine a world where Mary was in charge."

Mrs. Carmichael tilted her head, as if confused. Then laughed. "Did you hear that, Bertrand? I've found another suffragist."

"Worse, I'm afraid," said Genevieve. "A Bohemian."

"Hazel is an artist," said Mr. Carmichael. "Aren't you, Petal?" His declaration inspired such pink on his wife's cheeks that the entire gathering seemed to pause and admire it, her discomfort somehow refreshing.

"I like to draw," she said. "Though I am self-taught. And not yet sure of my technique."

"She's sending in a drawing to *Collier's*," said Mr. Carmichael. "For their magazine cover contest."

"Bertrand . . . please."

Mr. Carmichael smiled. "She's far too modest."

"Perhaps," said Genevieve. "Or perhaps too married."

A cough from Mr. Carmichael. From his staff, assorted looks.

"Whatever do you mean?" said Hazel.

"Only that it's easier for a wife—and for her husband—if she remains a hobbyist."

Mr. Carmichael's expression turned to irritation. One of his lesser aides stepped forward.

"Genevieve used to live in Paris," said Walter.

Instantly, the crowd seemed to forgive her. She was eccentric, a little foreign. How exotic! Hazel, more than anyone, appeared impressed, positioning herself by Genevieve's elbow, gazing at her with a flushed and upturned face. And so, it was to Hazel and only Hazel that Genevieve now spoke about the painters and sculptors, poets and dancers she had befriended as a patroness and, on select occasions, as a muse. An experience that inspired her to lean into Hazel in order to describe it, as if warming herself on the woman's sun-browned charm.

That gleam in Genevieve's gaze, that bedazzled tone of voice, Walter knew too well. There was no way to keep her from seducing the poor, provincial woman—in public, in front of her husband and his employer—not without incurring more exposure.

It was Mr. Carmichael, fortunately, who steered the conversation back on course. He had an idea. A fantastic idea. Yes, the Passion Play had been a success. But it had also been a bit depressing. Considering the sophistication of Walter's wife—not to mention her experience—couldn't she put on a theatrical? Something cheerful? Something fun and *avant garde*?

Walter cringed—visibly, already fearful of the word "wife" and its repercussions.

Hazel too looked stricken, for reasons that eluded Walter. But not Genevieve. Genevieve understood. Genevieve even sighed. "How difficult it must be," she said, "to be the wife of the head of the commission *and* an artist." How did Hazel manage? She must have so many commitments. So many invitations. So little time to herself. Were they to work on a production together, said Genevieve, she would handle everything. Hazel could design the scenery. Then go home—and voilà—attend to her husband and family.

"We have no children," whispered Hazel.

"All the more reason," said Mr. Carmichael, "to support the men in camp."

"Yes," said Genevieve, her arm now dripping over his wife's. "The men need entertainment. They work so hard."

"Yes," said Hazel. "I suppose they do."

"I have every confidence," said Walter, "that the two of you will astonish us all."

Wasn't her *husband* helpful? said Genevieve. She didn't know what she would do without him. Hazel laughed. Walter did too. As her husband, Walter had only one response. "Thank you, darling," he said, as if he'd said it all his life.

* * *

THE MORNING AFTER THE PASSION Play, Walter is still lying in his cot, trying not to openly stare at Genevieve. She is spent and rumpled, sitting up in bed with a pot of waxy rouge. He did not imagine her relieving herself earlier—nor will he forget it—but the expression on her face right after was so intimate, so impossible to match up to the wall of hardened features she now presents him with: eyes, nose, slightly bored smile as she looks into her hand mirror and applies a pinkish blush to her cheeks with the tips of her fingers. Did he dream it? Did she want him to see it?

"Five dollars," bellows the wash-and-fold man through the door flaps. Sacks sail through air and land in a poof of dust and lavender. Genevieve smashes a pillow over her eyes. Half-open books and toppled bottles of moonshine litter the floor. A crumble of graying chocolate.

Down on his cot, Walter longs for tooth powder. And dry socks. He thinks of his tent five hundred feet away. His desk. His drafting tools. His pencils. His surveying instruments in their tidy, plush-lined cases: his theodolite, transit, and an elegant, brass tachometer.

"If we're married," says Genevieve, swatting a mosquito on her arm, "we'll have to send a man to fetch your things."

"Or," he says, "I could keep my own accommodations. As a study."

Genevieve gives him a look. "Mr. Carmichael will ask questions."

"You mean Mrs. Carmichael," he says.

Genevieve digs through one of her trunks, pulling out a hookah, then a music box—the latter she tosses on a pile of wilted stockings.

"Married people," he says, "sleep in separate beds all the time."

"Yes," she says, "but in the same room, where no one can see their loveless marriage."

"Ours needn't be that way," he says—already wishing he hadn't.

"What way?"

"Loveless."

She only flicks a glare over her shoulder, then digs through her trunk, shakes the contents of a taffeta bag onto the bed. Among the contents is a ruby band that fits, just so, on her ring finger. "I do," she says, and wriggles her hand. "Now get out, will you? Hazel is due here in an hour. I don't have time for a fake-wife fuck if that's what you're implying."

* * *

THE FIRES ON THE BLUFF above Ship Creek burn all day. Forty square miles of spruce forest crashing and collapsing into white ash and wind. Take a breath and you taste burnt sap. Cough and a black deposit, the size of a lozenge, glistens dully on your handkerchief. Bald eagles scream through the smoke and skeleton trees. When the tide rolls in, bits of cinder fleck the surface of the water as if pieces of the midnight sky fell into the ocean, all their starlight drowned.

Straggling in from their fish camp on Point Woronzof, the Dena'ina trudge through the rows of tents, selling salmon belly or embroidery, bewildered by the destruction. The soldiers try to explain in their best White Man English: The bluff must be cleared. For the new town. For the railroad. The trains. Choo-choo.

Alaska City, the crew boys want to call this new town, and a general vote will soon decide the issue. In his office, Walter presses wet, rolled rags against the windows to muffle the smoke. The list of town amenities that Mr. Carmichael has enumerated in his most recent memorandum is substantial: a residential grid, five commercial avenues, a park (but not too large), warehouse facilities for freight and ships.

Walter is a surveyor. His job is to measure lots, verify acreage. It's not as though he didn't major in engineering and master the basics of architecture—though positions of that pay grade were filled by men with more established commission connections.

He allots a dockyard for the town. A residential building. A swimming basin. A park. Each meticulously placed on streets and lots drawn on quarter scale. His renderings, however, are less practiced, almost rudimentary: plazas, townspeople bustling down sidewalks. One features Genevieve, though he did not plan on drawing her and his better judgment calls for the use of his eraser. She is too handsome, too well coiffed. But she is smiling—shyly, as if she has just been told a secret. He gives her a fur collar against the cold and an escort to hold her arm. The escort is most pointedly not Walter's height, nor Walter's build, nor anything like Walter at all—save for his bowler, placed at an angle so that the shadow of the brim obscures his face.

* * *

DINNER AT THE CRESCENT HOTEL goes as Genevieve requires. He and Genevieve are seen together, comfortably married, at a window table in the dining room. Despite the dry laws of the camp, the waiter quietly offers them a "menu water." Genevieve orders two. Walter abstains. The theatrical planning, Genevieve says, is at a nascent stage. Hazel is charming. Hazel is delightful. But the only productions she has ever seen are the Passion Play and a vaudeville troupe last spring.

"You love vaudeville," says Walter, remembering a certain opening night in Helena, Montana, and a certain dazzling, tap-dancing Jewess.

Genevieve continues: Hazel grew up on a homestead and ran the café in the camp before meeting Mr. Carmichael. Hazel can split wood, milk a cow, shoot a long gun, and dress a caribou. Hazel makes something delicious and extraordinary, which she calls raspberry fool. "She's very genuine," says Genevieve. "No pretensions whatsoever. And my God, her drawings. She's actually talented."

"Enough so for a magazine like *Collier's*?"

"Possibly. But *Collier's* is so middlebrow. All those tidy illustrations. I believe I may have to influence what Hazel thinks of as success."

Walter nods and saws through the gristle on his chop. He notices how delicately Genevieve lifts her fish off the bone. He notices the sweat on her temples as she glances down at—but does not touch—her foot. Not once has she ever mentioned the pain it must cause her. "Was it a horse?" he says. "Some kind of riding accident?"

"A fall from a second-story window."

"Your nanny didn't leave the window open?"

"I was sixteen," says Genevieve. "I jumped. Trying to escape an institution meant to reform my . . . preferences." Her tone is light, her eyes blazing.

There is nothing comforting he can say that won't make her furious and accuse him of pity. When she quickly switches the conversation back to Hazel, he nods. Hazel needs more canvas for her backdrops. Hazel needs oil paints. Hazel should really see the catalogues from the shows at the Art Institute and the New York galleries. Hazel makes her own clothes, by the way. On a pedal machine. Hazel, Hazel, Hazel. Walter gestures for the check.

"Dear God," she says. "I'm boring you."

"You've got a crush," he says.

She blushes, but only slightly.

"Be careful," he adds, in a tone more bitter than he intended.

"I won't endanger your promotion."

He was not referring to his promotion. Seducing Hazel is one thing, worshipping her another. Doesn't she realize? "It can be quite painful," he says. "Caring for someone who will never care for you back."

Genevieve avoids his warning with a last, decisive gulp of menu water. Walter examines the bill, checking and rechecking the addition, pausing midcalculation—aware only now how his warning may have exposed him, if only to himself.

* * *

THE DAYS NOW BEGIN AND end with Hazel. The lovely, charming, exquisitely punctual Hazel. In she flits each morning with her willow basket packed with picnic sandwiches and charcoal pencils. By evening, she has finished with the sketches for what Genevieve has entitled "Alaskana: An Extravaganza in Two Acts" including those for "The Cleopatra Number," which features a less-than-Alaskan pyramid drawn directly on the canvas walls of their tent.

To provide a sense of scale, says Genevieve.

To save on drawing paper, says Hazel, a costly rarity that must be shipped on the officers' barge. Over the next week, she completes a Japanese temple for "The Mikado Number" and an oasis for "The Arabian Nights Number" behind the dresser and bed. Each is perfect in its details, down to minarets and date palms, rickshaws and straw-hatted drivers—all pieces of exotica that Hazel has never seen but has imagined into being based on the descriptions Genevieve provides. Genevieve, Hazel says, is an evocative storyteller.

Hazel, Genevieve says, can translate even an offhand comment into an entire picture. And her work ethic! She sketches right up to the moment that Walter arrives. Only to startle at the sound of his footstep and drop her charcoals.

"There is no need to go," pleads Genevieve. "Walter doesn't mind." But Hazel is too late already. Off she rushes to fix Bertrand's supper—leaving a pirate galleon behind this evening, floating over a Caribbean sea behind Walter's desk.

"Impressive," he says, only after she has left. Not that Genevieve seems to hear him. She is studying the tattered sails, the ragged, limp, windless menace of the ship. "Surely some of the credit is due to your direction."

"Well," she murmurs. "Hazel does excel at doing what she is told."

"Such an obliging nature," he says. "Might work to your advantage."

"Obliging," says Genevieve, "is not exactly how I would describe it."

"What other adjective would you have me use?"

"Frustrated. Ambitious far beyond a silly magazine. Aware she must disguise it." She points to the galleon, where the figurehead is, like most figureheads, a woman confronting the oncoming waves, her breast exposed, her hair windblown—but, in this case, an expression of such fury on her face. Her mouth is twisted into a howl, her eyes seething slashes of black pencil.

*　*　*

AT NIGHT, IN HIS ARMY-ISSUE cot, Walter no longer sleeps. Bottles crash, boots are tossed across neighboring tents. Someone believes a kid named Barstow has peed in his canteen and eaten his last fatty piece of salmon jerky.

Genevieve dreams on—immune or simply comforted by the mayhem.

After a few hours, Walter sits up finally and waits for dawn. Hazel's figurehead looms over him on the wall, rageful and knowing, as if to tell him that yes, his feelings for Genevieve are foolish, farmboyish, one-sided. A figment of his isolation.

Still, the things he knows about her that no one else knows, the things he has kept pinned to the inside of his mind like a catalogue of crumbling butterflies too delicate to ever touch: Her love of ice cream—but only vanilla and only when eaten from a glass bowl. Her hatred of harp music, but only in drawing rooms. Her weakness for calf's liver and Epsom salts and satin ribbon. He has seen her retch drunkenly into a potted palm and throw a strand of pearls off the deck of a ship, sober. Performing, perhaps, even then. But with a fearlessness that has always eluded him.

If only it were lust he felt. If only so much of love was not also self-loathing.

Outside, five hundred fresh arrivals argue and mutter by barrel fires, most of them lying on bedrolls spread out directly on the mud. Bootleggers hawk their jittering wares from wheelbarrows. Threats are made. Punches missed and delivered. Walter is almost grateful to the nightly chorus. Even the slurred steps of a drunkard who stumbles past their door flap, calling out to a friend in the distance for help with his own feet.

* * *

THE ENGINEERING COMMISSION, AS TEDIOUS as it is, is almost a relief. Walter's official project is to verify the boundaries of the train yards—a simplistic task that leaves him whole afternoons to return to the office and work in secret on his plan for the new town. He completes a tidy, commercial grid, each avenue identified by a number, each street by a letter. Then creates a linkage road between the docks and depot. Then adds a city hall, a chamber of commerce, and, almost against his own will, a theater.

Not that the building, however imaginary, would ever be completed in time for Genevieve's production—a production, as he is careful to remind himself, that also belongs to Hazel. Both women now fall silent when he enters, as if he has just tracked mud all over their tender discussions. More disconcerting is their laughter. Everything is funny. And delightful! The way that Genevieve botches their tea, the way that Hazel breaks her charcoals—pressing so intently against her sheet of paper.

The following week, when Mr. Carmichael calls him into his office, Walter half-expects to be confronted as to why his Petal is so constantly away from home, bewitched as she is by Genevieve's attentions. Instead, Walter is simply asked to take a seat. "I had no idea you could draft," says Mr. Carmichael. "And with such foresight, such precision."

It seems that a few days ago, while leaving a pound cake on Walter's desk to take home to Genevieve, Hazel stumbled upon his drawings—and suggested that Mr. Carmichael take a look, if he was going to be working so late. "That park," says Mr. Carmichael, swooning in his swivel chair. "That linkage road!"

He only has one question, about the double lot on Fourth Avenue.

"A theater," says Walter. "I was thinking of the upcoming production."

"I see," says Mr. Carmichael. "A theater." Such a thoughtful nod to both their wives. Romantic even. But as a member of the commission, Walter must think bigger, more expansively. With some vision, some planning, this new town of theirs may grow beyond its role as a railway destination. What the territory needs is a capital. A Chicago of the Arctic. A New York of the North.

Consider, if Walter will, the Marshall Field's in the Midwest or Penney's stores spreading through the Rockies. *That* is the kind of attraction they should reserve for an enterprise, one that shows off their modernity, as well as their potential for commercial investment. As for now, Mr. Carmichael would like to borrow Walter's layouts and designs. Just for a few days. Just to review them.

Walter nods and thanks him for the opportunity. That Mr. Carmichael will present his plans as Mr. Carmichael's is too distasteful for either of them to mention—though, as Walter consoles himself, not without its advantages. The following day, he is invited to a meeting with the senior staff. The commission needs such able-minded, self-starting engineers, Mr. Carmichael says. Walter is a young man of considerable promise.

* * *

RIGHT AFTER THE DESIGNING OF the costumes (the lace, the feathers, the silk, the parasols, the dressmaker's dummy), the final touches to the libretto (the ink, the notebook, the crossing out of lines, the recitations of lines, the midnight readings by lantern light), the insertion of "The Igloo Number" and the painting of a banner that will flutter above the camp reading: ALASKANA: AN EXTRAVAGANZA IN TWO ACTS, Hazel suddenly needs silence, Genevieve claims. Hazel needs to concentrate.

Why must Walter clunk around in his boots? His noise, his sighing is intolerable. Genevieve meets him at the door flap. She speaks to him in whispers. Even though Hazel hardly seems to notice if or when he enters, her slender hand moving so rapidly across a corner of a drawing, before flipping it over to a fresh page and beginning a new one. Then flipping it over to another fresh page. Each drawing, flawed, impossible, a failure once again. Or so it seems, from the slump in her shoulders.

Genevieve, meanwhile, is boiling water for Hazel's tea or heating up a brick to wrap in flannel for Hazel's cold feet. Six o'clock comes and goes. Still Hazel works on, until Walter is almost tempted to remind her of her husband and his supper—and her husband's

Dena'ina mistress, who will no doubt cook him that supper if Hazel doesn't hurry back home.

Not that he would risk such a comment. Especially not this evening, when he discovers that Hazel has prepared him one of her famous creek-cooled raspberry fools. She has left it on his cot, in a mason jar with a linen napkin. The fool is light, fluffy—a cloud of ripe, pink summer. "Hazel," he says, but only to thank her.

Genevieve glares at him. And whisks him outside. "I made it," she says. As a practice for the fool she is preparing for Mr. Carmichael tomorrow evening. Hazel works so hard. Hazel is so committed. The least Genevieve can do is relieve her from the drudgery of a few daily tasks.

"It's a theatrical," says Walter. "All she has to do is paint a few backgrounds."

"Oh, that," sighs Genevieve. "That was Mr. Carmichael's idea."

"Yes. And Mr. Carmichael likes his ideas."

"We have decided that Hazel should pursue her own ideas. Just for a little while." Hazel is working on a few, select drawings—which, if he can keep a secret, Genevieve is going to send to the Art Institute in Chicago, via a second cousin once removed who happens to sit on the board.

"So," says Walter. "There is a *we*."

Nothing from Genevieve, save a slight, knowing smile.

"I'd prefer," he says, "if you wouldn't fuck her on my desk."

Genevieve stiffens, but the expression on her face is strangely serene, as if she were drifting far, far above the wooden walkway and the mud and his petty ugliness—an ugliness that she no doubt believes stems from the threat to his position on the commission. "Hazel is different," she says. "Hazel is special. If she knew how I felt, she would only mistrust my encouragements."

"All you do is encourage her!"

"Of course I do. She has so little faith in her abilities."

"You're acting like her servant," says Walter—though "servant" is hardly the right word. She is too dutiful, too devoted, as well as long-suffering and ignored. What she is acting like is Hazel's wife.

* * *

THE CRESCENT NOW BECOMES A nightly refuge. Walter stops there after work for a menu water. The first of which tastes like lukewarm kerosene. The fourth of which also tastes like lukewarm kerosene. A game at the pool hall follows. Until he is too tired or drunk to do anything more than stumble back to the tent and sit on the woodpile.

Just for a little while, he tells himself. Just to see if Hazel is still there, which Hazel always is, her silhouette—like Genevieve's—backlit by the light of the lantern. To and fro the women move behind the canvas walls: the shadow Genevieve by the stove or the dresser, the shadow Hazel at his desk; the dark lines of the Japanese pagoda and Egyptian pyramid floating over them as if they existed in the kind of old-fashioned spectacle that traveling tinkers used to present to families after supper, using a candle and little figures cut from sheet metal.

More than once, as Hazel is feverishly drawing, Genevieve crosses the room to stand behind her. Her face is blocked by shadow, and—though she doesn't reach out to smooth Hazel's braid off her shoulder or caress the back of Hazel's neck—her longing is so glaringly visible in how still she stands, how much distance she keeps.

Perhaps, thinks Walter, that is what love requires.

The moon rises. Half-burnt trees hiss smoke into the darkness.

Down by the east end of the creek, fiddle music drifts over the roaring of the current.

Waits at the whore encampment have grown so lengthy, the pimps now hire musicians and give out tokens to reserve advance visits. The male-to-female ratio now stands at 24:1—a number that fails to factor in the Dena'ina women and girls removed by force from their fish camp by late-night gangs of railway humps and soldiers.

Similar incidents involving white women have never been reported. And yet when Hazel steps out of the tent tonight, at this late hour, Walter knows he should offer to escort her. He even steps behind the woodpile to avoid having to do so. But she sees him. She smiles. He does as decorum requires and holds out his arm. Their walk for the most part is silent, interrupted only by the firelight and laughter they pass by, the hunched backs, the occasional hungry, drunken glance.

The Carmichaels' tent is dark, the door flap tied down. No one, evidently, is waiting up for her. No one is even home. "I should join Mr. Carmichael at the commission," says Walter. "He always works so late."

"He is with his mistress at the fish camp," says Hazel. "She's expecting another child. Or so I have been informed." Her tone is as lovely and lilting as ever, her skin radiant in the dark.

Walter is so taken aback, he focuses on the ties on her door flap. For someone so lacking in innocence, how is he still so naïve? Of course Hazel would know about her husband. And why shouldn't she bring it up? It's not as if the entire camp doesn't also know.

"It makes me happy," says Hazel. "To see a husband so enamored with his wife."

The ties on the tent flaps are triple knotted. And half in shadow.

And not coming loose. Perhaps this why he says, with a little desperation, "Is it so easy to tell?"

"Not at all," she says, with a smile. "Besides, it *is* permitted."

Years from now, long after his ascendancy to territorial governor, long after his marriage to a young, buck-toothed daughter of a Seattle grocery store magnate who comes to Alaska for her grand tour, long after his young, buck-toothed bride befriends the eldest daughter of Hazel after Hazel dies in the birthing room of her downtown cabin, attempting to deliver her third child, he will try to forgive himself for what he says next. He was tired, he was forlorn, he was petty, and he was envious, and he couldn't undo the fucking knots on the door flap, which is maybe why he says, "No, Hazel, it really isn't permitted. At all."

She looks at him—confused. He keeps it simple. He keeps it factual. Hazel, for her part, seems neither shocked nor judgmental as she listens. About their pretense of a marriage. About the nature of his wife's affections.

"I suppose," she says, "I should have known."

"She does act very tenderly toward you," says Walter. "I tried to warn her."

"It's just," says Hazel, "I thought she was my friend."

"She is your friend," he says. Then pauses. "It's not as if her admiration for you would influence her admiration for your drawings."

The effect is immediate. Hazel's face drains of all expression. "No," she says. "Not on purpose. But she might overestimate my—"

Years later, Walter will wonder how he was able to say what he said next so quickly, with such agility. "Oh please don't bring up that cousin from Chicago!" he says. "The man is an idiot. You mustn't listen to his criticisms. I told Genevieve not to send him your work."

This time, Hazel tries to recover with a stricken little smile. And a lie of her own. Of course, she says, Genevieve told her the same thing. That her cousin in Chicago is an idiot. That it doesn't matter if he dislikes her drawings and won't show them to his colleagues at the Art Institute.

"You need to try New York," said Walter. "Or Europe! Genevieve will help you."

Hazel's smile quivers—a broken daisy in the middle of her face. She thanks him for his help in getting home. She is a little tired. She is quite used to being alone at night. She can undo the knots. Perhaps it's better that he goes.

Walter lingers outside, watching the tent fill up with lantern light, watching her figure as she sits down at a table—not hunched over one of her drawings, not moving at all, just sitting there. As if she had been snipped out from the shadows with scissors.

* * *

THE NEXT MORNING, HAZEL DOESN'T show up at their tent. Nor does she send a note. Perhaps she is sick, Walter tells Genevieve. He promises to ask Mr. Carmichael. There is no need to go to Hazel's tent and disturb her. Especially if she isn't feeling well.

At the commission, however, the entire office is astir. A memorandum has arrived. The memorandum is from the Department of the Interior, congratulating Mr. Carmichael on the approval of his layout for the new railway town, projected to accommodate up to seven thousand additional workers. Walter smiles. Walter applauds. Both are more difficult than he had imagined. His draftsmanship— his town—looks quite elegant drawn on vellum, certified with the commission's official stamp.

To celebrate, Mr. Carmichael invites the entire senior staff—and Walter—and their spouses to an impromptu gathering at his tent. He has ordered a jigsaw puzzle from Seattle. Jigsaws, he claims, are the latest craze in mainland America, the idea being to fit a boxful of tiny, broken pieces into a much larger and more appealing picture.

"Come at six," he says. "We'll raise a glass to the future of the territory!"

Inside, the Carmichaels' tent is only slightly larger than the standard-issue model. And yet the luxuries they possess: wedding china, a dry kitchen, a back-door flap that leads to a private outhouse. Hazel greets each guest at the door flap, a pink blossom of a hostess in pale calico. She is delighted. She is welcoming. Most especially to Genevieve, much to Walter's relief.

Genevieve, says Hazel, must come help her with the salmon croquettes.

Walter, says Mr. Carmichael, must come help him with his jigsaw. The jigsaw picture is of a racetrack, with horses, nose to nose, about to cross the finish line. Several different shades of similar blue complicate its assembly. Some belong to the sky, some to the silks of a rider, and some to places in the puzzle not yet identified.

Flouting the official dry laws of the camp, goblets of wild currant cordial are poured and passed around. Mr. Carmichael is so bedeviled by the piece he has chosen, he drains the entire contents of his goblet, pausing only to ask how the theatrical is progressing. "Hazel is such a perfectionist," he says. "She won't show me anything."

Genevieve glances over from the kitchen, a tray of croquettes in her hands. So does Hazel. "The Extravaganza?" says Walter. "It's going wonderfully. The last time I checked."

"Are they sticking to schedule?" says Mr. Carmichael. Now that's it's already August, is a fall performance possible? Just between the two of them, he says, the men in camp have gotten restless. What they need is distraction—a reminder that life isn't all work, work, work, and women of questionable character.

"A fall performance—" says Walter. Then with a pause that feels almost fated, he glances down at the jigsaw, spies the perfect curvature, and fits in Mr. Carmichael's piece.

"Would you look at that!" says Mr. Carmichael. All conversation stops as the head of the Engineering Commission climbs up on his chair, taps on his glass. "As everyone knows," he says, "Walter is a man who can get things done." He can survey a train yard. He can draft as well as an engineer. He can design as well as an architect. He doesn't mind if his wife and her best friend take over his tent with their artistic creations. Nor is he stymied by a jigsaw."

It's Walter who will serve as his deputy. Effective immediately.

A few men look at Walter with loathing, a few with envy and resignation. Genevieve comes over and places a hand on his shoulder. "Bravo," she says, in a tender voice, a genuine voice that for a moment sounds almost as if it has as much to do with his accomplishment as with his protection of her and Hazel's abandoned theatrical. She leans in, as if to kiss his cheek. She smells of lavender and cordial, sweat and cool pale skin. He doesn't breathe. Even when she stops, just inches from his face, and brushes back the hair on his forehead.

"To Walter!" says Hazel suddenly. The entire party, including Genevieve, swivels its attention to lovely, talented Hazel, who has raised her cut-glass goblet. She drains it. Then pours another and raises that one too. "To my husband," she says, opening the stove door and tossing in a handful of paper. "To a new town. And a fall performance!"

There is a round of slight, polite applause. Nods of approval. A nearby engineer offers to tend the fire for her, but she waves him off. "I love performances," says Hazel, tossing in another handful of paper. "Don't you, Genevieve?"

"Hazel?" says Genevieve. "What is that you're burning?"

"Some drawings, the ones that didn't quite work."

"Wait," says Genevieve, a note of panic in her voice. A note that at first Walter is slow to understand. There is a crate by the woodstove, stuffed with drawing paper. Not that he can get there, not in time. Nor can Genevieve, not with her ruined foot. By the time they cross the crowded room, Hazel is stuffing whole armloads of drawings into the stove, the drawing paper thin, delicate, unlikely to smother the embers.

Mr. Carmichael is still staring down at his jigsaw, obsessed. "Petal," he says. "Let's not build up the fire. Not with so many guests."

She ignores him—and leaves the door open. The draft whistles as it sucks up the overheated pipe, the drawings inside turning instantly to cinder. Faces, lines, trees. Genevieve tries to find the tongs, the poker, but there are no tools. She grabs for something with her bare hand. "Stop," says Walter. "Be careful."

Genevieve pulls out a still-burning scrap. She throws it on the ground and stomps it out. "How could you?" she says to Hazel, in a bewildered voice.

"They were charcoal to begin with," says Hazel. "Now they're charcoal again."

"Hazel," she says. "You're breaking my heart." The anguish in her voice is so unmistakable, Mr. Carmichael abandons his jigsaw puzzle.

"Petal," he says. "What is going on?"

"Genevieve is leaving," says Hazel. "She's not feeling well."

Genevieve bends down to pick up the blackened scrap at her feet, then stands up—blinking, her face a wreckage of features. There are so many people, though, so many skirts, such a little space inside the tent. There is no room for her to swing out her foot. She stumbles. Walter reaches to help her. "Don't touch me," she says. And limps her way to the door flap by herself.

"Hazel," says Mr. Carmichael. "You didn't really burn your pictures."

"If you'll excuse me," says Walter. "I think I'm—"

"Wait," says Hazel. "You haven't had dessert." She runs into the kitchen and brings him back a plate of raspberry fool—made by her this time, creek-cooled and topped with fruit she picked this morning. He should try it. Just a bite. Just to see what a proper fool tastes like.

* * *

"TOO MUCH CORDIAL" IS THE verdict in the morning at the *Anchorage*, the docked barge that serves as the camp's official post office. "Too much cordial" is also the verdict at the Crescent, though the fact that the Carmichaels did not order a case of menu water for their party may have influenced the gossip at the bar. Gossip that centers on a thinly disguised catfight by the woodstove. Involving Mrs. Carmichael and the strange, uppity, possibly foreign wife of Mr. Carmichael's top employee.

"Too much Genevieve" is the verdict at the commission. Not that anyone will articulate this verdict where Walter can overhear. But he can see it in how the staff avoids his eyes: It was Walter's wife who got him the promotion, kissing up the way she did to lonely little Mrs. Carmichael. Now that the ladies have fallen out—as ladies so often do—how will he maintain his position as deputy?

Walter shuts himself inside his new office and sneaks back to the tent after lunch. Genevieve has not left her bed or gotten dressed. Her face is puffy, her kimono ripped across the sleeve. "She knows," she says. "I know she knows."

"Perhaps," says Walter. "But it's not as if she exposed you."

"If she does know and she had any feelings for me—"

"Stop," said Walter. "There is no point."

"Maybe I did something," she says. "Did you notice if I did anything?"

"I noticed," he says, "how much more generously you treated her than she treated herself."

Genevieve fingers the blackened scrap on her lap with a motion that reminds him of the boys at Princeton, adjusting and readjusting the positions of the cards in their hand as if to magically change numbers into faces.

"Put it away," he says, gently. "And get some rest."

To his surprise, she listens to him, tucking Hazel's drawing under a pillow. Sunlight presses through the canvas walls. There is the sound of whistling, the soft, relentless roar of the creek. She stares up at the ceiling. "You would never send me away," she says, with astonishment in her voice, as if just realizing this.

"I'm your guardian," says Walter. "And as your guardian, I think you need some rest." There is something strange about her grief, though, something distant and removed. So much so that after she falls asleep, he checks the dresser and the trunks and even under the bed. Her syringes are dry, the vials empty, there is no smuggled bottle of menu water. He sits on his cot, looking up at

Hazel's figurehead until the sun goes down and silences her fury. This deep into August, the darkness starts much earlier, but not nearly enough.

* * *

WEEKS PASS. CONSTRUCTION BEGINS. THE lumber mill whines and buzzes until the last scrap of daylight falls off the end of the earth into the ocean. Clouds of windblown sawdust mute the colors of sunset, and seagulls drop dead from the sky—their stomachs exploded from eating fish who have eaten too many tiny bits of shaved wood, thinking they were minnows.

Hazel is seen shopping at the Mercantile, picking up her mail, and attending the Ladies' Guild luncheon, where no one with any knack for social acceptance mentions Genevieve or the now-defunct theatrical. All of which is relayed to Genevieve by the wash-and-fold man, for a two-dollar tip.

At the commission, Mr. Carmichael never discusses the jigsaw party or Walter's wife. Now that he has a deputy, he spends his days with his mistress or trout fishing in the foothills. Only when there is an announcement to be made does he show up at the office, asking Walter to gather the staff. The announcement must be kept confidential: Despite the popular vote of the Ship Creek residents, the name of the new town on the bluff will not be Alaska City. It will be Anchorage, after the camp post office, whose address is already established, thus ensuring that correspondence—especially correspondence with Washington— will not be disrupted.

Polite applause follows, after which Mr. Carmichael announces that there will be a lottery for lots in the new town on the bluff.

Senior staff members and their families will have preference. As deputy, Walter will supervise the assignments.

Walter, at this point, is supervising everything.

Much to his concern, Mr. Carmichael wants to see him for a minute in his office. It's been a long few weeks since Mr. Carmichael has been in his office, so long that his desk, his chair, his floor are covered in a layer of pristine sawdust. When a breeze blows through the gap between the windowsill and sash, the air thickens with tiny particles, gilding in the sunlight.

Walter coughs. Mr. Carmichael does not. Which may be a sign that Mr. Carmichael is about to mention the obvious: that Walter has claimed the double lot on Fourth Avenue for himself, ahead of the public lottery, ahead of Mr. Carmichael even. The J. C. Penney's has been moved to Fifth Avenue and, as a nod to Mr. Carmichael's admiration of modernity, Walter has been in talks to develop a talking-picture theater on C Street.

As designed, Walter's new home will have two identical, fully functional wings inside—one for him and one for Genevieve, allowing him a certain degree of freedom, which Walter will never question. Or restrict. Genevieve can do what she likes in whatever rooms she likes and with whom she likes, he will tell her. Soon. When she is able to get out of bed and think a little more positively.

Sitting behind his Army-issue desk, Mr. Carmichael does not mention any of Walter's breeches in conduct. Sweat glistens on his forehead. Each of his whalebone buttons worries against the snug fit of his vest. Walter is a good man, he says, a dependable man. Though there are so many employees in the commission, he wants Walter to be the first to know that "Hazel is with child."

"You must be very happy," says Walter.

"Well," says Mr. Carmichael. "I never thought I'd see the day,

I'll tell you that." After the whole blowup between their wives, Hazel all of sudden changed her mind about having children. For his part, he has always admired Genevieve and would never penalize Walter for his wife's behavior. But she did put a lot of pressure on Hazel. Not just about the theatrical, but about that Institute in Chicago.

Walter sits there in his Army-issue chair, studying a small golden pile of sawdust on the arm. He would like to leave. Mr. Carmichael asks him to stay. He has a question. It is delicate. "All that talk about Hazel's drawing," he says. "All that hand-wringing. You're a sophisticated man, an educated man, Walter. All I want to know is . . . was she ever any good?"

Walter leans forward, as if confused.

"I mean, good the way paintings in a museum are good," adds Mr. Carmichael. "The way people who get paid for their drawings are good."

Down the hall, there is the tap-tap of the office telegraph, the scratch of a pencil. Walter thinks of the figurehead on the pirate ship, the pagoda, the oasis—all drawn to please Genevieve, if not Mr. Carmichael. What did Hazel do when she was working on those ideas of her own? How was it that he had never looked over her shoulder as she worked at his desk? Or asked to see what she was drawing? Or picked up one of her crumpled efforts from the floor? Was he too distracted? Too intimidated? Too worried that she might be everything that Genevieve implied she was, which was everything he wasn't?

"I think," says Walter, "she has a baby on the way—and that's all that's important."

"Of course," says Mr. Carmichael, disappointment in his voice. He had always had such hopes for Hazel. She worked so hard at drawing, she loved it so much. His mother back in Montana had been similar. She played the piano very artistically, people in town always said, before she got married. The competitions she had won! In Helena and Big Sky and, once, in Salt Lake City. All his life, she played every afternoon before supper, the music so strange, so beautiful, he had the crazy idea that when her finger hit a key, it let loose a tiny, wild bird inside the instrument. Sometimes he even lifted off the top to look inside to check.

Then there was the year without rain, followed by the year where the calves got wasting sickness. His dad had to sell the piano to a neighboring rancher and his mother never played again. If you asked her, she would only say that she was just "a piano-teacher player." He thinks about that a lot. He wonders if it wasn't what made him so attracted to Hazel—even if she never really seemed to care whether or not he showed up at the café just to order from her.

* * *

YEARS FROM NOW, WALTER WILL realize that he needn't have ever told Genevieve about Hazel and her baby. Or about the house on the double lot he had designed for them. Or about the future that she and he could have together, not unhappily, if they tried—a future that would also include a thousand-acre property five miles south of what was soon to become Anchorage's downtown but, at the time, is so far away from the bluff it seems worthless, a wasteland of alders. Save for a creek that Walter will one day name Diamond Creek, after his father, Diamond Jake Livingston, the gambler turned chicken farmer, a creek that he will dam up into a lake and sell off in two-acre parcels of muddy, undeveloped shoreline.

The day that the men show up to drag Genevieve away, Walter is at the commission, sitting with Mr. Carmichael in his office. The men have Rocky Mountain horses, mules, and guns. She doesn't fight them or struggle. She doesn't try to run. She lets them bind her wrists and pull her onto a saddle. Walter did not send for them, though it was his name on the telegram that Genevieve sent the morning after the jigsaw party.

It is the wash-and-fold man who informs Walter of all this when he finds the tent empty. The wash-and-fold man—despite his name and bellowing voice—is only a boy. Walter asks him why he didn't stop the men. Why he didn't call someone. Walter is shouting. He is screaming. People hear him all the way down at the bathhouse. The boy runs away, terrified, without his two-dollar tip.

Inside the tent, everything appears the same. Nothing has been taken. Save for Hazel's drawing. Under the pillow where Genevieve hid it, Walter finds a bit of loose ash. He picks it up on the tip of his finger and—for reasons he will only understand later, long after he has retired from office, long after his wealth has ceased to either comfort or amaze him, long after his buck-toothed wife and his two unmarried daughters begin to spend their winters in Arizona for their constitutions, leaving Walter alone in his gargantuan home on Fourth Avenue the night that his only son, Gene, named not without penance after Genevieve, dies in a drunken car accident on Seward Highway—he eats that bit of ash off his finger. It dissolves on his tongue and tastes of blackened air, as if the fires on the bluff were still burning and he had forgotten and taken too deep a breath.

ACKNOWLEDGMENTS

TO NICOLE ARAGI, WHO CHANGED my life with her generosity, full-on faith, and encouragement.

To Kathy Belden, who notices all, tells the brave, complicated truth, and never quits.

To Nan Graham, Mia O'Neill, Zoey Cole, Lauren Peters-Collaer, and Jaya Miceli, for shepherding my book through the world of Scribner and beyond.

To Fiona Maazel, Molly Antopol, Rene Steinke, Libby Flores, Kimberly Cutter, Kerri Arsenault, and John Freeman, who read early and kept me writing.

To Michelle Wildgen, who answered every last-minute cry for help with the keenest advice.

To Emily Nemens, Hasan Altaf, Chris Brea, and Halimah Marcus, who edited me at all hours and in all time zones and celebrated the wacko joys of every sentence.

To Jeanne McCulloch, Julie Barer, Deborah Landau, Leigh Haber, Jeff and Dorothy Brady, who advised me and championed me and, in the case of the Bradys, let me hole up in their cabin.

To the city of Anchorage, the town of Skagway, the rivers, lakes, villages, and people of Alaska.

To Elisabeth Witchel, Rene Lassiter, Karina Beznicki, Richard Benjamin, Amy Brill, Hannah Tinti, Molly Fitzsimons, Mamie

ACKNOWLEDGMENTS

Healy, and Zibby Owens, who listened to my handwringing and offered belief and kindness.

To Dad, Anne, Mom, Patrick, Jonny, Lesil, and Lawrence. You made me. You love me. You forgive me. You let me clickety-clack into my little dream worlds with support and acceptance. Thank you.

To William and Wilder, my everything ever.

Thank you.

ABOUT THE AUTHOR

LEIGH NEWMAN'S memoir about growing up in Alaska, *Still Points North*, was a finalist for the National Book Critics Circle's John Leonard Prize. Her stories have appeared in *Harper's Magazine*, the *Paris Review*, *One Story*, *Tin House*, *Electric Literature*, and *McSweeney's Quarterly Concern* and have been awarded the Pushcart and the American Society of Magazine Editors' fiction prizes, as well as being selected for the *Best American Short Stories* anthology. In 2020, she received the *Paris Review*'s Terry Southern Prize for "humor, wit, and sprezzatura."